ALSO BY BARBARA D'AMATO

Hard Evidence

Hard Bargain

Hard Christmas

Hard Case

Hard Women

Hard Luck

Hard Tack

Hardball

HARD ROAD

A CAT MARSALA MYSTERY

Barbara D'Amato

*And an Essay by Brian D'Amato
"The Wooden Gargoyles: Evil in Oz"*

SCRIBNER

New York   London   Toronto   Sydney   Singapore

SCRIBNER
1230 Avenue of the Americas
New York, NY 10020

SCRIBNER and design are trademarks of Macmillan Library Reference USA, Inc.,
used under license by Simon & Schuster, the publisher of this work.

Text set in Fairfield

For information regarding special discounts for bulk purchases,
please contact Simon & Schuster Special Sales at 1-800-456-6798 or
business@simonandschuster.com

Manufactured in the United States of America

1   3   5   7   9   10   8   6   4   2

Library of Congress Cataloging-in-Publication Data
D'Amato, Barbara.
Hard road : a Cat Marsala mystery / Barbara D'Amato ;
with an essay by Brian D'Amato: "the wooden gargoyles : evil in Oz."
p.   cm.
1. Marsala, Cat (Fictitious character)—Fiction. 2. Baum, L. Frank (Lyman, Frank),
1856–1919—Essay—Fiction. 3. Women private investigators—Illinois—
Chicago—Fiction. 4. Chicago (Ill.)—Fiction. 5. Festivals—Fiction.
I. D'Amato, Brian. II. Title.

PS3554.A4674H356 2001
813'.54—dc21

2001031393

ISBN 0-7432-0095-0

To my father, Harold Steketee, who, like L. Frank Baum,
kept his boyish enthusiasm all his long life,
and who told wonderful stories, too—but, sadly,
did not write them down.

ACKNOWLEDGMENTS

This is fiction. None of these people exist. Nor does the Grant Park Oz Festival. But the Chicago area does have Oz festivals. During the first week of August, there is a festival in Lincoln Park which was previously held in nearby Oz Park, named for the books. This one is especially good for children. Another Oz festival takes place in September in Chicago's close neighbor, Chesterton, Indiana. In neither of these could any of the bad events of this book happen, but the good parts—the delight people still take in the Oz books—happen all the time.

My thanks to the people at the Harold Washington Library in Chicago for research help on an elusive fact about Chicago. Thanks to Mary Geneva Finn for showing me around the Lincoln Park Oz festival. And thanks to Mark Richard Zubro for attending the Oz Festival in Chesterton, Indiana, with me and especially for his criticism, which much improved the manuscript of this book. Also thanks to Tracy Reynolds Aleksy for her Oz quotation. And to Erik Wasson at Scribner for all his help.

Thanks to the 1939 MGM movie of *The Wizard of Oz*. There is probably no grade school class in the United States to which you could say "Lions and tigers and bears" and not get the reply "Oh my!" Think of phrases like, "We're off to see the Wizard" and "We're not in Kansas anymore"— practically every line of the film has entered our language. No other movie has so enriched the vocabulary of the world.

Oz fanciers will notice that many of the fictional people in this story bear the names of actual men and women connected with L. Frank Baum. This reverse roman à clef element is included just for fun. It may give some amusement to those who like to solve puzzles. Some references are very obscure. And some names are so obvious that they will be no puzzle at all. However, it is not necessary to know anything about the originals of these names to read this book. Also, lest any reader become frustrated trying to trace every single name, they are mostly, but not all, Baum-related.

Thanks, too, to the International Wizard of Oz Club. Founded in 1957, it publishes a journal three times a year about Baum, Oz, and the influences of Oz on our world. The club may be reached at P.O. Box 266, Kalamazoo, Michigan, 49004-0266 or Ozclub.org.

AUTHOR'S NOTE

When my father was a boy, his family had a summer cottage in Macatawa, Michigan, on the shore of Lake Michigan. L. Frank Baum had a cottage there, too, called The Sign of the Goose, because he had paid for it with the royalties from his first success, *Father Goose: His Book*. These cottages would seem very primitive by modern standards. Not only was there no air conditioning, there was no electricity, no central heat, and no running water. But the resort was heaven for a child—a small lake to fish in, a big lake to swim in, lots of children, and no cars or other hazards to watch out for. Baum had four boys. My father played with them, and he often told me the story of going to the Baums', where Frank, the father, would get right down on the floor and play with the children. My father remembered that Mrs. Baum considered this undignified.

Of course, when I was a child, I was given the Oz books to read, luckily at just the right age to read to myself and love them.

Then, in the wink of an eye, it's fifty years later and my granddaughter is in my living room watching the movie of *The Wizard of Oz*. Just a toddler, she is so fascinated that she views the entire movie—standing up!

Between my granddaughter and me, my two boys grew up reading the Oz books as well. How wonderful that words written down a hundred years ago could so delight generations of children! Thank you, Mr. Baum.

HARD ROAD

· 1 ·

WE WISH TO WELCOME YOU
TO MUNCHKINLAND

The Yellow Brick Road ran straight for about two hundred yards to the Emerald City Castle. There it split into two parts, circled the castle, rejoined, and went away on the far side. To our left was a clump of trees. There was a sign just before the little woods, shaped like a hand with a pointing finger. On it was written, LIONS AND TIGERS AND BEARS.

I read it to Jeremy, who was six and could decipher a few words but not very many yet. He said, "Oh, my."

The Yellow Brick Road ran down the approximate middle of Chicago's Oz Festival. The "road"—a yellow background with brown outlines of bricks—was painted on the central pathway through the Grant Park festival area, where Taste of Chicago and other big civic events take place throughout the year. At Taste of Chicago, held in July, restaurants from all over the Greater Chicagoland area rent booths and put their best foods forward. I absolutely love it—Chicago deep-dish pizza, Harry Caray's fried calamari, Chicago red hots, TNT chili and the Great Chili Cook-Off, fried funnel cakes, death by chocolate—I could live there.

But the new Oz Festival is even more lovable, partly because it's for children, partly because it's whimsical, partly because it's Oz. I'm an Oz fan. And this year—2000—was the centennial of the publication of *The Wizard of Oz*—a hundred years in September.

My little pal Jeremy is my nephew. He has red hair and freckles, a round face, a zippy personality, and if you gave him a fishing pole you'd be certain he was Tom Sawyer. My job today, on this warm Thursday in July, had been squiring him around Chicago from mid-afternoon until the 7 P.M. public opening of the Oz Festival. The opening ceremonies with Very Important People were to start at eight. His dad Barry, who is the second oldest of my five brothers, is an events coordinator. He makes corporate events, festivals, and conferences happen. Barry was busy with the festival preparations and Jeremy's mother, Maud, was at home, very busy with their three-week-old daughter. The name Maud sounds old-fashioned and sort of stately, which is charming in view of the freckly, bouncy, red-haired Maud I knew and liked, who had been Northern Illinois Women's Ping-Pong Champion three years in a row. Jeremy had not yet expressed any envy of the newcomer, but the hope was that having me show him some attention might offset future sibling rivalry problems.

Jeremy and I had spent the afternoon together and had gone on a carriage ride through downtown Chicago. The horses wear red plumes and pull nice, old-fashioned, leather-appointed buggies. The driver wears an 1890s cape and top hat. All right, it's kitschy, but Jeremy loved it, and I had to admit to a sneaking enthusiasm myself. It was horribly expensive, but Barry had handed me some extra cash to use in minding the child, including money for parking and unparking my car a couple of times, which in Chicago costs more than most events.

We stopped at two bookstores, looking for an Oz book Jeremy didn't have. *Glinda of Oz* was the last Oz book entirely written by L. Frank Baum. The stores didn't have it, and we decided that was okay because we didn't want to carry it around all evening anyhow. I took out my small pocket notebook and wrote down the title and "get some-place soon." Then I took out a red pen and underlined the note.

"Why do you write things down, Aunt Cat?"

"Because otherwise I'll forget."

"Why do you carry so many pens?"

"Because I'm afraid something important will come up and I won't have anything to write with."

"Why did you use a red pen?"

"To make sure I knew this was a really important matter. Some of my notes aren't as important."

"Why is this important?"

"Because it's for you."

That got him. He stopped asking questions. For a whole thirty seconds. Then he said, "What are we gonna do next?"

"I'll show you." I took him to the observatory at the top of the John Hancock building on Michigan Avenue to see the 360-degree view of Chicago. On a clear day, and this was an absolutely crystal clear day, you can see four states—Illinois, Wisconsin, Indiana, and far away the coast of southern Michigan. Lake Michigan is much too wide to see across, but this southern curve makes you feel you almost could.

Finally, having spent two hours minding a child, I took him to the restaurant area on the ninety-fifth floor of the Hancock, ostensibly to buy him a soda or a Shirley Temple. Actually, the point was to get myself a nice cold beer and to sit down. How do parents find the strength to do this job twenty-four hours a day?

My admiration for Maud rose a whole lot. I'd have to tell her so.

We arrived at Grant Park at six-thirty. And now we were in Oz.

Grant Park is big. Fifteen city blocks long, it lies up against Lake Michigan between Lake Shore Drive on the east and Michigan Avenue on the west, Randolph Street on the north and Roosevelt Road on the south—in other words, it bellies right up against the Loop. This makes it well over a mile in length, not even counting the "museum campus" running south from its south end, which includes the Field Museum, Adler Planetarium, Soldier Field, and the Shedd Aquarium. In the center of Grant Park is Buckingham Fountain. Eight months of the year this dramatic tiered pink marble confection with its fanciful sculpted sea creatures throws a hundred-and-thirty-five-foot water display. The fountain was modeled on the Latona Fountain at Versailles. However, in typical New World robber-baron style, the donor, Miss Kate Sturges Buckingham, daughter of one Ebenezer Buckingham, who made his fortune in Illinois Central Railroad grain elevators, ordered it to be twice as large as the one in Versailles. *That'll show those snotty French*, I can imagine her saying. It holds one and a half million gallons of water.

Jeremy and I could see Buckingham Fountain about a block away as we walked down the Yellow Brick Road. There is no entrance fee at Grant Park festivals.

"Where are we supposed to meet Dad?" he asked.

"At the Emerald City castle at nine P.M. That gives us about two hours to explore the festival."

"Yay!"

"If I wanted some popcorn—" I said, just to get him started.

"I'd go to the land of Mo!"

"And I do want popcorn." In Mo, it snowed popcorn. Jeremy and I, fellow Ozians, often played "can you top this?" with Oz trivia. I really should not call it trivia, but minutiae. Nothing about Oz is trivial. Our enthusiasm can be very tiring for those who are not aficionados. I have friends who are Trekkers who almost drive me around the bend with their force fields and "Who was Q?" "Who was Mr. Worf?" "Did Captain Kirk really ever say, 'Beam me up, Scotty'?" (The answer seems to be no, it was just "Beam me up.")

But kids love knowing things that very few adults know. Jeremy crows with delight when he beats me with a question, and the rest of his relatives have far less Oz info than I have, so I'm kind of the spiffy auntie.

I was sure there was a Mo popcorn stand someplace, because I had helped in the early festival planning, being a known Oz fan. At the festival, it was not actually in Mo, it was in Quadling country. I have written several articles on connections between Chicago and L. Frank Baum. Baum lived here for nineteen years around the turn of the century, taking jobs as an actor, as a newspaperman, later in a department store, finally as a full-time writer. He wrote *The Wizard of Oz* in a house on Humboldt Boulevard on the northwest side in 1899. I'm a freelance reporter, working in the Chicago area, and I was currently writing a story about the Oz Festival for a major daily, and a more scholarly piece on Baum himself and his work for *Chicago Today*. But even though I'd been here at the festival several times over the last few days, I did not know exactly where the popcorn was. The food stands had moved into place at the very last moment. That was okay. Popcorn was just a pretext. Really, Jeremy and I wanted to wander.

A lot of people only think of the *Wizard of Oz* movie when they think of Oz. The challenge for the festival was not only to use a lot of the most familiar movie elements, which would appeal to just about everybody, but also to include a lot of the wonderful characters and places L. Frank Baum invented for the other Oz books. My favorite was *The Land of Oz*. A stranger book has never been written. Those who have read it will know why; for those who haven't, I won't spoil the treat by revealing the plot. Or then again maybe my favorite was *The Magic of Oz*, where two friends, searching for a birthday present for Princess Ozma, arrive on an island where a magic plant grows. While admiring the plant, their feet take root. Jeremy's favorite was *The Royal Book of Oz*, begun by Baum and mostly written by another author, in which the Scarecrow searches for his family tree. I had read it to him four times and Maud said she'd read it to him so often she'd long since lost count.

Of course the movie elements were everywhere at the festival. There was a field of poppies, for instance. Grant Park is always lushly planted with flower beds, and this year they'd planned well ahead for the inaugural Oz Festival. Instead of going with geraniums or petunias, they had planted poppies. The Latin name for those big, bright red oriental poppies is *Papaver somniferum*, literally what L. Frank Baum intended—poppies that put you to sleep. He knew whereof he spoke. Unfortunately, oriental poppies tended to bloom in early June in this part of the world. Since the festival was in July, the planners had chosen a different variety, bright yellow-orange California poppies.

The farmhouse that Dorothy rode from Kansas through the sky sat on a slight but disorienting angle—or cattywumpus my uncle would call it—doing duty as a funhouse in the Munchkinland section. And somewhere a human Dorothy was walking around in ruby slippers, even though in the original book the slippers were silver. The 1939 moviemakers had figured Technicolor hadn't been invented for nothing.

In the Oz canon, the Land of Oz is divided into four small countries, with the Emerald City in the center. The land of the Quadlings is red. Winkie country is yellow. Gillikin is purple. And Munchkin country is blue. So the festival divided the big area the city had given them into four different-colored "countries." In the very center was the Emerald City, actually a very pretty little three-story castle with the festival offices inside and a gentle roller-coaster ride for the younger children going spirally around it outside. The castle and roller coaster were, of course, emerald green. From the castle pinnacle flew Princess Ozma's flag, a banner with an emerald green center, its four quarters the colors of the four lands, yellow, blue, purple, and red. From above the castle's green doorway, a speaker played the "Oz Spangled Banner."

The lights, decorations, and uniforms of the vendors in Munchkinland were blue, of course. And in Gillikin country the color scheme was purple. Even the snow cones in Gillikin were grape purple. The general effect of all the color was dazzling and cheerful in the late daylight. Once the sun set and night came on, all the lighting in each section would be the appropriate color. And then the festival should be really, really impressive. E. T. Taubman, one of the festival designers, had told me that lighting is the most effective, most evocative way to create mood at an event, and one of the least expensive.

"But," he said, "it's usually ignored."

It wasn't ignored this time. Or at any rate, Taubman hadn't been overlooked by the press. His innovations for the festival had formed the basis for a glossy magazine article. Two of the news channels, WGN and Channel Twelve, had produced preopening segments on the festival and Taubman's light schemes. The lighting designs were colorful and bright and full of motion, just what television loves to show. Taubman's efforts had paid off both for himself and for the Oz Festival.

We passed a Munchkinland stand selling fizzy blue drinks called Witches' Brew. I stopped, intending to sample some, but in the low yellow light of the setting sun the blue goo looked muddy and not very appetizing. Plus, we were heading for the rides. I may not be a parent, but hey, I'm a quick study and I knew that stuffing a child with sugary, carbonated drinks just before going on wild rides wouldn't be very smart.

At a ticket booth near the castle I bought a "giant size" strip of ride tickets (emerald green tickets, naturally), not wanting to have to come back for more. My guess was we'd use them all.

The first ride we hit, in nearby Gillikin country, was more experience than ride. It was called the Magic Turning Mountains. In *The Lost Princess of Oz* the only path Dorothy and her friends can take to get across the canyon and continue their quest is blocked by huge mountains that spin. Scraps, the Patchwork Girl, thinks they can cross the canyon by hurling themselves into the first spinning mountain, bouncing from that onto another mountain, and then a third, until they reach the far side. And since she's made of cloth and stuffing, she tries the plan first, before the "meat" people take a risk.

To make the magic turning mountains, the festival planners had modified a fairground Tilt-a-Whirl, building purple molded foam rubber up over the seats in conical shapes, like huge pyramidal Nerf balls. The "mountains" rotated very slowly—insurance liability worries, no doubt—but looked like loads of fun. Smaller soft balls in purple, lavender, mauve, and violet totally filled the floor and intervening spaces so that children wouldn't be hurt if they fell.

"No adults," the ride manager said. He pointed to an

arched signboard that read MAXIMUM 48" TALL in lavender letters on dark purple. You had to walk under the arch to enter the ride and if you were too big you couldn't go in.

Well, I could see why. If a large person got knocked into a small person it might do the small person some damage. "Want to go by yourself?" I asked Jeremy.

"Oh, yes!"

He ran in, shouting, throwing himself at a mountain, bouncing from one mountain to the next in total glee, the sort of utter, uncomplicated joy that only children can have. The little monster actually climbed to the peak of one of the mountains and stood there spinning and crowing at the top of his lungs. Another boy who was taller tried the same thing and rolled all the way back down. Jeremy crowed louder. He had triumphed.

You could stay in this device as long as you wanted, so he did. I shifted feet, sighed, shifted some more, but I really liked watching him enjoy himself. Finally he bounded out the far side.

I pretended to pout. "Oh, poop," I said. "That looked great and I didn't get to do it." Jeremy always thought "Oh, poop!" was the funniest remark you could possibly make. I suspected his parents disapproved of the expression.

He giggled. "You're fun, Aunt Cat."

When they say things like that, you want to buy them ice cream and popcorn and chocolate and not even ask them to wash their hands.

"Let's find a ride you *can* do, Aunt Cat."

We found the Kansas Tornado back in Munchkinland. This was the very tornado that carried Dorothy to Oz, although, luckily for us, it had been plopped down here in the form of a kind of racetrack that zoomed up and down through cloud shapes until it got going so fast that it could spiral upside down through a blue tube.

He loved it. I was the adult, presumably, but I had that mixed scared-thrilled feeling, as well as the don't-make-a-fool-of-yourself-in-front-of-the-child feeling, and when I got off I staggered for the first two or three steps. I was glad we hadn't gotten to the ice cream and popcorn yet.

Then we did the Flying Monkeys back in Gillikin country, where everything was purple. The Flying Monkeys was actually a merry-go-round with monkeys in place of horses, and the music playing was "Over the Rainbow." The merry-go-round was purple, naturally, highlighted with Day-Glo violet and lighted with both ordinary and ultraviolet light. The ultraviolet light on the violet Day-Glo made the highlights look practically radioactive.

We found a booth where you put your head in an opening and could have your picture taken as the Tin Woodman, Scarecrow, Cowardly Lion, Dorothy, or the Wicked Witch. I elected to be the Wicked Witch, which put Jeremy into fits of laughter while he watched me be digitally photographed. I put the photo in my pocket. He made me promise to give him the picture to take home with him at the end of the evening.

"Now I really need ice cream or popcorn," I said.

"Or both."

Laughing, I said, "Watch it, buster. With you it's always gimme, gimme, gimme."

There was an ice cream stand next to the Emerald City roller coaster. Fortunately, it had more flavors than just green pistachio. Personally, I have never understood why anybody orders anything other than chocolate ice cream, although chocolate chip, fudge ripple, and double-double chocolate aren't bad. We stood eating ice cream and watching all the fun things around us.

The festival security and info staff all wore gray-colored shirts with OZ on the back in big white letters. Except for the shirts' color they were reminiscent of the uniforms of the Wash & Brush-up Company in the movie. I had asked my brother Barry why the festival hadn't used green for the Emerald City, but he said that he wanted them to be obviously security, not theme-park characters. There seemed to be a lot of security people out here tonight. Maybe the whole staff was required to attend the opening, since the mayor and the superintendent of police and other Chicago big enchiladas were going to be here. Security would have to be good. Most likely the staff would be subdivided into smaller shifts tomorrow.

Each night of the festival featured a different special event. Tomorrow a performance of *The Wizard of Oz* would be held on the outdoor stage where the ceremonies were going on tonight. Then, over the week, there would be a Dorothy look-alike contest, a Toto look-alike contest, Scarecrow look-alike, and so on. One night was Munchkin tumblers with a prizewinning high school tumbling group starring as Munchkins.

The Horse of a Different Color passed us by. He was pink. I had been in the organization offices when Barry and the horse people had discussed this effect. The anticruelty advisers quite rightly would not permit horses to be painted. So the decision had been made to get three white horses, oil them lightly, and sprinkle them with vegetable-derived food colorings. They used beet powder for pink, turmeric for yellow, and something vegetable in origin that I can't remember for green. As far as I knew, they weren't doing blue or purple. The colors would wash off with a hose. I had wondered aloud what would happen if it rained and the little children saw a pink horse turn white.

"That'll just be the magic of Oz," Barry said.

It was exciting, being involved in the creation of a festival. I've always liked finding out how things work, and up to now festivals and fairs and such things just seemed to happen. Getting in on the mechanics of it had been a revelation. I liked the festival's creative people, too, with the possible exception of the public relations firm of Glitz & Slick. Okay, so that isn't quite their name. It should be.

Jeremy was thrilled with the pink horse, led around by a young woman dressed to look like Scraps, the Patchwork Girl. But he *really* giggled when the Tin Woodman appeared, wearing a suit of shiny, real metal, making creaky noises, and carrying an oil can.

"Can I oil you?" Jeremy asked.

The Tin Woodman said, "Yes, please oil my knee; it's very stiff today." He bent the knee, making a creaky noise, and handed Jeremy the oil can. Jeremy applied it to the knee and squeezed the handle. A small jet of what I assumed to be water squirted out. Jeremy jumped for joy.

By now it was getting dark. I glanced at my watch, and saw it was just past eight o'clock. Not yet time to meet Barry.

Jeremy was studying me closely. "Aunt Cat, can we play together again soon?"

"Of course, Jeremy."

"Like maybe tomorrow?"

I looked more carefully at him. "Why? Any special reason?"

"Not too much."

"Tell me, honey."

"Well, you know. Mom's been kind of sick. And Dad's been real busy."

His mother had had some clotting problems toward the end of the pregnancy and had been told to stay in bed. And now, of course, with the new baby—

"Jeremy, your dad had a lot to do preparing for this festival. There were last-minute important pieces of equipment that didn't arrive. Like the Flying Monkeys merry-go-round was on a truck in Omaha, and the truck broke down, and they didn't think it would get here in time. Which would have been awful. And then they had that big rain two days ago and some of the electric cables shorted out from getting soaked. I think he's going to have a lot more free time now."

I looked up from the child and realized that the formal ceremonies were beginning. Though I couldn't see from here, the schedule said the mayor would be over at the bandstand near the Emerald City castle, probably preparing to cut green tape. Festival-goers strolled toward the sound of trumpets. The Royal Army of Oz, which was composed entirely of twenty-eight officers, no privates because they had all been promoted, would parade past the bright green bandstand with its bright green bunting. The mayor would speak; the Park District Commissioner would speak. I think even the superintendent of police was going to speak. An Oz expert from the Harold Washington Library was going to speak. The ceremonies would end with a big parade.

I was planning to stay far away from the bandstand area if possible. No reflection on all the luminaries, but I've heard pretty much all the politicians' speeches I need for the rest of my life.

Apparently I wasn't the only person who felt this way. I saw three of the festival developers plus Tom Plumly hanging out at the side of the Mo popcorn stand in Quadling country as the crowds drained happily toward the bandstand. E. T. Taubman, the lighting designer I'd met during the early planning stages of the festival, who had been responsible for most of the great effects, stood chatting with Plumly, the festival's head of security, Edmond W. Pottle, a banker and a festival backer, and another man I hadn't met "personally" but knew to be Larry Mazzanovich. Larry was a contractor. He had built the Emerald City castle and a lot of the specialty items. I'd seen him around the area. I wanted to wave to Tom Plumly if he looked over our way, or go say hi and ask Jeremy to tell him with what great delight a kid responded to the fair. Plumly would like that. But Plumly's back was toward us and they were halfway hidden behind the popcorn palace and seemed very intent on their conversation.

"Yo, Cat!" Jennifer Denslow came striding up behind us. She's a tall, vibrant woman with red hair and a creamy complexion. When you're short and kind of middling in coloration, you notice these things. I liked her a lot and we'd become friends, hanging out a bit together. You know how occasionally a person seems like an old friend from the first moment of meeting. Jen was the computer systems designer for the festival. She had put together the sequences for the sound system and adapted a lot of theme-park software motherboards for the festival to use. Not only had she done it brilliantly, but she'd kept the costs down. After all, Great Adventure and Disney World and Renaissance Faire and maybe even Dollywood might be in existence for decades, or centuries, but the Chicago Oz Festival was a ten-day wonder. At best, it might become an annual event, but it would still have to pack up, fold its tents, disassemble its castle, send back its specialty items, and get out on July 15.

"Jennifer, this is Barry's son, Jeremy."

"Aha! Another *J*," she said, holding out her hand. Jeremy shook it in a very grown-up fashion, while I said, "Another Jay?"

"Jeremy. Jennifer. The finest initial letter in the alphabet," she said to the child. "Very graceful letter to write." She made a truly graceful sweep with her hand, with curlicues as it tailed off. "The only other letter that comes close to such outstanding elegance is S. Have you ever thought about that, Jeremy?"

"Well, no. But I will *now*." He smiled up at her. He looked as if he was falling in love.

"See," she said, "*A* is quite clunky. Up, down across. *B* is blobby, don't you think?" She gestured.

He nodded vigorously.

"*C* is not bad, but it ends awfully soon. Less than half of a well-made *J*."

"Hey!" I said. "I'm a *C*."

"Well, it's not bad. But *J* is excellent."

Jeremy twirled around three or four times, swinging his arms, just to show her a *J* in motion.

Then Jeremy said, "Hey! There's Dad!"

Barry was a little distance away, over near the Tornado, but kids can pick their parents out at a distance, just as parents can see their child in a big crowd of children. Barry was striding across the open space where the blue Munchkin-land Tornado ride terminated. Jeremy shouted "Dad!" but of course with all the noise and shouting and distant band music, Barry didn't hear us.

Just then Tom Plumly left the group and ran past us. He was heading toward Barry, and frantically calling his name, loud enough that I could hear him over the celebrations. Another Oz Festival emergency, I guessed.

Jennifer, Jeremy, and I followed Plumly. We weren't particularly worried about whatever was happening. It was just puzzling. Instead of halting and talking with Barry, Plumly caromed into him. Plumly clutched at Barry, or Barry grabbed Plumly (I couldn't quite tell which), and they struggled briefly. By then, Jennifer, Jeremy, and I were closer to them. Plumly sagged and fell limp to the ground. Barry stood there, stunned. He bent down over Plumly. Then he yelled, "Somebody get a doctor! Security! Help us out here!"

Nobody responded instantly, of course; people never

react that fast. There was no security nearby. They were probably all at the ceremonies. Barry got his cell phone from his pocket and yelled into it.

"I need paramedics at the Tornado. *Right away!* I have a seriously injured man here!"

Jennifer and I hurried up and leaned over Plumly to try to help him. I didn't stop to think that Jeremy might be seeing something unsuitable for a child, somebody very sick.

But it was worse than a sick man. A huge patch of blood stained the front of Tom Plumly's shirt, and a pool of blood was spreading next to him. As I reached out to pull Jeremy away, I saw a short knife on the ground near the security chief's hand, an ordinary jackknife with a handle of about five inches and a blade the same length.

Jennifer rose from a crouch. She said, "I think he's dead." With a look of horror, she stared straight at my brother Barry.

· 2 ·

PEOPLE COME AND GO
SO QUICKLY AROUND HERE

Barry looked at us and I could almost read his thoughts from the expression on his face. He was appalled that we were here. He started to come toward us, but must have realized that he was the only festival official on hand and he had a responsibility. And, of course, I was available to take care of his son. He waved his hand at me. "Get Jeremy away."

I had already picked Jeremy up in my arms and was backing away. Barry shouted, "I have to get help. But, Cat, don't let Jeremy see this. Go someplace!"

I couldn't agree more.

By then two security guys had arrived near Barry. Jeremy was twisting in my arms. "Is that guy sick?" he asked.

"I'm afraid he is."

"But he looked like he was dead. I mean, he was all bloody. Wasn't he?"

"Well—" I've never been an advocate of lying to children "for their own good," and even if his parents would have handled this differently, they weren't here; I was the person on the scene. "I don't know whether he's dead, Jeremy, but you're right about the blood."

Walking as well as I could carrying a rather large child, I finally staggered us around the Emerald City castle and the bandstand to the purple Flying Monkeys merry-go-round in Gillikin country. "Jeremy, could you get on and ride without me for a couple of minutes while I wait here and see what your dad wants to do?"

"Sure."

It might seem heartless to ride a merry-go-round while somebody dies forty yards away, but this was a child, and he had never met Plumly, and in any case, I had to think. I had to think really hard.

At the moment the merry-go-round started moving again, Jennifer caught up to me.

"We'd better talk," she said.

"Right. I know."

"When Plumly ran past us, I didn't see any blood on him. Did you?"

"No."

"And then he struggled with Barry. Right?"

Sadly, I said, "Right."

"And then after that he fell down and then when we got there he was covered with blood. Right?"

"Right."

"Barry's your brother. I feel really horrible about this, Cat. But I still can't cover up—"

I was trembling now, I was so scared. I knew what she was going to say, and I knew she had to do what she was going to do.

She said, "I have to tell the police."

"I know." After a couple of seconds, I said, "I will, too. I'm sure there's an explanation. But what am I going to tell Jeremy?"

*   *   *

Jennifer started slowly back to where Barry and the dead Plumly were. As she left, I called after her, "If you get a chance, tell Barry that I'll stay here for a while. No, wait. You'd better *make* a chance to tell him, please. Tell him I'll hang around the merry-go-round here for a half hour or so, and if he can't get away, I'll just take Jeremy home. To my place. I need to talk to Barry, but Jeremy shouldn't be around if there's going to be, you know, unpleasantness."

She nodded soberly and walked away. Then she turned and spoke in a normal voice, just loud enough for me to hear. "I'll have to pass on to the police that you saw it, too."

"I know that." At pretty much the same moment, a police car pulled up next to one of the equipment trailers. The squad car had its lights on, and now festival-goers who were not at the opening ceremonies were crowding in to see what all the fuss was. A couple of cops on foot came in from the other side of the castle.

Many, many minutes passed. I wished I had brought my cell phone. I could have called Maud and let her know what was happening. Still, given the precarious state of her health, maybe I wouldn't have called even if I'd had the phone with me. The next time the merry-go-round stopped, I handed two tickets to the operator and got on to ride with Jeremy. We rode and stopped, at which point I had to fork over two more tickets, and then we rode around some more. Round and round and round. Like the worries in my head.

"Cat!" a voice called. Jeremy had been riding a purple-and-white flying monkey for twenty minutes, and could probably ride an hour longer. I was standing in front of him, near the monkey's nose. As the merry-go-round revolved, facing us toward the center of the fairground, I saw that the person calling me was Jennifer.

"What's happening over there?" I asked, hoping she'd put the answer in a way that didn't upset Jeremy.

To talk with me, she walked alongside the moving merry-go-round. "The police are taking statements. Barry has given them a sketchy idea of what happened, and he's waiting in the management office for them to get back to him. He says to tell you he can't leave right now."

"Did you tell the police what you saw? What we saw?"

"Yes. I had to."

The merry-go-round was still moving, but Jennifer was young and had no trouble keeping up with it.

"So should we go home? Did you ask him?"

"Yes. He says for you to take Jeremy home to their house—"

"Not yet," Jeremy said.

We had planned that I would turn Jeremy over to Barry after the ceremonies, and Barry would take him home. To his place, of course. But now I would have to, which meant a longish drive to Oak Park for me. I said, "We can always come back tomorrow, honey. There's been a really bad accident, and they'll probably close down the middle part of the festival for a while."

"Aw—"

"And we've done a lot of the rides already." The merry-go-round began to slow down.

Jennifer said, "I'd better get back."

The merry-go-round began to turn away from her.

"See you tomorrow?" she called. She walked toward the Emerald City castle. As we moved away, I looked back and waved.

Her head exploded. A cloud of mist and particles burst out of her forehead. The merry-go-round still turned, very slowly now. For a moment I could hardly understand what had happened. Then I thought, Thank God Jeremy was facing forward.

"Jennifer!" I shouted.

The nose of the Flying Monkey that Jeremy sat on exploded.

I didn't understand at first, but my body did. I grabbed Jeremy, ducked under the forms of two monkeys ahead of ours, and jumped off the slowly moving merry-go-round.

We were now on the far side of the ride, away from Jennifer. With Jeremy pressed to my chest, his face in my shoulder, I ran to a food stand and, half hiding behind it, peered up over the counter. I wanted to help Jennifer, but I was very much afraid she was beyond help. I was afraid for our lives. I hoped the counter and the other equipment were enough to make us hard for the shooter to see.

I was pretty sure the attacker had been beyond Jennifer, toward the middle of the fairground, when the shooting started. There were booths next to the merry-go-round, and its mechanical center was solid. This meant we had been farther away from the attacker than she was. That, at least, was to our advantage.

I couldn't see much from here, so I peeked between the food stand and the fare booth. Jennifer was flat on the ground, maybe thirty yards away, all splayed out like a rag doll, none of the tension of life in her limbs. Although it was impossible to be sure at this distance, it looked as if part of her head was just gone. A man stood near her, rigid and screaming, which was stupid. The shooter could still be nearby and might shoot him, too. Besides that, he was doing Jennifer no good. But people do stupid things under stress. And, to be fair, the crowd couldn't have realized yet that there had been a shooting. For all they knew, Jennifer had fallen and hit her head. The sound of the shots had been masked by the noise of the festival, the horns and trumpets of the marching band, and the assailant wasn't in sight. Only the few people near Jennifer would even see her wound, although a couple of worried women were now hurrying toward her. They didn't yet realize what the problem was.

Two security men in gray OZ shirts ran up, one pulling a cell phone from his pocket. He was speaking loudly enough so that I could hear him. "Get that doctor over to the Flying Monkeys! Get paramedics!"

Jennifer had help. If she were still alive and in need of help, which I very much doubted.

My job was to save Jeremy.

· 3 ·

WE'RE OFF TO SEE
THE WIZARD

"Come on, Jeremy! We've gotta run."

Running would be a lot faster than me carrying him. The kid runs like a mink. Whenever we play keep-away in his backyard, he outruns me. And gloats about it shamelessly.

He followed, but not fast enough. "What's wrong, Aunt Cat?"

"There's a bad guy around here. *Please* come on!"

Jeremy picked up his speed, and we raced away from the merry-go-round, keeping it between us and the general area the shots had come from. We crossed the Yellow Brick Road into Winkie country, which was yellow. There were several refreshment stands here. We slipped behind one that claimed to sell "fried mangaboos." But the scent was of fried potatoes. Then, holding Jeremy's hand, I ducked between that stand and an equipment trailer.

"Let's stop here a second and let me take a look around."

I put Jeremy behind me and crouched down to peer under the trailer. It was one of those large squarish silver things that construction companies sometimes use as tool cribs. In this case, it had been brought in to store foods that didn't need refrigeration and supplies like paper napkins, straws, and cold-drink cups. We were now about a hundred yards away from Jennifer. Only a minute had passed since the second shot, although it seemed much longer. The crowd did not yet understand what was going on.

The strip of festival I saw from peering under the truck were some legs, grass, walkways, the bottoms of amusement rides, and the wheels of strollers and bicycles. Most people were still at the ceremonies. There were men's legs, men's shoes, some running shoes too big to likely belong to women. And children's little feet and legs. Also a few small women's shoes, of course.

Still, how could I tell which were threatening, or even whether somebody out there was really after us? Could the shooter have given up and gone away?

Looking between milling legs from a distance, I was also barely able to see two paramedics as they crouched down, working on Jennifer. The paramedics' unhurried body language made it sadly clear that she was dead.

I saw a pair of legs wearing dark pants, feet in ordinary men's black shoes. They drew near the EMTs—checking whether Jennifer was dead?—then did a sidestep, moving laterally around the downed woman. I could easily imagine the man's eyes scanning the crowd, searching for Jeremy and me. But I couldn't see any of him above the knees. While the other people were approaching Jennifer, curious to see what was wrong, these feet now backed away.

Moving in a slow arc, the feet were coming closer to where I hid. Then they vanished behind other figures.

More cops arrived. I heard sirens.

"Jeremy, let's get going."

"Where, Aunt Cat?"

I wish I knew. "Out of here, hon. Follow me."

Countering the man's direction, we crept away past the fried mangaboos stand, past a rare book and memorabilia dealer. The rare book table was brightly lighted and I turned my head away and thrust Jeremy on my far side as we slipped past.

Once beyond the book dealer, I walked rapidly, holding Jeremy's hand. Our best bet was probably to circle around and ask the paramedics for help. None of the security people or police were close enough—now when I needed them—but we'd just have to take the chance and run to the EMTs. They'd protect us. I hesitated for a couple of seconds only because I didn't want Jeremy to see Jennifer's ruined head, but I was terrified he might be shot. I inched closer, ready to run over to the paramedics.

"Let's go talk with the—"

A shot buzzed past my shoulder, striking the forearm of one of the paramedics and going through to hit the side of a food stand just beyond him, making a wooden thump. The man jumped up holding his arm. I heard the sound of the actual shot a fraction of a second later. I ducked back. Whoever it was, he had got halfway behind us.

Suddenly the crowd realized there was an assailant out there with a gun. They had been milling in confusion before, now there was confusion on the hoof. The instant the first person started to run, they all ran. People shrieked and then men, women, and children stampeded witlessly in every direction. They didn't know where the shot had come from, only that somebody was shooting. The EMTs threw themselves flat on the ground. The security men a little distance away scattered apart. Two cops pointed to where they thought the shooter was. But they pointed in two different directions. They yelled, "Get away! Get away!" The crowd stampeded.

This was the time to get Jeremy out of sight. Under cover of people running every which way, we ought to be able to get ourselves lost.

There was a narrow alley formed by a food booth and the side of a power shed. Electric cables crisscrossed it.

"Come on!"

I ran, pulling Jeremy with me, into the darkened space. Beyond was a forest of boxes. "Come on. Come on." We tore along among them.

One of the Grant Park garage ventilation cribs was ahead of us. These are rectangular concrete air wells, like squat, square chimneys. Many of them have stone benches built around them to make them look less industrial. This one was angled, with benches only on the lower side. They all have metal grates on top, but on this one the grate had not been replaced properly. It was slightly askew. I gave the heavy grate a huge push and managed to gain another few inches of space.

"Let me go first." I had no idea if the air well was deep. I had to be sure there was footing, so that Jeremy wouldn't fall.

The air shaft was quite clean, and it led into a downward-slanting tunnel. Though the angle was fairly steep, it was not impossible to walk down, and the slope led to a flat area beyond the opening that faded away into darkness. Darkness and invisibility looked very inviting right now.

"Come on, Jeremy. Hurry!"

"I don't like this, Aunt Cat!" He had squirmed in and stood about eighteen inches inside the air shaft mouth, half crouched and peering down. His head was above the level of the outside cement frame. I just hoped the shooter wouldn't see him. He would give our position away if he stayed there.

"I don't like this either, but I like it better than up there. Come *on!*"

He edged a tiny bit farther in, slipping one foot forward, then bringing up the rear foot near it, then crept farther in.

"Come on," I said. "Trust me. It isn't hard. I can do it and I'm *old*."

He giggled. I was getting scared for him. I pictured his head exploding. To myself I whispered, "Damn it, Jeremy!" Imagining a shadow looming up behind him, gun in its hand, I grated out, "Jeremy, don't be a big poop!"

That did it. He came the rest of the way in.

Holding hands, we half-slid down the slope to the level area. Light carried into the darkness farther below, and didn't diminish much as we went in, or maybe my eyes were adjusting to the dark as we moved. The slope had been clean but there was a lot of trash down here on the level, washed in by rain. The lower area was a jumbled mass of soggy stuff. Most of it was paper and plastic debris. Unfortunately, some of it looked like the dried corpses, furry lumps, or skeletons of dead birds and dead rodents.

I led Jeremy to a cement buttress that had a wide collar coming up about two feet from the floor. We could sit on the edge, and I needed a breather.

"What are we going to do, Aunt Cat?"

"We're going to have an adventure and then go home at the end of it. But I have to think for a minute, honey. Okay?"

"Okay."

It wasn't so easy to think. I knew my brother. I knew he wouldn't shoot at his own child. Or—I thought I knew him. But Jennifer had said that after being interviewed Barry was waiting in the management office, which suggested nobody had been keeping an eye on him. It was horrible enough to suspect he might have stabbed Plumly. Still, I had to face that possibility; I had seen Plumly before he struggled with Barry and he had looked okay, though upset. After the struggle, he was bloody.

Wait. The knife had looked like it had fallen from Plumly's own hand. Maybe he had stabbed himself.

Oh, sure! What wishful thinking that was. If he stabbed himself, why was somebody shooting at Jennifer and Jeremy and me? Plumly must have pulled the knife out of the wound at some point and it fell from his hand when he collapsed.

What a hideous thought—that Barry might have stabbed him! To me there is something much uglier about sticking a blade into another person, up close and personal, than shooting him, even though the effect on the victim may be exactly the same.

Why shoot me or Jeremy?

The killer had to believe we had seen something that was dangerous to him. Jeremy, me, and Jennifer.

Which led me right back to Barry. Hell.

And why Plumly? Really, the most important fact about a murder is *who* was murdered, isn't it? What had he done, or what had he found out?

Plumly. Why would anybody kill the security chief?

Suddenly, the light from the tunnel opening dimmed. A figure was standing in the mouth of the shaft, where the glow from the festival entered. Someone was looking into the tunnel.

He couldn't possibly see us. Please not. We were in darkness; he was in light. But I could see the outline of a person.

At that instant, he made me think of the Tin Woodman.

I whispered, with my hand cupped to his ear, "Jeremy, we have to be very quiet." I stood up. "Follow me quietly. Take my hand."

"I'm scared, Aunt Cat."

"Jeremy, do you remember in *Dorothy and the Wizard in Oz*, Dorothy had gone to California, and there was a big earthquake and Dorothy, and Jim the cab-horse, and the boy Jeb, all fell down a hole in the earth? And they had lots of adventures? And then finally they came to Oz."

"Of *course* I remember!"

"Well, this is a lot like that."

"Some of their adventures were scary, Aunt Cat. The Mangaboos, the vegetable people, were going to plant them. And they were chased by invisible bears."

That's a lot like this.

"We're going to have to be brave for a while. And resourceful, Jeremy, because I don't think we're in Kansas anymore."

· 4 ·

IF I ONLY HAD A BRAIN

Plumly. Why kill Plumly?

The last time I had seen Plumly before tonight was when I had dropped by the festival office in the Emerald City castle on Monday, three days ago. Actually, I had intentionally gone there, since the middle of Grant Park wasn't anywhere one would ordinarily "drop by." I was just curious to find out what was new, and didn't particularly expect to run into Plumly.

Plumly had been sitting at one of the two desks in the temporary little structure, filling out some kind of city permit. I said, "Hi, Tom."

"Cat! Nice to see you. Wanta do my job? I'm tellin' you, if I see one more stack of forms from the city, my joints are gonna seize up like the Tin Woodman."

"Aren't the forms all done by now?"

"I wish. They've got some idea that we didn't send in half the food permit sheets. You know, the health certifications for the food handlers. But we did. The city lost them."

"Well, did you keep copies?"

"Please! Every single piece of paper is copied three

times and filed in three different offices. My company office, the council offices, and Barry's office. God forbid one of the offices should have a fire."

"Well, send them the copies and prove you filled them out earlier."

He gave me a pitying grin. "Don't you think I've thought of that? Sure, I could prove to them we did it before. Wouldn't matter. They want an original. The actual ink on the actual paper they give you. With real pen dents. Nothing else is good enough."

"Oh."

"Sound like a Chicago municipal-style, moronic, pointless, unnecessary demand to you?"

"It really does."

"I gotta get out of here for a couple of minutes. Otherwise I'll freak." He slapped the pile of finished papers down next to the larger stack of unfinished ones. "Let me show you what's new."

I had not spent much time with Plumly and didn't know him well at all. He seemed pleasant but maybe a little harried. He had been a Chicago cop for twenty-five years, then retired at the age of fifty and formed his own security firm. That had been only four years ago, and yet he had landed this plum job, so I assumed that he had some clout someplace. While clout was a true Chicago phenomenon, I didn't much like it.

We walked out of the Emerald City castle into a beautiful sunny afternoon. In the three days since I had last been there in the park, a whole lot had been accomplished. Most of the extra landscaping was now in place. The paths were painted yellow, although the brown overlay depicting the brick grid pattern hadn't gone down on top yet. Several of the rides were up, and the Kansas Tornado was being tested. Like a theatrical load-in, the festival had to move in all at once. You don't tie up public space any longer than you have to.

"Been a lot of last-minute work, I suppose," I said to Plumly, just to get the conversation going.

"Oh, jeez, yes! Everything that could go wrong went wrong."

"What are you doing right now?"

"As you say, last-minute stuff. We're checking staff applicants' backgrounds through Lexis, Nexis, and public databases. Half of these vendors didn't know who-all would be working for them until this week. Their own staff is mostly needed at their regular stores. We *prevent* crime. I hope. It's not just clearing the employees, although that's big. You don't really want serial killer John Wayne Gacy working in the popcorn booth."

"No."

"These days there are a lot of lawsuits about what's now called negligent hiring. There's no national database of non-hirables yet. So you have to cybersearch every person individually on several databases. We also do preventive design. You can set up the physical space so that crime is less likely. For instance, I'm sure you realize the food stands are not part of the ticket system. The tickets are for rides. The customers pay for specific food when they buy it."

"Actually, I hadn't thought about it."

"Well, anyway. They do. So, unlike the rides, the food stands take in hard cash. I make the stands all keep their cash register more than an arm's length from the counter."

"Oh, I see. So the customer can't reach over and snatch cash out of the cash drawer."

"Right. It's perfectly simple, but people don't think of it. Especially restaurants that are used to doing it their own way on their own premises. They aren't always thrilled, either, when I tell them they have to do it my way here.

Tomorrow they'll be finishing the setup of the booths. Even though I told them several times, I'll go around and find out that half of them didn't conform."

"So you actually train the vendors."

"Sure. We do all kinds of things. Preplanning, for instance, so that the space is kind of cut up and foot traffic is organized for small groups, so that you don't encourage mobs. Fire prevention. We wander around eyeballing everything and asking ourselves, How could that particular booth or ride or whatever catch on fire? A lot of the hot-food booths have serious fire potential. There's LP gas for cooking and hot fat for frying and so on. There's huge barrels of wastepaper. We get somebody from the fire department in to take a look, of course. Other duties? We install security cameras. And once the festival opens, we'll get into the ever-popular policing of alcohol and drugs."

"You can buy beer at the BluesFest."

"But not at the Oz Festival. This is a child-oriented event. Still, there will be plenty of people selling prohibited substances under the table."

"A security firm must need multitalented people."

"We have to have a lot of different specialists these days. We even do corporate liability consultation. Security in the United States is a thirty-billion-dollar business. But it's like any other business. To grow, you have to have a track record, credits. Unfortunately, you have to have a track record to get hired and you have to get hired to develop a track record. We did the JazzFest. And one of the art festivals. And we've done a lot of smaller jobs around the Chicago area. But this assignment is very important for us as a company. The Oz Festival is going to be our biggest credit. It's gotta be perfect."

"So you're being extra thorough."

"Yeah. Check and recheck. Back and forth. Round and round. Man! I wish I had wheels like a Wheeler."

"You know about the Wheelers?" I said without thinking. In *Ozma of Oz*, Dorothy washes ashore in a chicken coop after an accident at sea. She finds herself on a strange coast, where the hostile natives have wheels instead of hands and feet. Naturally, they are able to pursue her faster than she can run, but she evades them by running up a rock-studded hillside.

Plumly studied my face. "You're surprised I know about Wheelers, aren't you?"

"Um, frankly, I guess I am."

He stopped in his tracks, standing on the Yellow Brick Road. "You're a reporter, Ms. Marsala. You know my company is relatively new. I'm sure you think I paid somebody off to get this job. Chicago politics as usual?"

"Well, it wouldn't be *un*usual, would it?"

"Nope. But I didn't. I got the job through nepotism; that's a fact. My brother's married to the— Oh well. You could look that up, if it matters to you, although I can't imagine why it would. I got preference, yes, but I didn't pay anybody off. I draw the line at payoffs. In fact, I hate them." From the clench of his jaw, I thought he was telling the truth.

"Just theoretically, what's the difference between payoffs and nepotism, morality-wise?"

"In one case money changes hands; in the other, it doesn't."

"I know that." Unfortunately, I couldn't stop myself from frowning.

"Okay. Maybe there's not much difference. But I think when you introduce cold cash into a situation, it's just more corrupting." He heaved a sigh and changed the subject. "Anyway, I suppose you think a former cop who gets a job through favoritism doesn't have the sensitivity to read books?"

"Oh, great," I said. "When I came here a few minutes

ago, I was just curious about what was new in Oz. Now I'm superficial, hasty, and biased."

"Know thyself."

I laughed. "All right. I guess that's fair in a way. So you tell me. What sort of person are you?"

"A person who admires whimsy. You know, of all the delights of L. Frank Baum, I think whimsy was the most important. Remember the Gump, from *The Land of Oz*? He was a flying creature made up of two sofas, some leaves from a potted palm, and the stuffed head of an elklike animal? Wonderful!" He smiled. "People rarely do whimsy anymore. Nowadays it's all plotting or characterization or—gasp!—social significance."

I said, "I would think a security specialist like you would prefer reality."

"If you can build a safe reality, you will have time and space for your whimsy. But I like this work. I'm very happy to have this job. My company needs it badly, if we're going to survive. Still, the festival is quite commercial. And there's something a little non-Oz about that."

"Commercial? Of course. Somebody has to pay for all this. How would you get people to put up Flying Monkey merry-go-rounds if they weren't at least being paid for their work?"

"I understand the problem. Somebody has to pay me and my staff, after all. I just wonder—"

"What?"

"Whether the right people are making the decisions."

The Oz Festival was going to be a big credit for his company? Oh, lord! Now he was dead and the festival had a killer loose. I suppose it's a good thing we don't know what's lying in wait for us.

Thinking about Plumly, I wished now that I could introduce Jeremy to him, to show him that, however commercial the festival might be, a child loved it. Too late.

Down in the tunnel, I cuddled Jeremy. The silhouette up in the lighted end, the vague figure that reminded me of the Tin Woodman, moved, his head angling as if looking into the shaft. He couldn't possibly see us, because we were in darkness, but he suspected we were here.

The figure was distorted by the odd perspective, us looking up through a tunnel at him. Also the shape was illuminated from the back with yellow Winkie-country light so it was impossible to see features.

I couldn't even begin to guess whether it was Barry or not, or even a man or a woman.

I whispered into the child's ear, "Jeremy, be very quiet, and take my hand. We're going to move out of here."

He did exactly what I told him. What a good little guy he was. We walked carefully, first along the level area, then down another slope, watching out for trash and mud, both of which increased in quantity as we went downward.

The slope was gentle, though, and even after five minutes of picking our way, we were probably only ten or fifteen feet below the ground surface. That was my best guess, but it was terribly hard to tell.

On a level floor again, Jeremy and I felt our way into a smaller tunnel that led off the big sloping one. There were concrete groins here, and they formed alcoves behind themselves that offered shallow hiding places. The light from the outside hardly reached us. The damp air smelled horrible.

"Aunt Cat," Jeremy whispered in my ear, "I don't like this place."

"Neither do I, but let's wait here just a few minutes and see if the bad guy gives up and goes away."

After a couple of minutes something altered. The distant light, now barely visible far off, changed in intensity. Someone was moving through the tunnel.

Jeremy and I slipped into one of the alcoves and found that it had a still smaller space behind it formed by an old iron pillar. These iron supports are all over Chicago—under Chicago, really—because the city was built on what had been a swamp. In the late 1800s, many of the downtown streets were raised above swamp level on cast-iron stilts, the roadways and sidewalks laid over iron grids. In the century since then, many of the tunnel spaces underneath have simply been forgotten.

We huddled behind the pillar. It was rusty and flaky and something damp was running down one side, making dripping sounds as it hit the floor, but I was grateful for the icky pillar's existence.

Very little glow of light reached into our alcove. But the dim light was a lifeline. I couldn't imagine how horrible it would have been down here if we had been in total darkness. When I saw the glow dim slightly, my heart sank. I squeezed Jeremy's arm, hoping he would be silent.

If it were Barry moving around out there in the tunnel, wouldn't he call out to us? Wouldn't he call for Jeremy?

And if he called, should I answer?

If he called, would I be able to stop Jeremy from answering?

· 5 ·

LIONS AND TIGERS
AND BEARS

If I caught sight of the man, and if it was Barry, I decided I
would cover Jeremy's eyes. He mustn't see his father trying
to kill him. And what we could do about it later, assuming
we survived, would just have to be decided when and if that
time came.

But, in my heart, I could not believe the killer was Barry.
He was a gentle man. He had never shown the least sign of
violence, beyond a certain childhood fascination with the
high school wrestling team. In fact, he was probably back at
the festival offices, handling the crisis and coordinating
with the police. He would assume we had left the park,
since Jennifer had told him we would. He would think we
were halfway home by now, safe and sound.

We held absolutely quiet and perfectly still. I was so
scared Jeremy might twitch, or call out, or sneeze, or just
whimper, that I felt nauseated. Then, when he didn't, I was
so proud of him, I kissed the top of his head.

*If we ever get out of this, kid, you can have all the ice
cream I can afford.*

Why, in heaven's name, had I left my cell phone in the car? How stupid could I be? Oh well, like sour grapes thinking, I decided it probably wouldn't have worked down here anyway. Of course it certainly couldn't work if I didn't have it.

We waited. The dim light had returned, but the stalker could still be very near. He could have come into this smaller tunnel. Then I heard something rattle nearby, something like a tin can. I tried not to tremble.

Whoever it was, he was certainly in our tunnel now, somewhere beyond the alcove. Had he come in silently and then walked beyond, passing us? If so, was he now turning and creeping back? He couldn't be sure where we were, could he?

Jeremy whimpered. I froze. Oh, gee! Had the man heard the sound? I squeezed Jeremy's arm, telegraphing, "Be quiet."

Something ran past my feet. A rat? I almost screamed. But I held the scream inside, and Jeremy apparently hadn't felt the animal brush past.

Whatever it was slunk across the floor. I saw it go, and it looked too big to be a rat, but in the darkness I couldn't really be sure. Then from a few feet away I heard a man whisper, "Shit!"

We held still. An eon later, I realized that I had seen no shadow shift, no change in light intensity, for quite some time. Had he moved away? Maybe. Scared of the rat? Or more likely, convinced the rat had been the source of the sound Jeremy had made. I had not heard him walk away. Had he slipped farther into the dark tunnel? Or gone back the way he had come?

Was he lying quietly in wait? Possibly inches away?

Did I know whether he was ahead of us—or behind us? No.

What now? We couldn't very well go farther into this smaller tunnel, if the stalker had gone past. He'd probably double back eventually, when he didn't find us. We couldn't go back the way we had come, to the larger tunnel. He could be waiting there for us to try to get out. Near us, somewhere to the south, was the Grant Park Underground, a very large, two-level subterranean parking garage that could house six thousand cars and had lots of guards and cashiers and real, live people. If we could find it, we might get help. For now, we had to hold still.

While we waited, the bigger-than-a-rat creature came padding back. This time I looked carefully, trying to make use of the thin, almost colorless glow.

It was a cat! Only the general shape and the slinky movement told me. "You may have saved our lives," I whispered to it.

It didn't care. It sat down and licked a paw.

When I decided that our stalker couldn't still be nearby or we'd have heard him, I whispered to Jeremy. "Come with me. We have to be very quiet."

If I'd been alone, I might have been able to hunker down silently here behind the pillar all night, and hope the pursuer would give up and leave. Or maybe that he'd have to give up because otherwise his absence from the festival would be noticed, and as a result he'd later have no alibi. But we couldn't wait any longer. I didn't believe Jeremy could stand it. He'd been wonderful so far, but he was a little child, and he was very scared.

Not without reason.

I peered around the pillar as well as I could, but unless the man was using a flashlight somewhere down deep in the tunnel, my chance of seeing him was pretty close to nil. I listened, and listened some more. Once or twice I thought I picked up very distant, very faint sounds. But face it, the sounds could be rats. There might even be traffic noise from up above. No question there were ventilation grates a lot of places along these tunnels.

Holding Jeremy's hand, I ventured out of the alcove. "Be careful not to kick any trash," I whispered directly into his ear. He squeezed my hand instead of responding aloud.

Must remember later, when we've survived, to tell him that he's not only brave but also smart.

We must have looked like two cats ourselves, our body language softly sinuous, as we slunk along the tunnel. I had decided to take the small tunnel into the unknown, rather than go back to the bigger tunnel, reasoning the stalker most likely would eventually return the way he had come. He would probably try to trace us back to the vent where we had entered. Also, I was quite sure that Grant Park Underground was somewhat south of where we went into the grid. At the very least, *most* of it was south. To the east was Lake Michigan and to the west was Michigan Avenue. I was pretty sure we hadn't gone far enough west to be under Michigan Avenue in the old freight tunnels, but why take a chance? South it was.

The cat followed.

With eyes completely adapted to the dark by now, I could see a very faint hint of yellowish light ahead. Maybe I'd made the right choice.

Holding hands, we tiptoed along the cement floor of the tunnel, toward the distant illumination. If our stalker was sneaking up behind, he'd see us against the glow. But what else could we do? We had to find either some people or a way out of here, and where there's light, there should be people.

Now I was hurrying, almost pulling Jeremy, although

careful not to tug on his arm, trying not to frighten him more than he was already.

The light grew stronger. The light at the end of the tunnel, I thought in my head—an oncoming train?—and I came close to giggling. I stifled it. That *really* would have freaked Jeremy.

There was a bend up ahead. When we reached it, I saw that the walls in this part of the tunnel were tiled with snow-white glossy ceramic squares. How weird! How useless! Maybe this was an abandoned subway stop. There were a dozen or more of those scattered under the city. As we came into the light, I saw—glory be!—cars! Parked cars.

"Come on, honey! We'll find a guard."

We ran. The cars were thinly scattered here, with a lot of empty spaces. We were at the far edge of this garage level, the less desirable parking spaces, and the few cars left must be the remnants of the overflow of the day workers who flooded into the Loop every morning. We would know as the cars grew more numerous that we were nearing the booths. People coming to the festival this evening would have parked as near the exits as possible. Which was exactly what I had done. Jeremy and I had parked on level one. My Jeep—so near and yet so far.

The tollbooths had cashiers, but the booths were at the top of the ramp, wherever that was. The place was just so damn huge! Guards patrolled on some random sort of schedule, though, and as we got closer to the center, finding one should be easy.

I heard footsteps. There must be a guard up ahead.

"Hurry, Jeremy!"

We ran. "Guard! Help!" I yelled.

My voice echoed off the tiled walls.

And so did the footsteps. They were an echo, too. In fact they came from behind us.

A shot spanged against one of the support pillars. "Quick," I said, pulling Jeremy along with me.

Maybe a guard would hear the shot and come running. Sure. But he'd get here after we were dead. Or be shot himself.

We ran flat out. Grant Park Underground has emergency call phones at intervals, installed here after a series of rapes several years ago. As we raced by, I grabbed one. I couldn't take the chance of stopping to actually *talk* on it, but I gave it a toss and left it hanging by its cord. Maybe that would bring a guard. Maybe each phone read out its location somewhere in a central security control booth. I hoped it did.

But I'd bet they'd get here too late.

We ran on, hearing slapping footsteps running behind us. I flipped another phone off its cradle as we pelted past.

There were access tunnels where drains and electric cables threaded their way out of the garage. They were much smaller than the tunnel we had been in before, but there were several of them. Maybe we could confuse the man pursuing us.

"This one," I said aloud, and then as Jeremy turned toward it, I waved my hand to another just beyond. A gamble, but maybe our guy heard me, and if so, would follow the wrong trail. We plunged inside.

As soon as we got in the narrow tunnel, I put a hand on Jeremy's chest, slowing him down. Then I walked rapidly, but with exaggerated care. He imitated me. There were bulbs in wire cages along here, but they were at best twenty-five watts and two out of every three were burned out. Very shoddy maintenance; what do we pay our taxes for? Twenty-five watts is plenty to see by, though, in an otherwise completely dark place. I was grateful for them but fearful that they would let our pursuer see us. When we passed into a dark stretch, I stopped and looked back at a light a hundred yards behind. No figure passed into that yellow glow. Maybe we were safe.

As long as we didn't get lost. We came to places where the tunnel branched. The first split was a narrow-angle fork, and it seemed a good idea to take the right-hand one, because it was smaller. Jeremy was a small child. I'm a short adult. Therefore the man who was chasing us had to be larger than we were, since virtually all adults are larger than I am. At the second, which was a T-junction, we took the left. Later a right. If we got completely lost and needed to come back, I should be able to remember that we'd gone right, left, and right again, alternately.

Something brushed against my ankle. I jumped in terror, hitting my head on the low cement ceiling.

The cat had followed us through the garage and into the new maze of tunnels.

Jeremy kept up with me. But he was making soft whimpering noises, quietly enough so I doubted he could be heard. The signal was clear, though. He was near the end of his rope. I could feel a buzzing in the hand I held against his back, as if his chest were full of bees.

The tunnel was not only cramped but extremely unsavory. The farther we walked, the more horrible the odor became. I had recently done a short article on nonlethal police crowd control devices. One of them was an odoriferous exploding pellet that delivered a stink so disgusting that any crowd hit with it dispersed fast. Skunks perfected this type of warfare eons ago. Horrible smells apparently demoralize human beings very quickly.

I knew this hideous moldy, fecal, vegetable-rot smell would eventually pull the heart and gumption out of

Jeremy. Me, too. There was nothing to criticize when he finally crouched near the wall. "Aunt Cat, I'm scared. I can't go any farther."

"Aw, honey. Hold my hand."

"I'm scared, Aunt Cat. I'm really, really scared." For the first time, he started to cry, big, big tears. He was gulping and on the verge of panic. Before now he'd been frightened and hair-trigger tense, but I'd been able to keep him focused. This was serious. I hoped we were far enough away from our stalker so that stopping a few minutes wouldn't be disastrous. With the choices we had made of branching tunnels, the killer would have to be very lucky to be anywhere near us.

I thought it would help to talk seriously with Jeremy, beginning the conversation actually as a sort of therapy.

"Jeremy, you're a brave person. You're my very best buddy. This has been a lot for anybody to put up with, and you're doing very well."

"Really, Aunt Cat?"

"Shh. Not too loud. Jeremy, I don't mind telling you that I'm as scared as you are. But I think we've lost our hunter, and I know we're gonna get out of here."

He hesitated. Then he said, "Right-o, Aunt Cat."

"Right-o? Why the British accent?"

"Saw it on a James Bond video."

"Oh. And a very nice accent it is, too."

"I like James Bond," he said, squeezing my hand. "But not as good as the Wizard of Oz. The Oz books are very, very creative."

I smiled. "Indeed they are." You smile when a child says something that sounds adult, but you shouldn't; you're being condescending. I switched gears and nodded soberly.

"And it's a good thing there's a lot of them, isn't it?" he said.

Suddenly I knew what he was doing. He was chattering
to *cheer me up!* To encourage *me*.

I said, "We really are having an adventure, aren't we,
Jeremy?"

"Like Dorothy."

"Right. Tell you what. I'm the girl. I'll be Dorothy. What
will you be?"

"The Cowardly Lion?"

"No, you're too brave."

"So was he. He just didn't know he was. But okay. I'll be
the Scarecrow."

"Good."

Jeremy looked behind me. "And *he* can be the Cowardly
Lion. He looks just like him."

"He who?" I jumped and spun around in fear, but—
thank heaven!—it was just the cat again. In this light I
could see that he was a patchy orange and white. Because
my household has a VIP, a Very Important Parrot, I haven't
specialized in cats. Was this color pattern called marmalade? If so, it was a very dirty marmalade cat. A marmalade tom? For the time being, we might think of him as
a male cat. He generously permitted Jeremy to stroke his
back.

I said, "Good. He helped us back there. He's got every
right to come along if he wants to." The cat seemed to be
getting used to us. After Jeremy stroked the cat, he picked
him up in one arm, still rubbing his ears. I was about to tell
Jeremy that strange cats, especially feral cats, don't like to
be touched, but the animal lay in his arms purring. Jeremy
relaxed visibly. Soothing the cat had drained the fear out of
him. There was a red collar with white diamond patterns
around the cat's neck, so dirty that I hadn't noticed it before.
No tag was attached that I could see. After a minute or two
the cat jumped down.

Jeremy said, "We have Dorothy and the Cowardly Lion and the Scarecrow, but we don't have the Tin Woodman."

"No, we don't have the Tin Woodman." A chill ran down my spine. I said, "I'm feeling better now. How about you? Time to go on?"

"Sure, Aunt Cat."

· 6 ·

CURSES! SOMEBODY ALWAYS
HELPS THAT GIRL

The three of us walked steadily on, taking a right at another place where the tunnel diverged. At this point, I really had no idea whether we were going north, south, east, or west, but if we ever had to find our way back, I needed to keep alternating choices in a regular manner.

Where were we now? We could be under Grant Park or under Michigan Avenue. Unfortunately, if we kept going long enough, we could be almost anyplace under the central city. Several years ago, a company driving pilings in the Chicago River broke through the roof of an abandoned freight tunnel that ran under the river. They flooded half of downtown. Millions upon millions of dollars of damage resulted. Why hadn't they known the tunnel was there? Because they didn't have good maps. Why hadn't the city inspectors checked the site before permitting the piles to be driven in? Well, the inspector who was supposed to inspect didn't get there when he should have because *he couldn't find a parking space!*

You gotta love Chicago.

Anyway, that was the first time many Chicagoans, myself included, realized how extensive the tunnel system under the city really was. If you had a decent subterranean map, you could go almost anyplace anywhere in the downtown area without ever coming up where the daylight shines.

Unfortunately, there was no map down here with me and my buddy.

We hit another split, where we took a left, and I could feel my stomach muscles tightening from fear, a little more all the time. The tension in my neck was painful. Responsibility for this lovely, brave little child was almost freezing my ability to think. Did he want to ask me, *Aunt Cat, do you know where you're going?* Probably he did, and was just too nice.

Thank God for the occasional functioning lightbulb.

"Jeremy, what's that?"

"That noise?"

"Yes. That rumble."

"It sounds like cars. Up there." He pointed at the stained cement roof.

"I think so, too."

We were under a street. That was good. People are on streets. Help was maybe just a few feet away.

Above us. Through solid concrete.

"Let's think, Jeremy. If we're under a street, sooner or later, there's got to be a manhole."

Hope I'm right. Very much happier, I walked forward. The best thing was that as we walked, the automobile rumblings continued, which meant that we weren't walking away from the street into some deserted backwater, but along under a major throughway.

The tunnel went on and on and on. And in this section

there were very few working lightbulbs. We could hardly see the bulb behind us now, and none had appeared ahead yet. The dark was wetly oppressive, the damp like being in a wet paper bag.

"Aunt Cat!"

I jumped inches.

"Aunt Cat. Look up there!"

In the almost total darkness, his sharp young eyes had seen thick, staple-shaped wire metal brackets, set into the wall to form a ladder. And where there's a ladder, there ought to be someplace it goes. "Great, Jeremy!" I climbed up.

What I saw was exciting and daunting at the same time. A round iron manhole cover was visible in the low light, primarily because it was a dark red-rust color against the gray cement. From the circular collar area around it depended stalactites of yuck. The yuck was probably a mixture of road salt and street cruddies. From the crisp, crusty look of the stuff, it could have been accumulating there for a decade, sealing the opening.

I pushed the round iron lid.

The manhole cover wouldn't budge. I pushed and pushed at it, but I was standing seven steps above the tunnel floor with my feet wedged uncomfortably onto a metal bracket. If I pushed up with all my might, the bracket cut painfully into the bottom of my arches. I tried standing sideways to the ladder, placing my feet along the bracket instead of across it, but that put one foot ahead of the other. I pushed up hard, but the awkwardness of the position reduced my leverage.

It was so frustrating I almost cried. Here we were within earshot of safety. I whispered a few choice words under my breath, and that took some of the frustration away.

Standing with my feet crosswise on the bracket again, I

took a deep breath, held it, and gave a mighty heave. The iron lid moved, ever so slightly. Then a rumble passed above and it slid back in place.

Damn! Damndamndamn! Still, I had broken the seal that rust and street goo had put on it. The second time had to be easier.

Somewhere I had read that manhole covers were made round so that they couldn't fall into the hole, as square ones could. Thank heaven. Picturing this thing that felt like a hundred pounds of cast iron falling down on me and Jeremy would have been enough to make me give up.

"Are you okay, Aunt Cat?"

"Reasonably okay. Here I go again."

One more *huge* heave. I felt the muscles scream in my back. There—the lid was off! A thin crescent moon of light showed between the lid and the cement. Warier now about it slipping back, I pushed it more sideways than straight up, and the stupid thing moved much more easily, sliding rather than being held up by my sheer force.

Air! The glow of streetlights!

Jeremy said, "Yay!"

"Damn right! Yay!"

With another big push, the cover slid farther off. Suddenly, there was a crash and a rattle as a truck tire the size of a Zamboni rolled over it. I lurched back and lost my grip. I tumbled down the bracket ladder and stupidly tried to catch myself with my left hand. The hand got hold of a bracket and the weight of my body pulled my elbow and shoulder joint so hard I screamed.

I slid the rest of the way down to the wet cement floor.

"Aunt Cat! Aunt Cat! Don't be dead!"

Jeremy shrieked and wept and patted my face. My shoulder felt dislocated. "I'm not dead," I said, although frankly I wondered. Of course, it wouldn't hurt this much if I were.

Slowly, lying in the muck, I made myself sit up. Years ago,

my third brother had dislocated his shoulder falling off a playground jungle gym. I remembered the doctor had said if it was dislocated, my brother would be unable to raise his arm above shoulder level. I tried raising my arm above shoulder level. It hurt a lot. Whimpering in pain, I nevertheless was able to raise it. Not dislocated. It needed ice. Cat Marsala, instant orthopedist. But my first job was to get us out of here. Ice could come later.

Above our heads the manhole cover was tipping and rattling back and forth in the traffic vibrations. It had better not fall back into place.

"Jeremy, we can get out. But that's a busy street up there, so we'd better do this really, really carefully. You follow behind me up the ladder."

Right. Up the ladder. One-handed, maybe?

I was afraid that I would edge my head up into the open space only to have it clipped by a truck tire. I wished I had a periscope or even a mirror. It was so exciting to be within inches of safety that I could hardly restrain myself enough. However, I waited at the top of the ladder, with Jeremy just below me, while cars and trucks rumbled and thundered above. Then came a pause. That ought to mean a red light down the street.

I peeked up. Yes, there was a streetlight half a block away. The traffic had stopped, but the light was changing again.

"Okay, Jeremy. Get ready. We're going out in about two minutes. When I think it's safe I'll jump out. Then you come just to the top of the ladder. But be ready to duck back down *fast* if I say so."

In the event, it happened more easily than that. The light changed. Traffic was thin, and we climbed out fast and walked from the street to the sidewalk. We should have pushed the manhole cover back, but I was just too drained. I found a cop instead.

I showed him the manhole cover problem. He called it in to Traffic Control. I asked him to page my friend, Chief Harold McCoo. "About the shooting at the Oz Festival. Tell him I'm Cat Marsala." The cop looked at me kind of funny, seeing an unprepossessing, bedraggled, smelly, damp woman wincing in pain and holding the hand of a bedraggled, smelly, damp child. But he paged.

Jeremy and I sat in a squad car, listening to the police radio and trying to feel warm. McCoo was on his way. As I tried to relax I suddenly thought, What about the cat? I looked over at Jeremy.

He was just taking the cat out from under his shirt.

I smiled.

This was all fine, and thank God we were alive. But an even harder problem lay ahead.

What should I do about Barry?

· 7 ·

WE'VE COME
SUCH A LONG WAY ALREADY

"It can't be only ten after ten!" I was utterly amazed. Apparently Jeremy and I had been down in the tunnels only a little over an hour. It had seemed like four or five hours.

We were in the District Commander's office in the brand-new First District police station. My friend Harold McCoo had come in and declared that, even though the detectives would prefer to take us to the Area, which is where detectives ordinarily hang out, the new First District would be better for Jeremy. We were here already, for one thing, and McCoo believed it would upset him more to move him. Also, the new station was clean and bright and had quite a dazzling selection of food and drink machines. And milk, which somebody had poured into a plastic plate for the cat.

One of the detectives was bringing Barry to the First District from the festival, where he had been questioned. Remarkably, McCoo himself was taking a statement from Jeremy. A chief of detectives *never* does this kind of thing.

They don't go out on cases. Commanders of districts, who are below McCoo in the hierarchy, don't go out on cases either. Nor, despite what you see on television, do the lieutenants who rank still further down. But McCoo loved children and he realized that Jeremy was fragile.

Harold McCoo was a very good man.

"My name is Harold," he said, holding out his hand. Jeremy shook it soberly. Jeremy was veering back and forth in emotions, between excitement and the teary residue of fear.

"I'm Jeremy Marsala," he said.

"That was very brave of you, going down into the tunnels."

"Yeah, I guess. But we had to. The bad guy was chasing us."

McCoo is a middle-aged black man of medium height and stately motions. He doesn't rush; he's never flustered. His main problem in life, seemingly, is a constant fight with his weight. He loves food. Now he must have decided Jeremy needed a little distraction.

"You want to get something to eat from the machines? I've got plenty of coins."

"Sure!" Jeremy went out with McCoo. I stayed in my chair, on the theory that bonding between McCoo and Jeremy would be good for both of them. Besides, my shoulder was shrieking in pain and the less I moved the happier I was. In a couple of minutes they came back.

"McCoo!" I said, when I saw Jeremy return carrying Twinkies, a Hershey bar, a can of Coke, and a bag of hard candy. There had to be a pound of pure sugar in the collection. His parents would freak. Under my breath I muttered, "That's right. Bribe a child."

"What?"

"Uh, nothing."

McCoo said, "All the adrenaline you two've been pumping probably sucked up his blood glucose. Glycogen. Whatever. I'm just trying to replenish it."

"Yeah, yeah. I know a cop with a marshmallow heart when I see one."

"Very funny. Now, Jeremy, tell me how the bad guy started to go after you. What happened right at first, before the chase?"

"You mean when the man ran to Daddy?"

"Yes."

"Well, me and Aunt Cat were talking with Je-Jennifer. And then I looked around and this guy was sort of grabbing my dad. And then the guy fell down. And, no, wait, we started walking over to Dad and *then* the guy fell down, I think. And Aunt Cat and Jennifer went over to look at the guy who fell down but Dad said, Get Jeremy away, because you know how grown-ups always think things with blood are gonna be bad for kids."

"Yes, I know. Grown-ups are like that."

"And so we went to the monkey merry-go-round. And Jennifer went back to see. She could tell you about that part."

"Um. Yes. She did tell one of the officers about it."

"Okay."

So Jeremy didn't know that Jennifer was dead. I had felt fairly sure that he didn't. He could find that out later, if he had to. There had been enough emotional stress for him for one night.

McCoo said, "So now tell me about what you did next."

Jeremy picked up the cat and held it in his lap. Surprisingly, it didn't struggle or claw, but just settled down and closed its eyes. "Well, Aunt Cat said run. I didn't know why, but I figured it had to be important, so we ran. And she saw something bad, I guess, because there were all these *gunshots!*"

"That's very scary."

"So she said, Let's go down this thing like a slide, but made of cement, see, and we did, into the ground. And we thought we were safe, but then—"

Jeremy went on at some length, explaining everything we had done. He indulged in a bit of dramatization, but not much. He dwelled a long time on how bad the tunnels smelled, and he had been quite impressed by, as he put it, "coming right up out of the street."

McCoo said, "I'll bet you're not allowed to go out in the street by yourself."

He was right, of course. I hadn't thought about it at the time, but that was one reason why Jeremy had been so thrilled about climbing up out of the manhole.

"So, Jeremy, tell me about this guy who was chasing you."

He stroked the cat. "Well, he was 'normously *huge.*"

"How huge?"

"Very, very, very, very, very."

"Did you see him up close? Or from the front?"

"Not up close. He was in the—where the tunnel opened. I saw him when he came to the entrance."

"The entrance to the tunnel? Did you recognize him?"

This was the big question, of course. Jeremy drew in a deep breath. "He was like a shadow. Because—because— we were where it was dark."

"The light was behind him? So you couldn't see him well?"

"Yes. Only I saw he was *huge.*"

"You saw a silhouette?"

"That's like an outline?"

"Pretty much. More like you cut the person out of a

piece of paper. So, maybe you could see whether he was fat or skinny?"

"Sort of medium."

"Mmm. Anything in his hands? No? Didn't see? Any hat on his head?"

But Jeremy just didn't know. And I was glad at least that he didn't make anything up. A lot of adults couldn't have resisted adding details. Finally he said, "All I know is he was *huge*."

The door crashed open and Barry came rushing in, trailed by a short Asian police officer, who said, "I couldn't stop him, Chief."

"It's okay," McCoo said, no doubt greatly relieving the mind of the worried cop, who had begun to sweat at the idea of screwing up in front of the chief of detectives.

Barry paid no attention to either of them, running to Jeremy and sweeping him up into his arms. "Are you okay?"

Jeremy squirmed. "Yeah, Dad."

"They said somebody shot at you!"

"Well, yeah. But Aunt Cat escaped us."

Barry set Jeremy back down in a chair and felt his arms and legs as if he were looking for broken bones. "I thought you were home. I thought you were safe."

"He is safe, Mr. Marsala," McCoo said.

Barry looked around, apparently realizing for the first time that McCoo was there. "Harold McCoo," McCoo said, holding out his hand.

"Chief of detectives," I added.

"Why wasn't I told right away?" Barry demanded. "Instead of holding me there, asking me all kinds of questions. Spending two hours!"

"Well, Mr. Marsala, we didn't know—"

"You kept me there. I should have been here to take care of my child."

"Actually," McCoo said, "Jeremy and Cat have only been here about half an hour and we sent for you as soon as they arrived."

"I don't understand."

"Maybe Jeremy would like to tell you what happened."

Jeremy did. He was quite proud of his escape by now and told it with even more gusto than before. I'm pleased to say, though, that once again, despite dramatization, his facts were accurate.

"Oh, lord!" Barry said. "You're really not hurt? They shot at you? Are you hurt?"

He pulled Jeremy to him, but by this time Jeremy was embarrassed. "No, Dad. Come on. They didn't even come close."

A female police officer was called in to stay with Jeremy and the cat. She brought along a box of checkers and a foldable board. McCoo beckoned me and Barry and another cop into an interview room. These rooms have heavy metal staples set into the cement block walls for attaching prisoners' handcuffs. It's a very unpleasant kind of place, despite the fresh, light blue paint.

"I'm sorry about the room," McCoo said. "But I think it's less disruptive to Jeremy for him to stay there and for us to come here."

"All right, all right," Barry said. "What's the problem?"

"Sit down, Mr. Marsala," McCoo said. "This will take a few minutes."

"Get going then. I have Jeremy to think about."

"Let me tell you what Cat and Jennifer saw."

And he did.

Barry had heard that Jennifer had been shot and killed. Apparently, unless he was lying and had shot her himself, he had assumed that her death had been unrelated to Plumly's. Then, after hearing that Jeremy and I had been shot at, he thought Jennifer's death had been a mistake; they had been shooting at us. But he couldn't imagine why. Finally, after McCoo told him what Jennifer and I had seen, and that he was a suspect, he sat there, apparently stunned.

After maybe a minute, which is a long time if you're waiting for somebody to speak, he asked, "Cat, you really saw the same thing Jennifer saw?"

"I saw no blood on Plumly when he ran past us. The first time I saw blood on him was when we got to you, after he grabbed you."

He shook his head. "Not possible. I didn't notice any blood when he ran up to me, but he grabbed me before I really got a look at him." There was blood on Barry's sleeve. The tech had taken a sample of it, but we all knew it was Plumly's.

"Barry, if it had been just me, just my impression, I'd think I'd been hallucinating or something. But Jennifer saw exactly the same thing."

"But, Cat, you *know* me," he said. "I wouldn't kill anybody."

He turned to McCoo. "And the shooting," he said. "I don't get it. Why would I carry a gun on me?"

"Well," said McCoo, "why would anybody?"

"If I shot anybody, where's the gun? I don't even own one. This is nuts!"

"Mr. Marsala, we don't know where the gun is. We've got people out searching for it. By tomorrow morning, we may have found and identified the gun. The park is a difficult area to search in the dark. If we don't find it tonight, we'll have more people out looking first thing tomorrow."

"Yes, Barry," I said. "They'll find it's registered to somebody else, and they'll find that person, and discover why this all happened."

"And what if they don't?"

I couldn't answer. In fact, it seemed very doubtful that whoever had fired those shots at Jennifer and Jeremy and me would leave the gun where it could be discovered by the police.

Barry thought for another long while. Finally, he said to me, "If you thought I killed Plumly, Cat, then you must have thought I shot at you."

"Barry, I saw what I saw. But I don't believe you killed Plumly. And I know you wouldn't have shot at Jeremy and me."

Riding right over my words, he said, "And if so, you must have thought I might be the person chasing you in the tunnel."

Not knowing what I could add that wouldn't make things worse, I kept quiet.

"You thought I tried to kill my own child."

Breathily, I said, "No. No. I just told you, no."

Turning away from me, he said, "So will you let me take him home, Chief McCoo?"

"Take Jeremy home? Of course. You're not under arrest. He's your son. I have no authority to stop you."

And now I knew McCoo had considered what I had been too stressed or stupid to think of. If Barry had been shooting at Jeremy, how could we turn Jeremy over to Barry? God, what a mess!

Barry suddenly looked drawn and old. "All right! If you're worried, I understand. But I don't want him to go home with you, Cat. I'm angry at you."

"I have the sofa. He could sleep there—"

"I'll call Dad and Mom. They have a guest room. They can come and get him."

"What will you tell Maud?"

"Maud! Oh, shit!"

Barry dropped his head into his hands. He said, "I'll call her. I don't want you to say one word to her about this until we get this straightened out. She's still hemorrhaging off and on."

"I'm sorry—"

"If it hasn't stopped by Monday, they want her in for cauterization."

"That sounds awful."

"They call it 'minimally invasive,'" he said, smiling without humor. "Which is like the saying about minor surgery. Minor surgery is surgery on somebody other than you."

Barry looked at me with loathing. He was exhausted. He'd had a lot to deal with even before tonight. Maud had to have help in the house after the baby was born. Her mother had come to stay for the first two weeks and had just gone back to Florida a couple of days ago because Maud's dad had a health problem, too. Maud had a day-help caregiver now.

Barry said, "If Jeremy goes to Mom and Dad's, he can't worry Maud by telling her what happened. Actually, this is a good idea. I should do a few things at the festival tonight. It's in an uproar."

Now he was rationalizing the decision to send Jeremy to our mom and dad's, but if it made him feel better, it was okay by me. I was feeling hideous enough for both of us.

Barry could only manage a short period of positive thinking, however. After a few more mumblings, he sank into a grim mood. Finally, sounding surly, he said, "I'll call Dad and Mom. But I'll call Maud first."

The phone call was painful for all of us. The phone wasn't really private, and we could hear him begging her. "Don't even think of coming into town. Jeremy is perfectly all right. He was nowhere nearby when Plumly died."

Not only was this not strictly true, but Barry had said nothing to her about Jennifer's murder, Jeremy and me being shot at, or our run through the tunnels.

"I just can't get away so soon, honey. Anyway, you know how he likes to play with Dad."

There followed quite a long period of Barry listening. Then he said, "One night without pajamas is not going to hurt him. Please, Maud, let's keep our eye on the ball here. If you get sicker, who's to take care of him? And the baby?"

Some more silence.

"Sure. I should be home by one A.M. or so. I want to find you asleep."

Pause.

"Well, *please* let her get up and feed Cynthia."

Pause.

"You know we agreed to have her take one bottle a day from the very beginning. All right. 'Night."

Then he called Mom and Dad.

Barry went someplace in the building. McCoo said he was finishing making his statement, which would then be typed up, and Barry would read it and sign it. He had left without saying another word to me.

McCoo said, "Cat, I know he's your brother, but we're going to handle this by the book."

"I never said you shouldn't. But Barry is not a killer."

"Whether he is or not, I believe Jeremy is safe with him, if he wants to take him home. You and Jeremy have told us what you saw, and he knows you have, so there's no reason for Barry, if he's the killer, to go after either of you."

"Barry would never hurt Jeremy."

"Not even to cover up two murders?"

Oh, lord. I didn't think so, but how could anybody claim to be a hundred percent sure of such a thing?

"Look, McCoo, he didn't have time. After Plumly was stabbed, Barry went to talk with security and then the cops."

"I know that."

"Then Jennifer came back to talk with me. She said the cops had temporarily finished with Barry, I admit that, and then she was shot. Immediately after that, Jeremy and I ran. And we were being chased almost from that minute to the time we came up out of the manhole. Lots of people must have seen Barry by then."

McCoo rubbed his face. He looked sad, but he was far too honest to fob me off with "Wait and see" or "We'll look into it."

He said, "From your description of your run through the tunnels, the person who chased you followed you until you headed out of the Grant Park Underground Garage. Maybe he followed you for another five minutes, but you have no evidence that he did, and if he did, you eluded him by taking random tunnels. You crept along for at least another thirty minutes after you left the garage, and in that time you never saw your pursuer. As far as you know, maybe he realized right away in the parking garage that he would never find you, so he simply turned back. Right?"

"I don't see why— Oh, all right. Maybe."

"You were on the run, so to speak, for an hour and ten minutes altogether. You can only be sure your pursuer followed you for the first twenty minutes. I'm sorry to tell you this, but nobody went back to the Emerald City castle to reinterview Barry for at least an hour."

"An hour! Why not?"

"Come on, Cat. We had a fatal stabbing and a fatal shooting at a big city festival. And more shots fired after that. And a paramedic wounded. The first thing we had to do was to button up the scene and try to find the shooter. Just doing the basics took far more than an hour. We had to get the addresses of all the witnesses to the two murders. We called in three evidence techs to do the site search. There was potential evidence all over the place if you count cups and gum wrappers and cigarette butts and footprints in dirt. We finally went back to reinterview the first witnesses about the same time you were coming out of the manhole."

"Somebody must have seen him in the Emerald City."

"He doesn't think so, and nobody reported being with him or seeing him there. He says he collapsed into a chair in the office after the first questioning. His impression was that pretty much everybody else had rushed out into the central area to see what was going on. At that point, he says, he thought you had taken Jeremy home and he didn't even know that Jennifer had been shot. He spent the time trying to figure out why *anybody* would be killing anybody else at the festival, and especially Plumly. He says Plumly was a really nice guy."

"He was. Very nice."

"And it's perfectly believable that Barry just sat there. He'd had a shock. That is, if he isn't guilty. For that matter, he might have sat there even if he had killed Plumly and let his confederate chase Jennifer and you and Jeremy."

"A confederate! That's very far-fetched."

"I wish. People have partners in crime all the time."

"If he wanted an alibi, and he had a partner, Barry would make sure somebody would see him at least at some point."

"Maybe. Assuming he wasn't flustered."

"What about the three guys who were with Plumly just before he was killed? E. T. Taubman, Edmond Pottle, and Larry Mazzanovich?"

"We're contacting them now."

"Contacting them? You mean you haven't talked to them yet? They just went home, or what?"

"Well, they certainly didn't come forward. We'll soon know where they went."

"Don't you think that's very suspicious, all of them disappearing?"

"Sure. But I also don't think it's unusual. A crime happens and suddenly all the witnesses vanish. Guilty or not."

"These are responsible citizens."

"Cat, grow up. Even so-called solid citizens act like that."

I shook my head, but I didn't doubt what he said. "McCoo, when you or your people talk with them, tell them Jeremy and I have told all we know. I don't want anybody trying to kill us. This evening was more than enough."

If you want support, understanding, consolation, and all that good stuff, you don't want my mother. She's much better at guilt. Fortunately, we have Dad to depend on. Mom berated Barry for the problems at the festival, even though she had no idea how deeply involved he might be. Nobody told her that Plumly had died practically in his arms, or that he was a suspect. Barry simply told her he had to stay here and help the police and that Maud couldn't come and get Jeremy because of the baby. So he said, "We thought maybe Jeremy could stay with you for a day or two." I think I saw Jeremy wince at this. His grandmother wasn't the most fun person to spend time with, although if he played his cards right, he might be able to get his grandfather to take him to the Brookfield Zoo. My dad loves zoos. He loves animals in general.

Then Jeremy, honest little kid that he was, said, "Aunt Cat and I escaped through the underground tunnels, just like Indiana Jones!"

"Escaped from what?"

"The bad guy who was shooting at us."

"Shooting? Catherine, you let somebody shoot at Jeremy?"

"No, I tried to stop somebody from shooting at Jeremy by getting him out of there."

"Into the sewers?"

"Not the sewers—"

"Catherine, you should have gone to the nearest policeman."

"Next time, Mother, I'll think of that."

As she was leaving she said, "And leave that dirty cat here, Jeremy."

"He's my friend."

I said, "Mother, Jeremy *keeps* the cat."

She was about to make it quite clear she was the mother and I was the daughter, and what she says goes, when my father said, "Jeremy keeps the cat. Tomorrow, Jeremy, we'll take him to the vet and make sure he's in good health. And we'll get him his shots."

Jeremy said, "He won't like shots."

"No, but it has to be done. You can help by consoling him afterward. After the vet, we'll stop at the store on the way home and get him some special sardines."

· 8 ·

FOLLOW
THE YELLOW BRICK ROAD

It was a relief when Jeremy and my parents left. Little kids are wonderful, but you use a lot of mental energy trying to protect them from hurt or worry. And even though I believe in honesty, you have to be cautious when it's not your child.

McCoo put in a call to the police in Mom and Dad's sub urb, asking them to swing by their house on patrol, just to check.

Barry had stayed in the room with me only long enough to see them go. Then he flung out again, white with anger, and presumably went back to whatever room he had been in while reading his statement.

"What a horrible night," I said to McCoo. My shoulder was killing me. Tears were forming behind my eyelids. And I couldn't imagine any way out of the hell ahead for Barry. "The only thing worse would be if that utter ass Sergeant Hightower was in charge."

McCoo's lips pushed out and then fell back into a sad droop. His gaze had flicked up at the door behind me.

Somebody said, "Utter ass, huh?"

Hightower strolled in. He was slim, he was straight-backed, he was handsome. His uniform was tailored and freshly pressed. And he was very pleased with himself.

"It's not Sergeant Hightower," McCoo said. "He's been promoted. It's Lieutenant Hightower now."

Hightower marched around from behind me to stand near McCoo. "I'll be handling this case from here on out," he said. "It's going to get a lot of media attention."

I sighed in resignation and tried to move my arm. It wanted to be left alone. Trying successfully not to say, "I didn't mean to call you an utter ass; I meant pompous ass," I actually said, "McCoo, I'd better go try to make up with Barry."

What a feeling of guilt! I felt ashamed of myself. I felt disloyal. A traitor to my family. Cruel to Barry—

When I walked in, Barry looked sick and old. Belatedly, unwillingly, I checked out his clothes. He was wearing dark pants and black shoes, like I thought our attacker wore. But so many people wore the same.

He had finished rereading his statement, I guess, because it was lying on the table in front of him. His elbows were propped on the table and his head hung down between his shoulders. The door closed behind me. He started as if somebody had hit him.

"Barry, please let's talk."

"How could you do this to me?"

"Barry, I know you're no danger to Jeremy." I didn't add that, even if he'd killed Plumly, there was no reason to kill Jeremy, now that he'd talked to the cops. I really, really believed Barry wasn't guilty. Didn't I?

My brother was built to be a cuddly kind of guy, not

exactly chubby, but far from lanky. One of my older brothers was huffy, self-important, and interested in looking gorgeous. He does constant muscle-building workouts. Scalp treatments. Hair transplants. Expensive clothes. That was not Barry. As a child, Barry was the one who didn't punch me. If you don't have older brothers, you won't understand this. If you have, we will have an instant meeting of the minds.

Barry got to his feet, and then he pointedly turned away from me. I walked in front of him, and he turned the other way. He didn't want to see me or even to acknowledge my existence. His face was red with suppressed anger.

"Barry—"

"Leave me alone. I can't believe you'd hurt me like this."

I pulled him down into a chair and sat in the one right next to him.

"Barry, *look* at me."

He wouldn't. I took his face in my hands and turned it toward me. He said, "All right, all right. But I'm still—"

"Just listen. Don't talk. Please, Barry, I don't believe you stabbed Plumly. I really don't. All I told them is what I saw."

"What you *think* you saw could get me arrested for murder."

"What I think I saw is what Jennifer thought she saw, too." He winced at that. "Barry, this is not my imagination. It's something we're going to have to deal with. I'm absolutely sure there's an explanation for all of this. Maybe Plumly stabbed himself. Maybe Taubman or Pottle or Mazzanovich stabbed him, and the wound didn't start bleeding until he struggled with you."

"He didn't *struggle* with me! He grabbed me, like he wanted help, and then he sort of sagged and he kept slumping down, and I tried to hold him up and then he just collapsed."

"All right. I won't call it a struggle. All I'm saying is that any vigorous physical activity, like grabbing you, or running, or whatever, could have made the wound bleed. Maybe he pulled the knife out of the wound as he was running toward you. The doctors always say never pull a knife out of a wound because that will cause a worse hemorrhage. The point is, I really believe somebody else killed him, not you."

He nodded but didn't speak and he looked away again.

"Barry, did Plumly tell you anything?"

"No."

"Nothing at all? What did he say?"

"He didn't say anything. He—gurgled."

I thought about that for a few seconds. "Mom doesn't know any details yet, but she'll be furious with me when she hears about what I told the police. And I know you're angry. But, Barry, I'm going to figure this out. You don't have any friend anywhere who's going to work harder than me to find out what really happened. I won't let the cops grab on to you just because you're convenient."

"Yeah, okay. Whatever." He was dismissing me, not agreeing. "Go away now. I don't want to talk with you anymore."

"Are you okay to drive?"

"They say I can go?"

"Of course. You're not under arrest."

"Then I can drive."

When I went in to tell McCoo I was leaving, he said, "I'll have a squad car take you to where your car's parked. And then follow you home." I didn't object. "Cat, what's wrong with your arm?"

"Nothing. I just wrenched it when I sort of fell off the manhole ladder."

"No, it's worse than 'just wrenched.' You're letting it hang limp."

"McCoo, nobody likes a know-it-all."

"And your point is?"

"What's more, nobody likes anybody who's so self-assured that he doesn't care whether people like him or not."

"Cat, stifle. You need a doctor to look at that."

"Not now. I'm just too exhausted."

"Now."

"Tell you what. I promise you, Chief McCoo, that I'll go to a doctor immediately if it's not better by morning."

· 9 ·

THE EMERALD CITY,
AS FAST AS LIGHTNING

It wasn't better by morning. It was worse, throbbing and hot. I made an appointment with my doctor. He could see me at 9:30 A.M.

The morning news boiled over with stories about the two Oz Festival murders. The Reverend Troy Carpenter, a Chicago minister who considered himself the conscience of the city, said, "The festival should close immediately, out of respect."

This, of course, would never happen. There were deaths at big functions all the time—heart attacks at the Bears games, fights at sporting events that occasionally terminated in manslaughter. There were occasional shootings, too. And although murder was rare, I don't think a Chicago function would close even if somebody mowed down a troop of aldermen. Or maybe especially not then.

The city council was in session—what a boon—and a number of politicians made statements on the floor that the festival should be closed out of respect to the two deceased.

These speeches were disingenuous, however. What? A Chicago alderman disingenuous? Surely not. The point was, they could look like they were all heart by saying this stuff. But they all knew it was in no one's interest to close the festival. There was nothing going into that space until next week. The vendors were in place and would lose money if it closed. Church groups were scheduled to bring whole troops of children. Entertainers were scheduled to sing on the bandstand. Even the restaurants up and down Michigan Avenue stood to gain from the crowds. The city council would debate this just long enough for the festival to run its course, and then there would be no point in closing. It's the cruel truth that the more days that went by, the less people would care.

It was a bonanza for the TV news crews, of course. Many mournful reporters remarked on the "irony" of such a crime happening in a setting where little children were supposed to caper and have fun. The reports from the scene showed the general area where the two had been killed. But the police, wisely, had not allowed the reporters in until the bodies were gone and had never showed them the exact location of the bodies. They were reduced to having vendors point to the "death scenes" and the vendors, when I saw them onscreen, were not terribly accurate.

So far, the focus on Barry as a possible suspect hadn't made the news. Lieutenant Hightower said to the reporters, "We're looking into several possibilities. We've got strong leads." I would have been grateful to him if I'd thought he was being kind or even judicious. But experienced detectives usually are pretty careful about sticking their necks out, in case they're wrong. Not for the suspects' sake, for their own. My mother, of course, would know by now the extent of the problems at the festival, but not my involvement. And since Barry wasn't mentioned, nor was Jeremy's and my run through the tunnels, Maud wouldn't yet be overly worried. Still, I hoped Barry had told her everything. She would know Jeremy was safe, which was the most important thing. The whole business of keeping information from other people for their own good makes me uncomfortable, as I've said before. If it were up to me, I'd have told her everything in the first place. But it wasn't up to me.

As I headed out the door, the phone rang. The readout showed my mother's number. Thank goodness for gadgets. I let the machine kick in, but waited next to the recorder. If there was any trouble with Jeremy, I'd pick up.

"Catherine! Barry told me what you did. I absolutely *could not believe it!* Your own flesh and blood! I always knew you resented being the only girl and the second youngest child besides, but I never thought you'd take it out on your perfectly innocent brother! Are you just doing this to annoy me? You call me back the minute you get in, and I certainly hope you have a good explanation, although what good explanation there could be I'm telling you I just don't know!"

She hung up.

Going to the doctor was looking better and better.

"Yipe!" I said when the doctor checked the shoulder. He claimed he had to "manipulate" it a little to find out what was going on. He asked how this felt and how that felt and everything he did felt hideous. Then he ordered an X ray in case of a fracture, which he doubted I had.

"Let me guess," he said. "You fell and landed on your shoulder."

"Yup. Off a ladder, sort of."

"What you have is not quite an acromioclavicular joint separation."

"Oh, one of *those*. I've always wondered about them."

"All that means is that you've pulled the collarbone away from where it joins the shoulder blade. The shoulder joint is very complicated. Three bones come together, the upper arm bone, the shoulder blade, and the collarbone, and the whole thing is held together by a bewildering network of ligaments. You can screw it up pretty easily. You've stretched but not torn some of the ligaments that hold your shoulder blade up against your collarbone."

"This is good?"

"It certainly could be worse. You could have had a complete separation. We might be talking surgery. Arthroscopic surgery or open surgery."

"And as it is?"

"You'll have to wear an elastic support. And don't fall again, even a little slip-and-fall. Don't let anybody pull on your arm. Don't climb trees or ropes."

"You're kidding. Climb trees? I'm having trouble lifting a frappemochaccino."

"Good. Baby it. Come back in a week. And call right away if it seems to be getting worse. Sometimes there's hidden damage."

"Frankly," said Larry Mazzanovich, "I don't give a rat's ass for Oz."

We were in his site office, a trailer in a sea of mud at a construction area on West Randolph. The whole block was a maze of wood forms, stacks of equipment, and very deep footing holes into which a pile driver was driving pilings. Some of the pilings were surrounded by lattices of rusty iron rebar. The rebar looked big enough to have been designed for the Space Shuttle launch site.

"Why not?"

"It's just bullshit stuff for kids."

"So why did you get involved with it?"

"The Oz Festival? Hey, if the city likes it, I like it. All I'm saying is I don't like it."

"Uh-huh. So what kinds of festivals do you like?"

"Taste of Chicago. Food from one end of the park to the other. Now that's okay. The BluesFest isn't bad, either."

This was getting me less than nowhere, so I said, "You're a contractor? And an alderman?"

"Well, alderman isn't a full-time job. Plus, suppose you're voted out? Gotta have something to fall back on." He shrugged. Mazzanovich was a shar-pei kind of man, all wrinkles. Not the dry, fine wrinkles of old age, but big rounded folds. His eyes hid behind folds, and plump cheek folds bracketed his mouth. His hair was coarse, medium long, and spiky. There was a thin layer of gray dust over his skin and hair, as if cement powder settled on him all day. He wore chinos and muddy boots.

"And you're building this place? A new hotel?"

"A major luxury hotel. I'm a contractor but I'm not a general contractor. I'm a cement contractor."

"Oh. Did you do cement contracting for the Oz Festival?"

"Don't be stupid. You don't pour cement for a Grant Park event. The city's real careful you don't do anything that would change the park. You can't so much as trim a tree. Can't trim the *grass*, for God's sake. Jeez, you have to get a permit to walk on it, practically. What they went through to get an okay to paint the walkways into Yellow Brick Roads, you wouldn't believe. It's *removable* goddamn paint, see? They're gonna run a solvent and a scrubber over it later! Like a vacuum Zamboni! All the world out there's trying to make paint more permanent, and we're lookin' for stuff that don't last. Shouldn't wash away in the first rain, but shouldn't last, either."

"So what *was* your role?"

"Advise the city board that advises the Park District."

"I see."

"Whattaya want, anyway? I don't wanta be rude, here, but I got a job to do. And the cops already wasted half my morning."

"I'm sure you realize that Barry Marsala is my brother—"

"Hadn't thought about it. I probably woulda guessed he was some kind of relative."

"And because you and he and Taubman and Pottle were all in the area when Tom Plumly was stabbed, I thought you could tell me something about what happened."

"Very good! Cute! Subtle! You wanta ask me if I stabbed him, ask me if I stabbed him. Listen, I don't have any objection to a girl being loyal to her brother, but you're not gonna start some rumor that I murdered the guy. Because I didn't, and I would take it very, very amiss if any slander got going. See what I mean?"

"I only want to understand what happened."

"And you think I'm gonna tell you?"

"Why not? You talked with the cops, didn't you? And it's not a secret, whatever you told them, is it? If it's the truth, why not tell me, too?" He didn't look impressed. "Get me off your back."

He smiled unpleasantly. "You're not on my back, kid. You're not powerful enough. This is Chicago, remember, and there's people in this city who can *really* get on your back."

Still, he hadn't said no, so I asked, "Was Plumly okay when he left you and the other two men?"

He looked at me with just a whiff of respect. "Persistent, aren't you? Yeah. He was just fine. When he left us, he was just fine and dandy. He was walkin', wasn't he? He went over to your brother."

"You're right. He ran over to my brother. Had you said anything to make him run away?"

"Nope. Musta needed to talk to him real bad."

"What had you been talking about?"

"The festival, of course. Two of the food stands hadn't done what we told 'em. One was using hazardous cooking fuel. There's rules about that kind of thing. One had dancing girls on the banner. Unclothed dancing girls. Not right in a kids' festival."

"I see. The cops told me last night they couldn't find you after Plumly died."

"Musta not looked very hard. The traffic getting out of there was a goddamn bitch. I mean, everybody musta charged outta there at the same time."

"When they heard the shots."

"Can't exactly blame 'em, can you? It took me half an hour to get outta Grant Park Underground and an hour and a half to get from there to my house."

"You parked in the Grant Park Underground?"

"What did I just tell you? Sure. It's the closest place." He didn't show any sign of guilt, but then he'd brought up the subject. Maybe he'd done it intentionally in order to act as if the underground brought back no special memories for him.

I said, "Why didn't you stay around after Plumly was killed?"

"Why would I? Didn't know anything helpful. Also, didn't want to get involved."

"So it took you two hours to get home? Where do you live?"

"Northbr—uh, North Side," he said.

"An hour and a half to the North Side! It ought to take you twenty minutes."

"No shit. Talk to IDOT."

IDOT is not idiot, although people have been known to

make the mistake intentionally. It stands for Illinois Department of Transportation.

Underneath the trailer the earth began to tremble. I had to stop myself from grabbing the edge of the desk. Mazzanovich perked right up. "Hey, kid," he said. "Gotta go. Here comes the mud truck." A gigantic bright red cement mixer lumbered down the dirt ramp, looking like a pregnant fire extinguisher. "See, when you're doing footings, the batch of cement has to be poured while the batch underneath is still wet, or it won't bond. You get a truck caught in a traffic jam and you maybe have to dig out a whole piling. So you basically don't hang around with your thumb up your ass."

Mazzanovich was out of the trailer, down the wood steps, and on the ground in seconds, shoving his hard hat onto his head.

I walked away from the construction site. Looking back, I saw Mazzanovich waving his arms at the cement truck driver, and a second man standing near one of the pilings, also gesturing.

I wondered what it was that was so different about Mazzanovich now. It was the hat. The hard hat had covered that crest of spiky hair. The hair that stood up on top of his head. If he'd been running his hands through it, would it stand up straighter? And if he had, would it, in the right light, remind a person of the funnel on top of the Tin Woodman's head?

· 10 ·

A WHIZ OF A WIZ

"I expected to see models and mock-ups," I said to E. T. Taubman, the lighting designer who had lit the Oz Festival so magically.

His studio covered the entire fifth floor of a converted warehouse building on Chestnut west of State. Actually the studio was only half a dozen blocks from my apartment, which was in an old warehouse building near the El. Six blocks and maybe 2.5 million dollars away. This was a primo postgentrification zone.

The studio's floor was that very, very heavily varnished original wood with all the grooves, chinks, scars, and stains preserved as if set in amber. It fairly screamed "artist." The area was divided into two large rooms and one huge one. I had entered directly off the elevator, although there was a sliding metal door that could be bolted to keep people from just jumping off the elevator at the fifth floor and walking in uninvited.

Taubman said, "Yeah, I used to have analog models of the sets, but I couldn't stand dealing with them anymore. Nobody does it that way now. It's all CAD."

By which he meant computer-assisted design. If I'd
thought about it, I would have realized that cybertech had
eaten lighting design the same way it had overwhelmed
architecture or animation or basically anything. By "analog" I guessed he meant "real."

Taubman walked into the farther room, the huge one. I
assumed I was to follow. Taubman was a tall, very thin man,
who walked with a kind of rambling awkwardness. "Thin as
a one-sided board," my grandfather would have said. He
had reddish-blond hair, so short that his pale scalp showed
through, and an angular, bony face. He wore a white silk
shirt, beautifully cut navy pants, and black shoes.

"Here," he said. "Models."

One corner of the room was filled with a sort of shoal of
computer tables, the kind with swing arms for monitors and
slide-out low trays for keyboards. There were several printers, including two color printers and one extrawide. Also, of
course, he had a fax machine, and a little monitor and key-
board that looked as if they continuously ran his e-mail. A
twist of fat cables led out of the clutter to a trio of big Pioneer plasma screens hung like paintings in a row on the
plain brick wall. Taubman folded his long bones into a com-
plicated-looking desk chair. Everything on the chair that
could possibly adjust adjusted. It didn't just go up and
down. From the levers on the side I could see that the seat
tilted, plus you could tilt the back separately from the seat,
and after Taubman sat, he nudged the arms with his elbows,
clicking them into an apparently favorite position. The
chair had wheels, of course, a lever to control the seat
height, a back-tilt lever, gears that locked the arms in place,
and an adjustable lumbar pad. There was a half-keyboard
attached to rods protruding out of each arm, like the sort of
thing you might have if you were a very rich paraplegic. You
could work lying way back if you wished.

Taubman took all this technology as a given, and simply flicked a mouse ball. A buttoned list called STUDIO came up on the left screen. He clicked one button and the lights went out. He clicked another. Hunter-Douglas blackout shades slithered down smoothly over the windows. Because the shades ran in steel frames, the huge room became almost completely dark. Then he clicked again, and the right-hand panel lit up. SETS, it said, at the top of a long list.

"Check this out," he said. He scrolled down the list to the words "Mourning Becomes Electra Steppenwolf" and hit two keys.

A giant all-white log cabin appeared in the middle screen. At the tap of another key it opened like a dollhouse. Inside were four cutaway rooms with 1890s-looking rustic furniture, also all in white.

"Is that all generated by the computer?" I asked.

"Sure."

"Why is everything white?"

"It's easier to see what you're lighting that way. You can always restore the colors and textures later." He typed another few letters and the set went dark, with a single oil lamp on the digital table casting flickering shadows on the nonexistent walls. Two more keys and dawn rose outside the windows.

"Oh, my!" I said. I was really enchanted. "This is a lot better than dollhouses." Morning sunlight was already slanting in through the hazy air.

"I didn't design the sets, though," he said. "I just light them." He let evening fall in the Electra cabin and then quickly flipped through at least twenty more all-white sets. There were Empire drawing rooms, medieval inns lit only by the fireplace, beaches, a tree house, many, many period rooms. And in all of them you could tell the time of day and the mood, just from the lighting.

"You don't *just* light them," I said sincerely.

"Oh. Thanks."

"These can't be exactly like the actual stage productions, though," I said.

"Nothing is. This software actually lets us get closer to what the final production's going to look like than the old miniatures did."

I made him show me more. There was a craggy moor, a Scottish castle, and a stone-flagged courtyard with a gallows. Each was bathed in a different sort of light. The moor was soft and bluish, the castle was bathed in harsh, full, cold daylight, the courtyard was sad, very early morning, with a tinge of red at the horizon. It wordlessly proclaimed "the morning of an execution." For each he pulled up photos of the real productions. They looked almost the same, except not so good as the digital ones.

"This is amazing. Is this your principal business?"

"I wish. By rights, there ought to be enough money in theater lighting in Chicago for a person to survive. But there isn't. It doesn't matter how talented you are."

He clicked the room lights back on.

"So do you mean you'd rather do theater than festival lighting?"

"Usually. The Oz Festival was more fun than most, because it was more imaginative."

"More profitable, too, I would think."

"They pay reasonably well," he said, a bit sourly.

"Well, that, too, but I meant the publicity. You got a huge media boost from it."

"Yeah. Wasn't that color spread in *Chicago* magazine excellent? I do edgy work, but the magazine really picked up on the best parts. The Day-Glo, and the neon tubing on the merry-go-round. The cover photo *rocked*! Very discerning, weren't they?"

He certainly didn't seem uncomfortable about the fact that a woman had been killed near his edgy merry-go-round. Suddenly he remembered he was supposed to be modest. "Of course, the Oz Festival caught a lot of PR because this year is the hundredth anniversary of the publication of *The Wizard of Oz*. It wasn't all just because of my lighting."

Hey, no kidding.

I said, "Do you do music festivals? Or rock concerts?"

"The major rock stars have their own lighting people. I do some of the Grant Park music festivals. I do some industrials."

"Industrials? You mean like factory lighting?"

He snorted. "God, no. Like restaurants. Sometimes lobbies, like corporation lobbies. That stuff is mainly a matter of designing just the right mood. For a restaurant, the mood you set can make or break them. Imagine cafeteria lighting in L'Heure Bleu, for instance."

"I see what you mean."

I wandered around the room, looking at his stock of equipment various lightbulbs, several dozen different types, socket styles, holders, mounts, pedestals, clamp-ons, plus small light boards with computerized circuits that did the same job huge boards used to do, and piles of rolled wire. When I was a child, there were only a couple of dozen kinds of lightbulbs in general use. My dad told me that when he was a child there were only four—twenty-five watt, fifty watt, hundred watt, and hundred-and-fifty watt. He was exaggerating, but not by much. Now, judging by Taubman's shelves, there were hundreds upon hundreds—not just different wattage but par count and focus angle and filament type, and more and more and more.

"Do you keep all these to use?"

"No. Wouldn't pay. You need very large numbers for

installations. There's no point in my being a lightbulb warehouse. I just have a few examples here if I need to check one out."

"A *few* examples?"

"Yes. Just to look at. Then I try to duplicate that light on Softplot. That's the main software I use. Anyway, let's see what I can show you about the—um—the Oz Festival." He played around with a couple of swift keystrokes and the screen filled with an aerial overview of Grant Park.

"Okay. Look. The streets and permanent paths and Buckingham Fountain and so on are obvious here. These contour lines show the elevation of the ground. You know there are little rises, and some flat, low areas—"

"Yes. I know roughly where they are. And I can see them there."

"We wanted to take advantage of nice things in the terrain. This is an early sketch version. At this point we hadn't even thought of putting in the castle. The first plan was to have a central vendor area that was all green and to call it the Emerald City. But then your brother said we had to have a small on-site office and—uh—somebody said everybody loves castles. So we made the office a castle."

The plan changed. It no longer looked like a sketch. Like all CAD design, it looked a bit too polished. The terrain map showed the placement of booths and rides and light sources.

"Orange is my designation for the existing park lights. All the other lights are installed specifically for the festival."

"Does your data include underground plans, like tunnels and Grant Park Underground, and so on?"

As I said this, I watched his face to see if he showed any guilt. If he'd chased Jeremy and me in the tunnels, he ought to react. But I could see no distress or change of expression.

He said, "Well, Grant Park Underground, for sure." He typed in a couple of commands and a dotted line appeared, showing the outline of the underground. "Tunnels—mm— I don't think even the City of Chicago knows where all the tunnels are," he said. "Some of the drainage tunnels ought to be in here. And maybe power cabling."

Another set of lines showed up on the map. The display was getting crowded and confusing, since at my request he had just superimposed one thing on top of another. But even so, seeing those tunnels gave me a chill. There were a *lot* of tunnels. One of them ran practically under the Flying Monkeys merry-go-round, or at least its planned location in this early sketch. It was disconcerting to realize that the park was so honeycombed underneath, and even more upsetting to understand that you could be down there underground, right under the feet of potential rescuers, but without any way to get their attention or to escape.

Taubman said, "Okay, let me show you how we use this software. Do you live in a house or apartment?"

"Apartment."

"Describe it. How big is it and what shape?"

"Well, it's about twenty feet long and about fifteen wide, not counting the bathroom and an eight-by-ten kitchen."

"That isn't very big."

I've often described it as being about the size of an average Chicago bus. It's a little wider but not as long, so it really does have about the same square footage. I said, "Freelance reporting is not a way to get rich."

"Okay," he said. By now the shape of my apartment had appeared on his screen with size markings along the sides. "Look at the bulb in the track fixture above you."

"I see it." It was a tiny bulb, half naked, held only by its power points and a clamp. My mother would hate it. She just *loves* lampshades, the bigger the better and some still in their store wrapping.

"That's a halogen bulb with a twenty-five-degree beam. I use that because I want to bathe this desk area in task lighting so I can read papers. The degrees just mean that part of an arc. If I wanted more of a narrow spotlight, I'd pick a fifteen-degree bulb. If I wanted a wider wash of light, I might pick a forty-degree light beam. You understand? Now what in your apartment would you like to spotlight?"

"Well, I have a parrot who's extremely fine. Long John's perch is right about here."

"Okay." Taubman clicked and a symbol representing a bulb appeared above Long John Silver's perch. Then an area of concentric circles grew around it.

"The center," Taubman said, "is where the light is strongest. The others just show you where the scatter goes and how intense it is. Now tell me where you have your furniture."

I did. A big pool from a wide-angle beam appeared over a reasonable simulacrum of my thrift-shop sofa and a medium twenty-five-degree pool of reading light over the really comfy chair that I had found discarded on the street and had slip-covered. He threw in a medium-beam light near the front door, which would be nice to have.

"Now you say you have a parrot?"

"Yes."

"Would he like this?" A boxlike shape representing just my living room appeared, then rotated, so that instead of looking down at the place from the ceiling, we were now looking at the back wall. He punched some buttons, muttered "macros" and "cyan" and some other incomprehensible stuff, and suddenly on the wall appeared a jungle! It was a projection, of course, and beautiful! But not beautiful enough for Taubman. He muttered some more, scrolling through menus on his left-hand screen. "Most of the furniture and whatever is canned," he said. "I don't have to build much from scratch anymore. This is actually one of the jungles they used in *The Phantom Menace*." As I watched, magenta-and-pink butterflies popped into existence on several leaves. Then yellow highlights flickered along the edges of the vines.

"My goodness. That's great!"

He played around with colors for a while, turning some of the larger leaves bluer, augmenting the leaf veins, just doing riffs to impress me. Which was fine. But still, I was here for a reason.

I had a suspicion about one thing he mentioned. "I hate to change the subject, but you said earlier that 'somebody' thought everybody loves castles. Who was it?"

He shrugged his sharp shoulders, but I kept looking at him and finally he said, "Well, it was Jennifer. Oh, lord. Poor Jennifer."

"Yes. That was a terrible thing to happen."

He nodded. He looked genuinely sad. I said, "Mr. Taubman, do you know who killed her?"

"Of course not. I would have told the police if I did."

"Or who killed Tom Plumly?"

"No."

His bony face was not very expressive. But he shifted uneasily in his chair. All I could do was press him more. "Plumly was right there with you and Pottle and Mazzanovich. And then he ran away. Why?"

"I guess he wanted to see Barry." Taubman looked away from me.

"What had you been talking about?"

"Oh, the festival. What else? One of the food stands was doing something dangerous with its cooking fuel. And one had something inappropriate on its sign. Naked ladies. Pot-tle was all upset about it. As if kids are gonna care that you've got nude dancing girls on a banner! Probably love it."

Well, I had asked, but I also got the feeling he was trying to distract me.

"Did you stab Plumly?"

"Listen, Ms. Marsala. I realize your brother is in trou-ble. I sympathize with what you're going through. I under-stand that you're willing to be rude in order to get the job done. But I didn't kill Plumly or attack him or stab him or anything, and that's the last I'm going to say about it."

"Could he have stabbed himself?"

"Could he? I suppose anybody *could*. But I can't see why he would."

Nor could I. "What kind of a person was he?"

"Reasonably pleasant, I guess. Rather intelligent, really. Seemed to be interested in the festival's artistic elements, which was surprising. After all, he was an ex-cop. And he ran a security service." I reflected briefly on what choice words McCoo might utter if somebody told him a cop is not supposed to be interested in artistic elements. Then in a fit of shame I remembered that I, too, had been surprised that Plumly was an avid reader.

Taubman said, "He actually had a sense of what fun the festival could be." Rather grimly, he added, "Not every-body involved cared about that."

"Like who?"

"I don't want to bad-mouth anybody. There's been enough unpleasantness already."

Jeez, you could say that again.

· 11 ·

I AM OZ,
THE GREAT AND POWERFUL

It is just *so* great to be able to go home for lunch. Working freelance I don't make much money, but there are other benefits, like this. When I was working at That Big Important Newspaper, I routinely ate at my desk so that my supervisor could see I was working.

My shoulder ached worse. Time for aspirin and a sandwich.

Not time to call my mother.

As I mentioned, my apartment is not any bigger than a Chicago bus. No dining room. No office. The word processor lives on the kitchen table. And my roommate, the African grey parrot who is called Long John Silver—this is the parrot's name, and despite a recent problem, we're sticking with it—lives all over the apartment. Because the bird flies loose while I'm out, there are a few little cleanup chores. Also for reasons of sanitation, I leave the kitchen door closed when I'm out.

As a young bird, Long John had been owned by the cap-

tain of a Louisiana shrimp trawler. When the captain
retired, he moved to Chicago, thinking there was no water
here. Imagine his surprise when he discovered you can't see
across Lake Michigan. When the captain died, he left Long
John to an English professor who taught at Northwestern
University and who lived in my building. Long John lived
with the professor for twenty years, learning to speak
Shakespearean phrases almost exclusively. When the professor left town, the result of a bit of a misunderstanding
with the dean about the dean's wife, he left me the bird.

African greys are not beautiful. They're a gunmetal gray
color with splotches of what looks rather like dried blood
on the tail. But they are absolutely the best talkers in the
bird world. LJ knows more Shakespeare than I do.

I settled down now on my thrift-shop sofa and LJ flew
down and sat on my shoulder. My good right shoulder, fortunately.

"Here, LJ. Banana. Your favorite."

Long John took it gently as always. Standing on my
shoulder on one foot, the bird rotated the other foot as if it
were a hand, so as to eat delicately.

"LJ, I'm in big trouble. I may have landed my brother in
prison. Do you remember my brother Barry, LJ?"

Long John Silver said, "'I have shot mine arrow o'er the
house, And hurt my brother.'"

Oh dear, very apt. I inadvertently hurt my brother. But
not truly inadvertently. I had known my evidence would
make things look bad for him. This was terrible. Was there
any way out?

Was Plumly a suicide? I thought back. As he ran past us,
could he have been concealing a knife? I pictured as well as
I could what he had been wearing. There was the OZ staff
shirt, nothing much more than a T-shirt. It was probably big
enough and loose enough so that a knife could have been

slipped into his belt underneath. But why would he do that? Why would he run away from Taubman, Pottle, and Mazzanovich with a knife stuck in his belt, pull it out, and stab himself while running or just when he reached Barry?

The idea was ludicrous. Why would he or anybody do such a thing? Even if the knife had been short enough to keep hidden in his pocket, the explanation didn't work. While the four of them had been in a tight little group, I hadn't seen him well. He'd had his back to me. But I had observed him from the time he left the three men, and he hadn't stopped to take anything out of his belt. Nor had I seen him stab himself while running.

And if he had run up to Barry, pulled out a knife, and then stabbed himself, wouldn't Barry have tried to stop him? And wouldn't I have seen it? Maybe not. They were so close together as they struggled.

Or *had* Barry tried? Was that why he and Plumly were struggling? Was Barry trying to stop him from hurting himself?

But then why on earth wouldn't Barry just say so?

What had Plumly been doing with his hands while he ran? Come on, Marsala, think back.

Picture it. Night has come on. I see Plumly standing with the other three men, around the side of the popcorn stand. I think he was gesturing, or they were, or both, but they were in their tight little grouping and I only glanced at them, then chatted with Jennifer, then Plumly ran away.

Ran away. *They* must have stabbed him. But then why didn't he bleed until he got to Barry?

Don't get distracted. What was he doing with his hands when he was running?

Focus, dammit. All right. The shirt was flapping a little bit as he ran. He tried to hold it with his hand. Was that right? Yes, I was sure I saw him put his hand to it.

Stabbing himself? No, I don't think so.

Pulling a knife out of a wound?

Well, that was possible. But he wasn't bleeding. Maybe wounds don't always bleed right away. No, wait. If the wound was serious enough to kill him in two or three minutes, he must have bled a whole lot. His shirt was soaked with blood when I reached him.

If the wound bled a whole lot, he could not have been stabbed before he got to Barry or I would have seen the blood. If Barry didn't stab him, he must have stabbed himself. Damn. Why on earth would he run away from Pottle, Mazzanovich, and Taubman and then stab himself when he got to Barry?

To make some sort of point? Had the three men threatened him with exposure for some crime? Or did Plumly want to make a point to Barry? Had Barry discovered that Plumly had committed a crime? Had Barry threatened him with exposure and so Plumly stabbed himself right in front of Barry as if to say, "See what you drove me to do."

Barry hadn't claimed any such thing. But if Barry had driven Plumly to kill himself, maybe he wouldn't want to say so. Barry could be a little bit self-righteous at times. He might have been ashamed of himself for being judgmental.

But even if he reproached himself for accusing Plumly of a crime, would Barry keep silent about it in the face of an accusation of murder?

Could Barry have accused Plumly of a crime, then found out he was wrong, that Plumly was innocent? Then if Plumly killed himself before Barry could set the record straight, Barry might be steeped in feelings of guilt.

And then, I suppose, he might be so ashamed that he didn't want to talk about it. Conceivably, he might be so utterly ashamed that he was willing to submit to a suspicion of murder.

And if so, I would just have to make him talk.

The doorbell rang. Rather than walk down to the lobby, I went to my front window and leaned out. "Who's there?"

"I am," said a very firm, but snotty voice. *Oh, jeez. Lieutenant Hightower.*

I buzzed him in.

"You are interfering in a police investigation," he said.

"No, I'm not."

"And you're going to have to stop it."

Hightower is the most impossible, rigid, unsympathetic detective I've ever met. He's unimaginative, too, which makes him a poor administrator. Most of the detectives in Chicago are pretty savvy people, and experience teaches them they have to be flexible. Very few of them care more about their appearance than about solving the case. Hightower is ramrod straight, haughty, and slender, and dresses to emphasize that. I have never seen his pants without a razor-sharp crease. Really, he looks like a tin soldier. The CPD ought to issue him one of those red coats and a saber.

"Gee, Lieutenant, I was almost going to say thanks for coming over, but you haven't exactly gotten off on a good foot."

"I'm going to tell you this just one more time. You may not go around interviewing my witnesses."

"Good. That's certainly the last time I want to hear it. You can't do anything about it. Courts can impose gag orders when there's a case under judicial consideration. But you're not a court and there's no case yet. My understanding is that I could get in real trouble if I told a witness to change his or her story. Or if I gave away a fact you were trying to withhold. But I'm not doing that. And possibly I'd be in trouble if I withheld important facts from you. But actually I'd like to give you any facts I come up with, and you'd probably run from them as if they were poison ivy. Is it possible that you didn't want to chat about this at the station because it's so foolish you don't want anybody else to overhear?"

He looked apoplectic.

"Maybe you'd better sit down," I said.

Hightower remained standing as straight as a flagpole. Just then, LJ dive-bombed, grazing his cheek with one wing. Hightower jumped back and made a grab for his gun. Then he saw his attacker was just a pet parrot and tried to cover up his alarmed overreaction.

"Think you're duck hunting with a handgun, Hightower?"

"That's an ugly bird."

"You—" I was about to say "strutting popinjay" because it fit Hightower so perfectly. But nobody says popinjay anymore, if they ever did. What was a popinjay, anyhow? Whatever—Hightower couldn't walk normally. He was always on the parade ground.

LJ said, "'Out, out, brief candle! Life's but a walking shadow.'"

With a condescending smile, Hightower said, "That's a cute trick you taught him."

I didn't bother to respond to his calling LJ "cute." "I didn't teach LJ anything. A former owner did."

Researchers say that African grey parrots are very intelligent, probably as intelligent as three-year-old children. Still, LJ doesn't know the meaning of these quotations, really. Or so I've always told myself. LJ hears a word and associates it with some line from the professor's vast well of Shakespearean lines.

Sure. Then what was this? Let's deconstruct it. Here was Hightower, the world's most pompous man. One I'd just thought of as a strutting popinjay. And what was the next line, the one LJ didn't get to?

"'A poor player that struts and frets his hour upon the stage and then is heard no more.'"

Apt, LJ. Eerily apt.

"You ought to clean up after him," Hightower said. Yes, there were a couple of bird droppings on the wood floor.

"I'll get to it," I said.

"Birds are dirty."

"People are dirty. You ever catch the flu from a parrot?"

LJ squawked, "Braaak! Aawk!"

"Good bird," I said. LJ flew up and sat on the curtain rod. Why didn't the silly bird dive-bomb Hightower's hair and pull out a nice clump? Maybe with little bits of scalp attached.

Although, why don't I try harder to start a dialogue with Hightower?

"Lieutenant, *please* sit down. We're not getting anywhere this way. Do you have a car downstairs with a driver? If he'd like to come up, I'll give you both coffee."

"No, he wouldn't like to come up." However, Hightower did sit, taking the only comfortable easy chair. Well, heck. That's what I have the chair for, right? To make my life easier.

"Look," I said, "we don't have to like each other. But you know I'm not going to stop trying to figure out what happened at the festival. Not without a court order, anyway, and I don't think you can get one. I know my rights and responsibilities. I've been a reporter for fifteen years. Now, you probably want to hear about what I observed when Plumly and Jennifer were killed. And I want to know just two simple facts that you certainly can tell me."

He didn't specifically agree. "Tell me what you saw during the murders."

I told him. In full, and fully honest, detail. When I was finished, he just nodded, acting as if he knew it all already. Ass.

I said, "Now, you can answer two questions for me."

"Maybe."

Don't grind your teeth, Marsala. Think of the dental bills. Don't clench your jaw; it gives you a headache.

"First question," I said. "You've had the autopsy done by now." He nodded minutely. "Where exactly was the wound? Or to put it another way, how fast did he bleed to death?"

"Hoping to save your brother, huh? Plumly was stabbed in the right upper abdomen, just under the ribs. The knife entered the liver and as they phrase it, 'transected the hepatic artery.' You bleed fast from one of those wounds, but it's not like you got your aorta cut. It's possible he was stabbed half a minute or a minute before he collapsed. The ME says running would make him bleed out faster, but he couldn't have been saved unless he was already in a surgical suite."

"Oh." Hightower had been more forthcoming than I had expected. But since I didn't like him, I assumed that he was just showing off.

"But," he added, "the bleeding would have started immediately."

"Oh. So when he collapsed, was he dead?"

"Probably not. They say he probably lost consciousness, lay there bleeding internally and externally, and died several minutes later."

"Oh."

"That's two questions," he said nastily.

"Not really. Whose fingerprints were on the knife?"

He smiled. "Plumly's." He paused, just to upset me. "And your brother's."

· 12 ·

I AM DOROTHY,
THE SMALL AND MEEK

"LJ," I said when Hightower had left, "we've got a problem. Barry touched that knife when he clutched at Plumly. He must have. He might not even remember doing it. The knife didn't fall to the ground until Plumly did. That's gotta be the explanation."

LJ didn't speak, but instead sat on my knee and looked directly at me out of that bright right eye, then swiveled that flexible birdy neck and looked out of the left eye.

"I can*not* believe that Barry would shoot at Jeremy. But somebody certainly did!"

LJ waved a wing out to the side, then hopped on one foot, which often means a speech is coming. Finally the bird uttered, "'So may the outward shows be least themselves.'"

"That's a big help. It's precisely the interpretation of the outward shows that I'm having trouble with. I know it can't be right."

"'So may the outward shows be least themselves.'"

"Now don't get stuck in a loop. I need to think, and you're distracting me."

" 'So may—' "

"Stop it! Here, have a grape." Next to banana, grapes are LJ's favorite things.

Wait.

Why did I think the stalker was shooting at Jeremy? Because I was so worried about protecting Jeremy, that's why. "The outward shows." Classical misdirection, as in a magic performance. The audience will focus on what it thinks is important. Jeremy was my most important job.

But what were the facts?

When the shot hit the nose of Jeremy's merry-go-round monkey, I had been standing near the nose, closer, in fact, to the nose than Jeremy was. The monkey's head and neck were maybe twenty-four inches long and Jeremy was even farther back than that, sitting on the saddle behind the brass pole. Probably three feet from where the shot hit. But I was right there, close enough to be clipped by a fragment of nose.

When the next shot had buzzed past me and hit the paramedic, it passed close to my left side. Jeremy was standing on my right.

In the Grant Park Underground Garage, the shot again came close to me. Not Jeremy. Maybe the guy wasn't a sharpshooter, but he was consistently missing Jeremy by a mile.

So maybe whoever it was had no intention of shooting Jeremy. Jeremy's presence could have been incidental.

And if somebody wanted to kill me but not Jeremy, did that make it more possible that it was Barry? Is killing your child more difficult than killing your sibling? Well, Cain and Abel might be a case in point.

The killer shot Jennifer because he assumed that she

had witnessed something important. He assumed I had, too, but that Jeremy hadn't. Or that Jeremy, being a child, hadn't noticed, or wouldn't be believed if he told what he saw, whatever it was. Or at very least, that Jeremy couldn't convincingly testify to a jury about it if the case ever went as far as a trial.

Which meant, of the witnesses the shooter had been trying to kill, maybe I was the only one left alive.

· 13 ·

AND YOUR LITTLE DOG,
TOO

"These are your observations, Cat," McCoo said. "How can I know what you saw?"

"I just want your take on it. The more I think about it, the more certain I am that the gunman was shooting at me, not Jeremy."

This issue was just too important for me to decide by myself. McCoo understood that, being both smart and sensitive. Eventually, he would tell me what he thought. Now he swung his rolling, swiveling, reclining chair away from me and scooted to his stainless steel coffeemaker. It was already perfuming the air. The aroma of great coffee calms me down.

"From Maui, I have yellow caturra, red catuai, moka, and typica, but under the circumstances, I started typica when you came in the door."

"McCoo, do you ever wonder whether you drink too much coffee?"

"Certainly not. Coffee is good for you. Millions of people

safely self-medicate for mild depression with a cup of coffee. Coffee in moderation may even help prevent Alzheimer's disease. There's a slight inverse correlation between coffee drinking and Alzheimer's. This may be the result of caffeine increasing dopamine levels, but no one is quite sure."

"Good heavens."

"In moderation, of course. Like anything else, in moderation. Now, try this brew. Typica is considered rich and rejuvenating."

I watched him take real cream from his tiny refrigerator. His coffee grinder showed flecks of brown bean residue in the hopper, not that I would ever have doubted that his beans weren't fresh-ground. Not McCoo. On my own, I've been known to nurse a mug of instant coffee with cream substitute, but McCoo would be horrified, and frankly, I do know the difference.

Sputtering noises signaled the end of the brewing process. McCoo poured coffee, and passed cream, knowing that I didn't take sugar. He watched as I tasted it.

"Oh, my," I said. "Oh, my."

For a highly caffeinated beverage, it was very soothing.

McCoo said, "About your question. I'm not trying to duck it. On the whole, I would say that I would trust your observations. In my opinion, you always pay close attention to details. So yes, probably they were shooting at you. If you think Jeremy is safe, why not relieve Barry's mind and tell him so? Anyway, you've both told what you know."

"Can I call from here?" This was not going to be a fun phone call, but it had to be done.

"Go ahead."

But Barry wasn't in the festival office. I didn't want to call Maud, for fear of having to explain more than I wished to, so I called my folks' house, hoping he was there.

"Mom?" I said, when she picked up.

A spate of indignation greeted me.

"Mom, let me talk for a second. I was just telling what I saw—Mom, is Barry there—?"

My mother had hung up.

"What happened?" McCoo said.

"My mother already took Jeremy back home. Him and the cat. Right after he and my dad got back from the vet this morning."

The two major papers, the *Chicago Tribune* and the *Chicago Sun-Times,* both run what-to-do-around-Chicago sections. Both published reviews of the Oz Festival. They had been written during a preview, before the murders.

Benjamin Ward in the *Tribune* "Tempo" section said:

> . . . with your best choice for parking being, of course, the Grant Park Underground.
>
> Despite the charm of the festival for a child, we can't help wondering why so much emphasis is placed on the all-too-familiar MGM movie elements.
>
> L. Frank Baum wrote thirteen Oz books, with a fourteenth published posthumously and written partly by another author. The series was taken up by several other authors with permission of the Oz estate. Over the years a total of twenty-six additional books were written. These forty books are filled with inventive characters and exciting, colorful events. While the Chicago festival does not entirely limit itself to characters from the movie, it fails to use as many of the other wonders of the Oz *oeuvre* as it might.

George Hill in the *Sun-Times* wrote:

. . . running through next Saturday in Grant Park.

In a festival that is in every other way a delight for children and adults alike, in terms of the Oz canon, the organizers are trying too hard. Most people derive their knowledge of Oz from the Judy Garland movie. But the Chicago Oz Festival struggles mightily to include the lesser-known works. There is a Gump ride, for example, made of sofas and ferns, and a pleasant but odd child-participation ride of rotating rubber mountains.

Possibly a festival with a through-line similar to the movie, in which festival-goers could walk among the movie events in the order in which they happened, would have had more universal appeal.

All in all, though, a pleasant way to spend a day with a child.

The banker Edmond Pottle said, "You're not a cop. You can't question me."

"Sure I can question you. You just don't have to answer, that's all."

"I'm glad you realize that."

"But I don't see why you wouldn't." I used the same line I'd used on Mazzanovich. "Is your information a secret?"

We were in Pottle's office in the Lake State Bank, Pottle's bank. The walls were dark walnut. The floor was an even darker parquet on which a Tabriz rug near the desk glowed like a stained-glass window.

Pottle's desk showed me how he saw himself. It was eight feet long, with a heavily carved base, in other words, important. Pottle was important.

Too important to do secretarial work. Not for Pottle the row of faxes, keyboards, monitors, and printers that most people today had in their offices. His sideboard held only cut-glass bottles filled with amber liquids, of which he offered me none. A glass—faceted, heavy, blocky, and no doubt very expensive—stood on a felt coaster, a few drops of liquid at the bottom. Pottle himself was slender but gave an impression of portliness, probably because he held himself as if his arms and legs were ever so valuable. His eyes were light green and reminded me of peeled grapes. The suit was navy blue summer wool, so light and soft-looking that you'd think the fabric could float on air. It goes without saying he was wearing black shoes.

He thought over my question for several seconds, his words being ever so valuable, too, and then said, "No. I have no secrets. But I'm very busy."

"Humor me. Just a couple of questions."

"Well, hurry it up."

The questions I had asked Taubman and Mazzanovich had stayed in my mind, although except for the obvious one, whether they'd stabbed Plumly, I wasn't quite sure why these questions resonated with me. Anyhow, you have to start somewhere. "What kind of a guy was Plumly?"

"I was extremely disappointed in him. His security firm is rather new, and therefore we thought it was generous of us to choose him."

"Generous? Hiring Plumly was charity? Or did he have connections? Did he know somebody?"

"I have no idea."

"Chicago is famous for its patronage problems."

"The reputation is overblown," he said firmly.

"Why were you disappointed? Did he do a bad job? He seemed to be working hard whenever I was there."

"He worked hard enough, I suppose. But he stuck his nose into parts of the project development that weren't his business."

"Such as?"

"Artistic decisions. It turned out the man was an *Oz* fan!"

"Uh—is that bad?"

"It's childish. I am not saying there's anything wrong with having an Oz Festival. It's quite appropriate for a city the size of Chicago to produce events for children now and then. Certainly the principal festivals, such as the Blues-Fest and the GospelFest, are adult-oriented. But a security specialist ought not to be distracted by fantasies such as the—the Gump."

"Oh yes. He told me he liked the Gump."

"The Gump was made of flying sofas! With palm leaves for wings. This is a fantasy for three-year-olds. A creature like that *would never fly*. It's not aerodynamic."

"I think that was sort of the point. That's why it's whimsical. What did Plumly want done about the Gump?"

"We have a perfectly nice Gump ride for the youngest children. That's all right. It's made of sofas that move around on tracks. With elk-like heads on the front ends." The way he said this you'd think he was saying "with botulism."

"Well, that's good, I guess."

"But Plumly wanted real palm fronds. In fact, the plastic ones were much superior. You can't have real fronds dropping pieces off all day long—" He coughed, grabbed an asthma inhaler, and sucked medication. He sat back, catching himself. "Why am I troubling myself with this? Plumly was good enough in his way. He was just too *childish*."

I absolutely did not know what to say to that. The argument sounded like the battles that rage over tiny decisions in theatrical productions. I once saw an entire cast come to blows, real physical blows, over whether the skull in *Hamlet* should be gleaming bone-white or caked with mud and disgusting. So Plumly meddled in things? That was interesting.

"Mr. Pottle, Plumly ran away from you three men over to my brother. Why did he do that?"

"I haven't the slightest idea."

"Had one of you said something to upset him?"

"Certainly not."

"Did he say he was going to go to Barry for a reason?"

"No."

"What had you been talking about right before?"

"We were talking about some of the food booths. One of them was using dangerous fuel and one of them had the bad taste to have a sign with nude women on it. Can you imagine! With children coming to the festival? Some people have absolutely no sense."

As I headed home, my cell phone rang.

"Hello?"

"Cat? It's McCoo."

"What's happening?"

"Hightower is bringing your brother in this afternoon. He's going to caution him."

This meant Barry was formally a suspect in the murder. They'd "give him his rights," which meant reading the Miranda warning to him. It didn't necessarily mean they were arresting him, though. "Why now?"

"The fingerprints on the knife."

· 14 ·

SOMETHING WITH
POISON IN IT

The idea of going to my parents' house for Sunday dinner, what with Barry having been called in for questioning last evening, made me practically nauseated. My mother's cooking ought to take me the rest of the way to truly queasy.

It was now Saturday morning. Yesterday being Friday and all. Why does my family have Sunday dinner on Saturday? It wasn't always thus. We started to do this when my mother, who insisted on everybody going to church before Sunday dinner, started fighting with one of my sisters-in-law who didn't want to go to church at all. Then my third-oldest brother—there are four older than me and one, Teddy, who is younger—converted to Catholicism, which sent my mother into fits of upset. She didn't see any reason to keep her distress to herself, which meant that every Sunday dinner became a proselytizing session, and if arguments didn't work, she moved swiftly to "Oh well, don't listen to me. I'm only your mother!"

My father was a peacemaker. He didn't often decree

anything, but when he did, it stuck. He ordered that discussion of religion could only take place on Sunday. Then
he decreed that Sunday dinner would happen on Saturday.

And that's why.

There was a square casserole in the oven with a red topping. I asked, "Lasagna?"

My mother had not spoken to me when I came in, which
wasn't surprising. However, now she went so far as to say,
"Tuna casserole."

"Why is it red?"

"I put tomato soup on it for topping. It makes a change."

That was for sure.

"What you did to Barry is utterly unforgivable," my
mother said.

"Well, that's up to Barry. To forgive or not." Hoping to
get a genuine discussion going, I said, "Don't you believe
people should tell the truth?"

My mother has always managed to duck real issues. She
talks all the time, but she won't really *talk*. She speaks in
clichés. The number of times I've tried to sit her down and
just chat like two friends is legion. Nothing comes of it.

Right now she was saying, "Family comes first."

"First before honesty?" I asked.

"Family always comes first."

"My country right or wrong," I muttered. Unfortunately,
the problem wasn't just a matter of honesty alone. Suppose
Barry really had killed Plumly? Suppose some confederate of his killed Jennifer and followed us? If there was even
one chance in ten that Barry had killed Plumly, I had no
right to protect him by lying. But I couldn't say that to Mom.
My waffling on Barry's guilt was surprising even to me.
The Red Queen in *Alice in Wonderland* could believe six

impossible things before breakfast, but I thought I was more logical. Two contradictory things—Barry must have killed Plumly and Barry would never have killed Plumly— two mutually exclusive ideas, and I believed them both.

At this point Roxanne swept into the kitchen from somewhere in the backyard. "Cat," she said. "Terribly disappointed."

By which she meant "I'm terribly disappointed in you." Roxanne has started talking this way for reasons known only to her. I've asked Douglas, who is my brother and Roxanne's husband, and he just says, "What way?" Personally, my guess is that she thinks it's upper-class Brit, and I suppose we can be glad that she hasn't yet added the accent.

Roxanne is a lady of leisure. Her one and only job was eighteen years ago, a short stretch as Customer Sales Representative for Pesky Telemarketers.

"How's Dougie?" I asked.

"Oh, Douglas is mad at you, too. Awfully shabby behavior."

"Yes," I said. "Deciding against a person without hearing the facts is truly shabby."

She stared at me blankly just as Douglas entered, my father in tow. They were carrying a discarded bathtub. My folks had remodeled their bathroom two years back and Mom never throws anything out.

"That crooked contractor just wants me to let him take it so he can sell it," she had told my father. "I want you to carry the tub out to the shed." Unfortunately, the house had no garage.

"And plant geraniums in it?" he said. But she scowled at him. Now she shrieked, "Don't bring that thing in here! It's dirty. We're going to eat in a minute!"

Dougie said, "Dad says the Elfridges are having a cookout and they want to borrow it."

"Bathing before barbecuing?" I asked.

Dad said, "They want to put the stopper in and fill it brimful of beer and ice."

"So why bring it in here?"

"To clean it. I can't give it to them this way."

"Why not clean it outdoors?"

"What? And let it get all dirty again?"

This was not the first time I suspected Dad of doing something odd solely to distract my mother, and I was sure of it when he winked at me. "We'll put it in the laundry room," he said to Douglas, who reluctantly held up his end and kept walking.

Dad also thought Douglas could use a little loosening up.

My father truly loves my mother. That's gotta be it. He's not a masochist. He believes that she can't help her negative attitude, and he may be quite right. He believes that, underneath, there is a lovable person. And he may be quite right.

My father is supportive to her and to all of us. He's kind of a large elf, with a puckish sense of humor, which he's careful to keep under control most of the time, because my mother is very quick to believe she's being made fun of.

And she may be quite right.

The front door opened and Barry, Maud, and Jeremy walked in. Maud looked white, drawn, and very tired. She was carrying the baby, wrapped to its neck in a pink blanket with blue polka dots. The kind of blanket you get from a friend when you won't tell them whether it's going to be a boy or a girl. Actually, of course, it already is a boy or a girl, but you know what I mean. Jeremy was carrying the marmalade tomcat, wrapped to the neck in his Cubs jacket. Both baby and cat looked sweet.

Now, if this isn't the way to deal with a child's worry that his mother is consumed with care of the new baby, I don't know what is. Barry saw me in the group and pointedly moved to the other side of the room.

Everybody cooed over the gorgeous new little morsel of humanity. The baby's name was Cynthia. After about ten minutes of the best baby in the world and how's the little sweetie, and look how good she is (my mother said, "Of course she's good. She's sleeping."), my father changed subjects.

"Now, tell the folks about your cat, Jeremy. He was a very good boy when we went to the doctor, wasn't he?"

"He was very brave."

Roxanne said, "Does he have a name, sweetie?"

"I'm going to call him the Cowardly Lion."

She said, "Kind of a long name."

"I can call him Lion for short."

"Or Cow," said Roxanne.

My mother broke into this exchange, saying, "Maud, I wouldn't think you'd allow this."

"Allow what, Mom Marsala?" Maud was always cheerful to my mother, which told me she found her heavy going.

My mother said, "Cats can smother babies."

"Don't worry, Mom," Maud said. "When Jeremy told me you'd suggested that to him, I decided to call our pediatrician, and he said that was nonse— Uh, he said it really wasn't true."

"Oh." Mom was stymied. Briefly. "Well," she said, "I certainly hope your doctor knows what he's talking about. Who recommended him to you?"

"He's the dean of the Northwestern University Medical School."

Things didn't improve when dinner was served. Roxanne and I set the table and then I brought the casserole from the oven to the table. We all sat down, including

Jeremy, but not including Lion the cat, who was closed up in the bathroom, with a bowl of milk. Oddly enough, he didn't complain. The baby also missed the meal, having blinked a few times and fallen back asleep in a little yellow carrying cot.

Foodwise, neither the baby nor Lion the cat missed much. Mom had bought a tub of coleslaw from the local deli to go with the tuna casserole. She passed around a jar of instant coffee and permitted Roxanne—"I'll let you do it"— to carry in the teakettle and pour boiling water into everybody's cups.

"I don't hold with all this fancy coffee talk," Mom said. "Big companies with lots of smart researchers have put millions of dollars into developing instant coffee."

Barry said wryly, "And very highly advertised, too." He had thereby used one of her favorite phrases and robbed her of a comeback should anybody object to the flavor.

Mom said, "The main thing is to use a very small amount of instant and stir it briskly. Don't make it too strong. Just the tip of a teaspoon is fine."

Conversation lagged for fifteen minutes after that. Which was about the time it took for everybody to finish eating. I reflected on what Chief McCoo would say about Mom's coffee recipe. Probably nothing; he'd be speechless. Dessert was canned apricots, exactly two per person.

"Can I take Lion out in the yard?" Jeremy asked.

Dad said, "Sure."

Jeremy's absence made it possible for everybody to start berating me again. Well, not Dad or Maud.

Barry said, "I have to leave in half an hour. They want me to come back to the police station."

"Why again?" Mom asked.

"I don't know. For more questioning."

"This is your fault, Catherine," she said.

Barry said, "They cautioned me, you know. That means they think I'm a serious suspect."

Maud said, "But they can't really think you killed that man! You're not that sort of person."

Looking directly at me for the first time, Barry said, "Cat, you could tell the police you made a mistake."

"That I didn't see what I saw?"

"That you're not sure. That the lighting wasn't good." He noticed Dad studying him soberly. "It *wasn't* good. She can't possibly be as certain as she says she is."

"What about Jennifer?" I asked.

"Jennifer is—well, after all, Jennifer can't testify."

Dad sat up straighter. "I don't like this line of talk," he said.

Okay!

"Well, it's not your life on the line," Barry shouted. I looked more closely at him—his nostrils were pinched and the skin below his eyes was tight—and realized what was making him so unpleasant. He was terrified.

My mother said, "Hush!" Then to me she repeated, "This is all your fault, Catherine."

"All I did was tell the truth. There has to be some explanation; I know Barry wouldn't kill anybody."

"Well, maybe you ought to mind your own business!"

"Mother, should people tell the truth or not?"

"You shouldn't have talked about it."

"Wait a minute here! I'm getting pretty damn sick of this. Who was shot at? Me!"

Maud opened her eyes wide, with some sympathy, I thought. But Barry was still frowning at me.

I said, "Who was protecting *your* child, Barry? *Me!*"

Nobody said a word. "Who had a bullet practically rip out her arm? Me. Who grabbed Jeremy and took what was maybe the only safe way out? Who talked Jeremy into thinking of it as an adventure instead of a really, really dangerous race against death, which it was? Me. We could have been killed, but I convinced him we were having an exciting time. Have I heard *one word of thanks?* From you, Mom? No. From you, Barry? Nope. Okay, you're under stress, but Jeremy is the most important person to all of us, isn't he? One word of thanks? No! From you, Maud? No."

Maud said, "I'm sorry, Cat. I have been thinking about what you went through. And I realize that Jeremy's safe because of you."

"And let's not forget, that since Barry didn't kill Plumly, which I firmly believe, there was a real, live assassin following me and Jeremy. This was not my imagination. I hope I'm safe now—if I am—because I told the police everything I know. But I'm not going to be able to relax as long as there's a killer out there."

My dad said, "You're right."

I said, "Barry, you may be furious at me for telling the truth about what I saw. But it's time for you to say to me, 'Oh, thanks, Cat. We owe you. You helped out with my festival, and then you probably saved the life of my child. You put your body between him and a bullet.' And what I want to know is *why do I have to ask for this? What is wrong with you people?* Is there one human being here who would like to say 'Thanks, Cat'?"

· 15 ·

NO HEART?

I left the house.

I felt so alone. My family hated me. McCoo was busy, and the cop in charge of the investigation—the investigation that could potentially free my brother from suspicion—was a haughty, rigid idiot. As if that weren't enough, I put my hand in my pocket and found the picture Jeremy had had me take at the festival—me as the Wicked Witch.

McCoo would probably talk with me if I went to his office. And he'd probably be there even though it was Saturday. But there wasn't much point. He'd only have to check with Hightower to find out what had developed. And he'd owe it to Hightower and his own principles not to give too much information away to a relative of the leading suspect.

I called Sam. Dr. Sam Davidian, my semi-significant other, is a trauma surgeon working in the ED at University Hospital. He'd probably be my significant other if our schedules let us get together for more than four hours or so in a given week.

He was on duty. No surprise there.

I said, "Sam, I have an ethical dilemma. Are you getting off work anytime today?"

"Matter of fact, no. It's Saturday. Rush hour in the trauma unit. Head trauma. Motorcycle accidents. Drunk drivers. Domestic violence. Alcohol poisoning."

"But you have other staff members."

"Yes. But we're low on people tonight. We had a little unfortunate accident."

"What happened?"

"You know Freddy? The new senior resident? He'd been on the floor twenty consecutive hours, truly beat, takes a shower, wants to sleep in the cot room, but there's only three beds and they're all in use. So he pulls on a johnny and goes and lies down in an empty exam room, Number Twenty-one. One of the docs has a call to start an epidural on a patient in Room Twelve. He and a third-year go into Twenty-one and find Freddy dead to the world, swab him, try to start the epidural, but he fights them. They've already been told that the patient is combative, so they wrestle him down and get the epidural in and flowing. About this time the attending is looking for them. Why haven't they started the epidural on the patient in Twelve? He finds them. Everybody is horrified."

"Especially Freddy, I would think. Sam, don't they always look at the wrist bracelet? He wouldn't have had one on."

"Of *course* they're supposed to look at the wrist bracelet. Unfortunately, they'd been on the floor thirty-six hours and were exhausted. You know, in this irrational world airline pilots can only fly a certain maximum number of hours, because sleep deprivation is a brain-killer. Planes could crash. But somebody who has your life at the end of a syringe—oh no!"

"But why didn't they recognize Freddy?"

"He'd just transferred in from another shift. They'd never seen him before."

"This sounds absolutely impossible!"

"Right. Is. It also happened. When you've got layers of safeguards, every accident that gets by sounds impossible."

"So they must be in hot water."

"Boiling water. They're both on suspension. Freddy, by the way, is perfectly all right, but he's taking two days off to recover. And he deserves it. So I'm working two shifts. If I'm lucky, it won't be three."

"But I need your advice."

"Can I give this advice over the phone?"

"It's too complicated."

"Then I guess—gee, I'm really sorry, Cat, but is tomorrow okay?"

"Is that like take two aspirin and call me in the morning?"

Blast!

Nobody loved me. As we used to say in high school when we were feeling excessively sorry for ourselves, guess I'd better go eat worms.

And then I realized there was one person on this earth I could go to who would care and who would *be there*.

Hal Briskman is the editor of *Chicago Today*. He is a constant buyer for my stories, which, of course, makes him a saint. Hal is not only a great editor, but often gets ideas that brew up into interesting long articles for the "think-piece" section. And he knows everything about Chicago politics.

Like McCoo, Hal is always at work. Saturdays, Sundays, plus all night as far as I know. Hal's only drawback is his affection for antique slang. A good story, for example, is "spiffy." Unless it's an extra-great story, in which case it's "spiffarootie."

I love him.

*   *   *

"Cat!" Hal said. "Light of my life."

"I brought coffee." I had brought really good gourmet fresh-ground fresh-brewed extra-strong coffee, not my mother's.

"So you want something."

"Yes. You know everything and everybody."

"Silver-tongued devil. Ask away."

"I've been working on the Oz Festival, as you know. I should have the material for the article about the Oz-haters for you soon. You know, no matter how you look at it, it's very strange that people would particularly pick on the Oz books."

When they were first published, the Oz books were immediately popular with children. They were also hailed as the first real American fairy tales. Earlier stories for children had been either heavily moralistic fables or the grisly stories of the likes of the Brothers Grimm, with children taken to the woods by their parents and left to starve.

But in the 1930s a librarian in New York City named Anne Carroll Moore had pulled the entire Oz series from the Children's Room of the New York Public Library. Since she was the doyenne of American librarians, librarians all over the United States followed her direction and pulled the books.

"She would never explain why," I said to Hal.

In the 1950s, I told him, a Detroit librarian eliminated all the Oz series books from his system because there was "nothing uplifting or elevating" about them. Somebody else said they were "a cowardly approach to life," whatever that may mean. How could Dorothy's brave search for a way back home be called cowardly? A librarian from Florida said they were "untrue to life." You want to say, "Hello? True to life? These are whimsical stories for children."

"So why," Harold said, "did this happen?"

"I don't know. To be fair, not all librarians agreed with these stick-in-the-muds. Some people called the Baum style flat, but it isn't. It's humorous and lively. People thought librarians might have been worried about the expense of buying a whole line, but there were other series like *Little House* and *Doctor Dolittle* that they bought."

"And so?"

"Some said it was because the Oz books were commercialized. It seems strange to us today. I mean, look at Disney. Every new movie spawns product spin-offs. But in the early 1900s this was all new."

"Can you get me the story on this within a few days?"

"I think so. There were Wizard of Oz musical comedies, during Baum's lifetime, some written by him, and movies and toys later. He made several movies himself. Later on, a critic of the critics suggested that librarians might have objected to the 'commodification' of Oz. I wouldn't be surprised if that was it. I think we could do an article on Oz as the first case of product sales on this scale based around a children's story. And it all ties to Chicago, of course."

"You're saying Oz laid the groundwork for Walt Disney enterprises."

"Right. And suffered for it."

"I'll buy that."

"But will you pay me for it?" I asked.

"Up to a point. Commodification only goes so far."

"I expected that."

"Cat, are you avoiding talking about the festival murders?"

"Not really. Delaying, maybe." He'd heard only that I was there as a witness. I told him what had happened to Jeremy and me in the tunnels, extra details that he wouldn't have gleaned from the police reports, his own reporters, and his extensive gossip grapevine.

When I finished, he said, "Dang!" It was his latest favorite word. "Makes me wish we were a daily."

"Hal, you realize I couldn't write you an on-the-spot about it, even if *Chicago Today* were a daily. I'm not going to do anything to focus attention on Barry."

I asked him, "Tell me about those three guys, Edmond Pottle, E. T. Taubman, and Larry Mazzanovich."

"You think the three got together and stabbed Plumly?"

"Honestly, Hal, much as I'd prefer that, I don't really see it. If three guys are gonna kill somebody together, wouldn't they do it in secret? Do Pottle, Taubman, and Mazzanovich have any kind of common history?"

"Like they all went to school together, went out behind the barn, cut their fingers, and swore in blood one for all and all for one?"

"Yeah, like that."

"I hate to have to tell you this, Cat, but I doubt they even knew each other before the Oz Festival. They're totally different types of people from totally different backgrounds, and as you well know, doing totally different types of jobs."

"I was afraid you'd say that."

"Take Taubman for starters. I've known E.T. slightly for years. He grew up in Winnetka, which as you know is one of the highest-income suburbs in the country."

"Or the planet."

"Or the planet. But his family wasn't especially rich. There are a lot more modest houses in Winnetka than most people realize. He went to New Trier High School, did a lot of theater, which New Trier is known for, did art, and went on to Swarthmore. I'm told he's always been a real culture-vulture. He's also had a tendency to hang around the rich. He finally married one, sort of."

"Sort of married somebody? I've heard of that."

"No, sort of rich. Her name is Stephanie Mathilda Sotor.

Her parents have a lot of money, but their idea of raising children is to deprive them of as much as possible for fear of their becoming 'spoiled,' so Stephanie won't have any serious money until the parents pass on to their reward."

"I'm not sure that approach really works. I mean, when it's very artificial, the kids just think they're being punished."

"Well, in Stephanie's case, it produced some odd behaviors. She married E.T., knowing he didn't have serious simoleons, either, but nags him incessantly to make more. She, by the way, works as a travel agent to the snazzy. Sends people to St. Tropez or whatever's the in place of the day. Brings in a small but for them significant amount of commission. Enough to keep them in brown rice and Chablis. Anyhow, she goes to the opera, the theater, classical concerts. In other words, she never goes to hear music that young people like. They both donate time to cultural causes. And she pushes people to hire E.T. as lighting designer. For concerts and galleries. Which I think embarrasses him. I don't know him well, but I've seen him wince sometimes when she's talking to a potential customer about how great he is."

"I saw some of his work. It's good."

"He *is* good. That's the heck of it. She makes him look like a fool. He could make it in the lighting design world better if she'd leave him alone and let him have at it."

"He's got a huge studio on Chestnut Street that has to be pricey."

"Yup. She insisted. In case a prospective client wants to do a 'studio visit,' she wants him to look successful."

We drank coffee and contemplated the folly of Stephanie Sotor-Taubman for a few minutes. Then I said, "What about Pottle?"

"Different story altogether. He isn't originally from

Chicago. Has family money. Went to Princeton, unless I misremember."

"Which has never happened yet as far as I know."

"Butter me up. I'll give you work. To continue: he came here to extend the family's banking empire. I don't mean he has world-class money. He's not Henry Ford, much less Bill Gates."

"Bill Gates indeed! Microsoft has a larger GNP than Canada!"

"I know. But Pottle is very, very comfortable."

"Came here from where?"

"Family's in New York. Illinois used to have a law against branch banks, but no more. You know, to found a bank, you apply to the Federal Reserve and get a charter, demonstrate you have assets, demonstrate you have no criminal record, and then you can open a bank. Banks lend money, and naturally, politicians who can dispense favors are among the borrowers."

"Do banks really lend money to politicians? I've never thought about it. Of course, they must."

"A politician can go to a bank and say, 'I need money for my campaign,' and borrow it. But suppose the bank is *so* friendly it doesn't press for repayment right away? Or suppose it sort of forgets about asking for interest?"

"Isn't that illegal?"

"If it's found out, sure. Now, Pottle himself I don't know much about. He's only been here ten years or so. There was a rumor he was maybe a tiny bit fast and loose in business dealings, but who knows? Humankind loves rumors, whether they're true or false."

"You'd better hope they love rumors. You run a newsmagazine."

"Hoist by my own petard. In any case, Pottle isn't from here, didn't go to New Trier High School, and lives in a

Gold Coast penthouse on North Michigan Avenue. I don't think he likes theater or opera, or any of that kind of thing. His path doesn't really cross Taubman's."

"Damn. Or as you might say, dang. What about Mazzanovich?"

"Ah, a whole different kettle of fish. A kid from a poor family who worked his way up. With his fists, so the story goes. He was a big supporter of the alderman from his area, became a ward heeler, went around to get out the ward vote, drove elderly voters to the polls and so on, and when the man in office retired, Mazzanovich stepped into his shoes."

"Drove dead voters to the polls?"

"Cat!"

"Never mind. How'd he get into the cement business?"

"Well, now, that's a story. There was a cement business called Bio-crete in his ward, owned by an older gentleman. Nice old guy, been in the business for decades, but he made the mistake of backing the wrong person for mayor, despite Mazzanovich warning him it was a bad idea. Anyhow, after the election, city inspectors just kept finding all these problems with Bio-crete's work. Profits fell."

"As one might expect."

"Finally, the man decided to sell out. Mazzanovich just happened to be able to put cash on the barrelhead to buy it."

"Gee, I hate to hear stuff like that. This is my hometown."

"And you want it pure? Cat, influence is everywhere. Payoffs. Vigorish. Connections. Example—a major city organization recently had its annual parade and cookout. Doesn't matter which organization, firefighters, cops, sanitation workers, whatever. You don't need to know. But the young man who was designated to make the refreshments arrangements happens to be the son of a friend of mine. So he called up one of our major fast-food retailers. McDonald's, Wendy's, Burger King, White Castle. This is another thing you don't need to know. He gets a price per person for a sandwich, side dish, and drink. They say they can provide a choice of two sandwich types, three side dishes, and about a dozen different drink choices. And the price is pretty spiffy, he thinks. Fine. Goes to his boss with the glad news. Boss is horrified. 'You can't use them! You have to use XYZ Catering.'

"So he calls XYZ Catering. They'll provide just one 'choice' of sandwich, a burger. One side dish, coleslaw. And hot coffee. Bummer, thinks my young man. But maybe they're really cheap. And the punch line? No way, José. The cost was three times the cost of the other company! Was XYZ connected? Your choice, Cat, is (a) yes, (b) yes, or (c) yes."

"But in this particular case, the Oz Festival is a city event. The city has always bragged that it tries to make most of the Grant Park events free. Like the lakefront fireworks are free and the GospelFest and all. How would somebody like Mazzanovich influence the festival?"

"Let me count the ways. There are so many I don't know where to begin. Let's suppose there are thirty Little Toto Hot Dog Stands around the city that all want to have a booth at the festival. Obviously, you can't let all of them in. You'd have too many hot dogs and not enough ice cream. So somebody makes a decision. Choose Barky's Dogs. The point being, *every time somebody makes a decision, somebody can influence that decision.*"

"But it's a group decision, isn't it?"

"Then it takes *more* influence. Listen, I'm not saying that all these events are influence-driven. I really believe that there's a lot of honesty in Chicago. But where there's money to be made, there's influence to be peddled."

I got up, stretched, and succeeded in not yelping as my shoulder screamed at me. "Hal, can you keep an ear to the ground on this? I've got myself into a horrible position. Barry is innocent. Truly. He's just not the sort of person to shoot a defenseless young woman like Jennifer. There's got to be someone out there who had a lot to lose if Plumly talked about something he discovered. And don't look at me that way. I know people always say 'he wouldn't do anything like that' about their relatives. But I'm not naïve and I'm sure of this."

"Roger-dodger. Will do."

"I'll have the Baum story to you by Tuesday."

"What's wrong with your shoulder?"

"Fell."

"Oh."

There was really no likelihood that Mazzanovich, Pottle, and Taubman had any mutual history. Add to that the unpleasant nature of Chicago politics, and I had gotten so depressed I went out for a drive,

· 16 ·

PAY NO ATTENTION TO THAT
MAN BEHIND THE CURTAIN

Early in his life, L. Frank Baum wanted to be an actor. He came to Chicago briefly when he acted in his own play *The Maid of Arran* in October 1882.

Theater was unpredictable and low-paying. The more things change, the more they stay the same. For a while, as a young man, he tried to make a go of business enterprises, but he was just too nice a guy. He opened a variety store called Baum's Bazaar in Aberdeen, South Dakota—then Dakota Territory—in 1888, and although he worked hard at it, he could not bear to take money from the very poor. By the time the store went bankrupt, there were over a hundred and fifty nonpaying customers on the books. He tried running a newspaper in the same town, but that went bankrupt, too.

Finally, in 1891, Baum moved to Chicago with his wife and their four boys, the youngest one just a baby. He had secured a job at a newspaper, the *Chicago Evening Post*, and earned $18.62 a week. This was so little, even then, that he finally quit and took a job as a traveling salesman, working on commission, selling china and glassware, which he had to transport in large trunks. With four children, his income still wasn't enough, and his wife supplemented it by giving embroidery lessons at ten cents each.

They lived at 34 Campbell Park, a site that is now renumbered 2233 Campbell Park, changed during the Great 1909 Chicago Street Number Rationalization, but the house is gone. No wonder; it was primitive. There was no electricity in the place, of course, which given the year was only to be expected, but also no running water, and not even gas for gaslight or heat. In the evenings they read by kerosene lamp, and if Baum wanted to write after sundown, he wrote by kerosene lantern or candlelight. If you tried to live like that today, with no heat or light or running water or indoor plumbing, the health department would close you down. For that matter, if you tried to raise children in an environment like that, you'd be arrested for felony child endangerment.

Several days earlier I had driven past the site where the Baums' first house had stood. Campbell Park is a bit south of the Loop and fairly far west. But there was nothing left to see except the general environment, which is totally different now.

Today I drove to his second house, which is still in existence. All the way, I checked the rearview mirror. Nobody had tried to attack me today, but there was a killer out there who thought I'd seen something incriminating to him. I hoped he knew I'd told everything to the cops.

In 1895 Baum and his family moved to this somewhat more livable building at 120 Flournoy Street (now numbered 2149). More livable by their standards, anyway, even though most of us today would consider living like this the equivalent of camping out. This house at least had gaslight

and a coal-fired range. The house was near the old Cubs
Park at Wolcott and Polk. Baum loved baseball, and went to
the park whenever he could afford it. When Baum's wife's
mother, a straitlaced old lady, came to visit, she was offended
that they could hear the cheering from the park on Sundays.

During all this time, he was writing, and sometimes publishing, stories for children. *Mother Goose in Prose* sold
fairly well. *Father Goose* sold very well indeed.

As Baum became more prosperous, he moved the family
to 68 Humboldt Boulevard, now renumbered 1667. It was
only a mile or so from Tripp Avenue, where Walt Disney
would be born a couple of years later. In this house Baum
had a study of his own for the first time. The family liked to
bicycle in Humboldt Park and picnic on the grass. It was
here he began work on *The Emerald City*, which eventually
was to become *The Wizard of Oz*. He couldn't sell it. Publishers considered it too radically different from children's
stories of the time. It was very "American" in flavor. That
was not considered a good thing. It didn't draw a specific
moral. That was a serious deficiency. It was quirky. That
couldn't be fixed. Finally, a small Chicago publishing house
agreed to bring it out, as long as Baum and his illustrator
were willing to pay all the expenses.

And then a miracle happened.

There were a few copies of *The Wizard of Oz* produced
in August 1900, but distribution of the ten thousand first-
printing copies did not begin until September. There was so
much demand that another twenty-five thousand were
printed in October, thirty thousand in November, and by the
new year, ninety thousand had been printed. It was the
best-selling children's book of the year. Christmas 1900 was
the first year children found an Oz book under their tree.
Since then the holiday giving of Oz books to happy children has never stopped.

*   *   *

With evening coming on, I drove from Humboldt Boulevard to Grant Park. It took me three complete turns around the area, up Michigan Avenue, then east on Balbo to Lake Shore Drive, south on Lake Shore, then west, and back up Michigan, to get up the nerve to park in the Grant Park Underground. I hadn't realized how cowardly I was until now. Each circuit ate up about twenty minutes, with the worst of the rush-hour traffic just coming to an end. Yes, there's a rush hour on Saturday evening, although it tends to be in both directions, into town and out of town, unlike weekdays when it's out of town. It was hard to imagine amid the exhaust fumes and bumper-to-bumper cars that the automobile had been considered a great boon to Chicago when it was invented. City planners were thrilled to get rid of the problems of horse manure and dead horses on the downtown streets.

Getting out of the car in the underground was a mental trip in and of itself. It was all I could do not to glance around for the chipped concrete block where the shot had hit near us on Thursday night. This time I didn't leave my cell phone in the car. Live and learn—and if you learn well enough, you may stay alive.

And finally I was back at the Yellow Brick Road. My notebook was in my pocket. A dozen pens were ready in my other pocket.

Certainly looking at the place Plumly died would tell me something more than I knew now. It had to. On Thursday almost all my attention had been focused on Jeremy. Without him to care for, I should be able to see much more. And maybe remember more.

The Yellow Brick Road ran east-west through the festival, from Michigan Avenue, around the Emerald City castle, to Lake Shore Drive on the far east side. Because I had come out of the Grant Park Underground onto Michigan Avenue, the west entrance was in front of me.

The place was full of cops. The police department calls flooding an area with uniforms "showing a presence." And they were doing it here. The likelihood of a third murder here had to be around zilch, but the mayor was making sure that nobody could say he took the killings anything but seriously.

I made a short right turn into Gillikin country, which was all purple. Here were purple snow cones, several booths of vendors, including books and memorabilia, plus knick-knacks like china Scarecrows, Tin Woodmen, Cowardly Lions, Dorothys, and Wicked Witches. A rare book dealer had a booth called "To Please a Child," after the biography of L. Frank Baum written by his son Frank and Russell MacFall. Now that it was dark, the purple Gillikin country lighting made it difficult to see his wares, forcing him to bring in two hooded high-intensity lights so that customers could actually examine the books.

The Oz lighting plan, which was dramatic, and which had received such good coverage in the media, certainly had a few drawbacks.

Without intending to, I had come into the festival near where Jennifer had died. The Flying Monkeys merry-go-round was turning, its music playing "We're Off to See the Wizard." The purple and ultraviolet lights, and the Day-Glo paint on the merry-go-round, gave an otherworldly glow to the monkeys. Jeremy had loved that merry-go-round. The lights and the monkeys made it unlike any he had ever seen. Fortunately, he knew nothing about Jennifer's death and wouldn't have any bad memories of this ride if I brought him back here.

Who was it who said "nothing to it but to do it"? Taking a

deep breath, I handed over a ticket and got on the merry-go-round, and while it was still stationary, I went to the same spot where I had been when Jennifer's head exploded. I could see the event horribly clearly in my mind. She had been walking toward the Emerald City area, which is to say, roughly east. Most of the festival-goers, still unaware of Plumly's death, had wandered over to watch the opening ceremonies at the Emerald City. The band had been playing. Not too many people had stayed here. But even with just a thin scattering of people, the assassin would hardly have stood out in plain view holding a gun, if he was smart. There were only a few places he could have been. He could not have been behind the merry-go-round because he wouldn't have been able to see Jennifer through the solid paneling in the center that covered the machinery. He hadn't been on the merry-go-round. Not only would he have been easily seen, but the shot had not sounded that close.

Several booths and equipment trucks blocked other possible sites—the fried mangaboos stand just north over the border in Winkie country, the snow cones to the southeast. Three or four of those silver equipment trucks were in the way, too, especially a few yards to the north. For a moment I toyed with the idea that the killer could have been inside a souvenir booth or an equipment truck. But the equipment trucks had no windows. The booths were possible only if the owner of the booth was in on the killing or if the owner himself had been the killer, because the booths had solid backs that you couldn't see through.

I hopped off the merry-go-round. Could one of the booth operators be the killer? Well, not the killer of Plumly. The only booth near where he was killed had been the popcorn stand and it was too far away for the operator to stab Plumly. If there were two killers, possibly one could be a vendor, but if so he would have had to have left the booth unattended when he had chased us down the tunnels.

Unless there had been a second staff member in the booth to hold the fort. If so, the vendor and his assistant both probably would have to have been in on the crime.

I could ask.

Half an hour later, I was convinced that hadn't happened. One of the book dealers said he and his wife had been present all day, every day of the festival, had not left the booth all the evening of the murder, and had only seen the aftermath of the shooting. Of course, they could both be lying, but that was extremely unlikely. I seemed to remember seeing them there.

The snow cones staff consisted of two kids—well, all right, they may have been eighteen, but they looked like kids to me. "We were here," one said.

"Yeah, but shit," the other said. "We missed all the good stuff. Didn't have a clue until the cops came. Never even saw the body."

They were disappointed to have missed it all. But they were telling the truth, unless they were the greatest actors of recent times. Frankly, they didn't seem to care that much, not about the customers, the cones, or the killing.

As far as background checks on all the vendors went, that was something the cops could do better than I could. They had the personnel and resources. I assumed they had done so and had also searched for ejected shell casings, which had to have gone somewhere if the gun was an automatic. I'd get McCoo to tell me whether they'd found any. But for now, my guess was the shooter must have been lurking in the space between the popcorn stand and the ice cream stand in Quadling country, or between the ice cream stand and the Emerald City castle, or near the Magic Mountain in Winkie country.

In other words, close to the center of the festival grounds.

In other words, pretty much where Barry was last known to have been.

Outraged as I was to see some of the festival-goers pointing to where they thought the murders had taken place, I had work to do and couldn't let myself get distracted. However, when one of the tourists flopped down on the ground and gurgled, I felt like stepping on him. He was in the wrong place, which made it only slightly better. The woman with him took a photograph. From the television reports, I knew that curiosity seekers had been like locusts at first. They had obviously decreased in number. It was sad, in a way, that interest had tapered off to these two moral morons.

Ignoring them, I pulled out my notebook and drew a plat of the area, marking the booths and trucks and rides and castle and all. Then in red I drew a sad little *X* for the spot where Jennifer had fallen and drew lines back to each possible hiding place for the shooter. It seems elaborate, but there is really no substitute for *getting things written down*. If you don't do it, you lose it.

And last, before moving on, I walked to the place where Jennifer had died. There was very little sign that anything so hideous had happened there. I knew the place on the grass only because it was burned into my memory. The grass was trampled, of course, but not any more so than places in front of popular food booths, the ticket booth, or the entrance to the merry-go-round.

The earth was damp. Somebody had washed away the blood.

Now for the sight lines where Barry, Plumly, Mazzanovich, Pottle, and Taubman had been.

The area formed a kind of triangle. The Emerald City

castle was at the top if you looked from the Yellow Brick Road, halfway toward Lake Shore Drive. The left point of the triangle was the Mo popcorn stand in Quadling country. The right point of the triangle was the Kansas Tornado ride in Munchkinland. From a position on the Yellow Brick Road I could see all three at once.

We had been standing near the castle, and the three men and Plumly had been near the popcorn vendor. In fact, from where we had been that night, they were half-hidden. Thinking about it now, I wondered whether they were intentionally keeping out of sight. At the time, it seemed to me that they were just getting away from the hoopla and noise of the opening ceremonies. But now I doubted that. There were more comfortable places to go hang out than the side of a popcorn stand. Why not inside the festival offices in the castle, for instance?

As I stood here, the Kansas Tornado swooped to a finish, riders screaming, metal wheels shrieking. When it came to a halt, the music began to play "We Wish to Welcome You to Munchkinland."

The Tornado, of course, was blue, as was all of Munchkinland. About twenty feet from the Tornado was the spot where Barry had been standing and Plumly had fallen. Nothing marked this place, either, except the trampled grass. I carefully sketched a plat of the larger area, the view of the popcorn stand, castle, and Tornado, and then a frontal sketch, the way I saw it from where I was now, halfway between the Tornado and popcorn stand. Then switching pens to red, I drew on the plat a stick figure of Barry as he had been when Plumly fell, leaning slightly forward, maybe reaching for the crumpling man. I drew in Plumly as well, folded up a bit on the ground, holding his stomach or abdomen with both hands.

Having done what I could to recall the scene exactly, I

walked to the spot where Plumly had lain and I stared down at the ground. The site didn't bring back any additional memories, just the one I already had of the knife near Plumly's hand.

Waiting for inspiration didn't work, so after a couple of minutes, I gave it up and started over to the popcorn stand. It was in Quadling country.

The popcorn stand was the usual county-fair type, generally squarish, with a wide counter at about chest height to an adult. It was sided and "roofed" with canvas and the front part of the canvas roof hung down a couple of feet from the top, displaying the words POPCORN SNOW OF MO in big white letters on a red background. Since this was Quadling, the counter, sides, and concessionaires' uniforms were all red.

The four men, when I first noticed them, had been standing in a tight little group, talking, around the side of the concession. To the best of my recollection, Plumly had had his back to me at first. Then he had turned, so that I saw who he was. And then I think he turned back. The other three had been gesturing, and I think Plumly had waved an arm, too, as if he were replying. Jennifer came over. I remembered thinking of calling out to Plumly, but then Jeremy yelled that he saw his father. Briefly, I had looked over to where Jeremy saw Barry. When I looked back, Plumly left the group and ran away from the three men toward Barry.

The people working in the popcorn stand would not have seen Plumly, Pottle, Mazzanovich, and Taubman because the side of the booth was in the way. But if the music had not been too loud, maybe they would have overheard what the men had been saying.

While the police certainly must have talked with the popcorn stand staff, it wouldn't hurt for me to do the same. It might make Hightower angry, but hey, that wasn't like actually hurting anything important. Hightower was entirely too uptight for his own good, anyway.

I walked over to the stand. Thinking I had better turn to a new page to take some notes, I checked my pad of paper. Yes, this was the page with the sketch showing the relationship of Barry and Plumly to the Tornado.

But Barry and Plumly were gone.

· 17 ·

SOMEWHERE
OVER THE RAINBOW

Mystified, I stared at the page. My mind must be falling
apart. There was no doubt my sketch had included the two
men, was there? I flipped a page back and a page forward.
Forward was a blank page. Back was the plat of the place
where Jennifer had died.

And the X was gone.

So then I knew.

I took one last good look at the sheet of paper under the
red Quadling light. Then, hardly able to contain my excitement, I walked over to Munchkinland, to the place where
Barry had stood holding the crumpling Plumly.

And the X reappeared.

Just as the bloodstain seeping into Plumly's gray shirt
would have seemed to appear when he ran into the blue
Munchkinland light from the red Quadling country light
that had masked it.

*   *   *

The operator at the CPD said McCoo wasn't there. I called the Area and asked for Hightower.

"It's an emergency," I said.

"I'm sorry. Lieutenant Hightower is out of the office."

"My name is Catherine Marsala, and I'm a witness in the Oz Festival case. This is urgent. He'd want to see me."

This last I wasn't so sure of, but what the heck.

Generally desk officers and operators will not tell you where a specific cop is. And you'd probably have to threaten to run them through a trash compactor to get the cop's home address—which makes sense—or even home phone number. But when they are actually on-scene on a case, finding them can be easier.

"Well, you're in luck, Ms. Marsala," she said. "He's at the Oz Festival right now. I can't tell you exactly where, though."

You know how life can slap you down twenty or thirty times in a row, then hand you a couple of real boons in immediate succession? Well, this time it did it to me. I wondered where Hightower would be and assumed he was interviewing witnesses again. But I could see over to the Flying Monkeys merry-go-round from where I stood. Not well, but enough to know he wasn't there. And I was practically on top of the scene of the first murder. Not here either. So I tried the offices in the Emerald City castle.

Not only was Hightower there, with two other officers, so was Chief of Detectives Harold McCoo! His big brown face looked as bright as the sun to me.

"McCoo! I've got to show you something."

"Cat, this is Detective Poul Ubagahara and Detective Hop Tomlinson. Cat Marsala." McCoo was always courteous, practically courtly, but this time he was going to drive me nuts.

"Detectives, good to meet you. Come and see some-thing, Mc—uh, Chief McCoo."

Hightower said, "Miss Marsala, we're busy."

"How much is it gonna hurt you to give me four min-utes?"

"Lord only knows how much," he said.

But McCoo said, "She's a friend, Hightower. We can do this."

They followed me out toward the popcorn stand. Oh, thank God. I would be able to tell Barry he was off the hook! Even that I'd accomplished this wonderful result for him. My family would think I was okay again. Nobody would hate me! I wouldn't feel so horribly guilty anymore, or so *wrong*.

There was a T-shirt booth over near the Witches' Brew beverage stand in Munchkinland. I quickly bought one that came close to the color of the OZ security people's shirts, the kind Plumly had been wearing. "Wait here a second," I said, and ran over to a hot dog stand nearby. I swiped a packet of ketchup fast and ran back.

"Hurry it up, Miss Marsala," Hightower said. Idiot.

"Look." I smeared some ketchup on the shirt and walked the four men, the two big important guys trailed by the two detectives, who, picking up on Hightower's skepticism, were trying to look interested but not committed.

Near the popcorn stand, under the red lights of Quadling country, I held out the shirt for them to see. It looked all one color. Red. The ketchup was not exactly the same darkness as the shirt, so if you looked closely you could tell the shirt was stained. But only if you looked closely.

"Now follow me."

I folded the shirt enough so that they didn't keep their eyes on it on the way to Munchkinland. It was only a distance of thirty feet or so. Once under the blue lights I unfolded it, fearful that this might not be as dramatic as I thought.

"I'll be damned," McCoo said.

The ketchup stood out as a distinct reddish-black blob against the now bright blue shirt.

"So you see, Jennifer and I only *thought* the blood appeared when Plumly got to Barry."

"I understand that," McCoo said.

We were sitting in the castle where the business office of the festival was located. Barry's desk was on the far side of the little room. The whole building was temporary, and the thin plywood walls let in the sounds of the festival. I wondered where Barry was. I wanted to tell him the good news.

McCoo looked thoughtful. Hightower actually had the nerve to look glum.

"What's the matter?" I asked Hightower. "Did I take away your favorite suspect?"

He shrugged, but McCoo caught my eye.

"Well, my problem is," McCoo said slowly, his voice a rumble, "my problem here is, this doesn't help."

"Of course it helps. Now you have to look at Pottle, Taubman, and Mazzanovich. It proves Barry didn't do it."

"I'm sorry, Cat. It doesn't prove Barry didn't do it. It shows the shirt *could have been* bloodstained when Plumly ran past you. Not that it *was* bloodstained. It still could have been perfectly clean until Plumly reached your brother."

Oh hell. In my enthusiasm I'd leaped too far too fast. He was right.

Hightower actually brightened up. "Yeah, I was just thinking that," he lied.

· 18 ·

DON'T CRY;
YOU'LL RUST YOURSELF AGAIN

When I got home, I phoned Barry, trying the Oz castle office first, hoping he'd arrived back there after I'd left. I didn't try his home first for fear of waking up the baby. Fortunately, he was at the castle.

"Barry?"

"Oh, it's you."

"Barry, don't sound so cold. I have good news."

"What is it?"

I described to him in detail what I had discovered. It took a little while to explain; Barry is more the organizer type than the visual artist. Finally, he said, "Oh. Okay."

"Okay? Is that all you can say? This is great news. It means there's no more reason to suspect you any more than the other three guys. They can't possibly arrest you now." I was forgetting about the fingerprints on the knife, but even if I'd remembered, I would have assumed they'd gotten on the knife when Barry grabbed at Plumly, trying to keep him from falling.

"Yeah, fine," Barry said.

Patiently, I said, "Barry, I'm not saying I'm a hero here. But the fact is they would not have thought of this without me."

"Sure."

"Please, Barry. Let go of your anger."

"Cat, you gave the police information that could have put me in jail."

"We've been over this. So did Jennifer. It was the truth."

"You admit now it wasn't true."

"It *was* true. It was a misperception, but it was an accurate description of what we saw."

"Whatever," he said, and he hung up.

When you're busy and involved in what you're doing, you forget that you have a persistent pain. But as soon as I let down my guard, the agony in my shoulder came rushing back. If anything, it was worse. I gobbled two aspirin with a glass of water.

Discouraged though I was, this was no time to get sloppy about procedures. By midnight I was sitting droopily at my kitchen table, where my computer lives, copying all the notes I had made during the day, including the ones in red. If you don't copy them immediately, they start to look like "wmf fggl wt thorgal." My hopes had been so high. Still, the bottom line was that it was no longer *only* Barry who could have killed Plumly. If he ever went to trial, I would testify that what I thought I had seen was dependent on the lighting.

After making sure the notes were in order, I took two more aspirin, the first two having made no dent on the shoulder pain, and went to check the messages on my answering machine. The first was from Hal Briskman:

"Cat, I've got a little more on Pottle for you if you want. Let me know."

The second was a click-off. Probably a telemarketer. I haven't programmed my phone not to accept calls that don't identify their number, because some anonymous calls could be from people involved in stories I'm doing.

The third was Jeremy. He had just recently learned to dial several phone numbers, like his dad's office, and his grandparents', and 911 of course, and mine. He had called, according to the time stamp, four hours earlier.

"Aunt Cat? I guess you're not there [pause]. Well, um, the reason I called [pause] um, Gramma says, um, Gramma said that you said something really bad about Dad [pause]. That's not true, is it?"

In the background Maud's voice said, "Who are you calling, Jeremy?"

"Um, nobody."

"Well, don't call Tokyo. We can't afford it [click]."

He hung up.

· 19 ·

IF I WERE KING
OF THE FOREST

"We think we see real things, a real world that's 'out there' and solid," E. T. Taubman said. "But we don't. All we see is light."

"You're right. I know that from high school physics class, but I don't think of it that way."

"We see just the middle of a long spectrum of radiant energy. Only what we call the visible spectrum, from violet through blue, green, yellow, and orange to red. Beyond red is infrared, and we feel infrared energy as heat. Beyond violet is ultraviolet. Some animals, like bees, see ultraviolet, but we don't. When the colors of the visible spectrum are all present, we see it as white light."

I had gotten Taubman talking, in hopes that he'd give himself away. If he hadn't killed Plumly himself, he was right there when Plumly was stabbed and he must have seen something. And a man with his sophistication about lighting must have realized the red light made it so we couldn't see the blood. So far, though, he seemed innocently happy to talk about light.

"When you see an object that looks green," he said, "you're actually looking at a thing that reflects green light. In a way, it's not green at all, it's sending all the green back to you. It's the *least* green an object can be. If you hit an object that reflects blue with a light that is pure yellow, with no blue whatsoever in it, it will look black."

"I think I understand."

"Let me show you." He flicked the light switch and the room was plunged into total darkness. I stepped slightly away from him. It was just a little bit creepy being in pitch darkness with a man who was possibly a double murderer and who might also want me dead. But before I got really worried, a blue light came on.

"Look at that," he said. "It's the fabric for a drape in a stage play the Bell Theater is producing next fall."

"It's just a lot of blue triangles."

"Not really." He clicked off the switch and clicked on another. The triangles vanished and red circles appeared.

"Wow."

"You can get really interesting effects that look like motion, just by changing light."

Taubman reached out one of his lanky arms and turned on a rotating gadget that threw blue and yellow light alternately at a painting on the wall. The painting depicted a stylized fish, and as the blue and yellow light hit it alternately, the fins and tail appeared to move.

"I like that," I said.

"If you've seen *Yellow Submarine*, there's a whole scene with fish that appear to move, but what appears to be flickering motion is just color alternation.

"The reason theater work is so great is that you can totally control the light. The whole audience is inside a black box and they only see what you allow them to see. If you want the characters to look ill, you cut down on your reds and

increase your greens. You can give the audience high noon
or evening or an approaching storm just with light alone. I
do corporate lobbies and, uh, things like the Oz Festival, but
you never get the same amount of control in a situation like
that because there are so many competing light sources."

He had been charging along happily with his description
of his work, right up to the moment he thought of the Oz
Festival. This was not my imagination. Oz bothered him.

I really liked that.

Edmond Pottle was much the same as before. His desk
was as opulent. His suit was as beautifully tailored. His
personality was just as sour.

"Mr. Pottle, as you know, I'm writing an article on the
festival."

He didn't know. He had probably heard that I was writing something, and he was too egotistical to admit the purpose wasn't clear. However, he said, "I thought you had
come here to try to clear your brother."

"Yes. But I still have my own work to do."

"I don't have much time. What can I tell you?"

Just like before. His time is valuable. "How does the city
decide on a festival? I mean, there must be lots of sugges-
tions, and there are only a limited number of weeks in the
year."

"Public benefit."

"Well, sure, but what does that mean?"

"We have a GospelFest because there's interest in gospel
music. A BluesFest because there's interest in blues and
because Chicago was one of the ancestral homes of the
blues. Blues singers came up from the South, particularly
from New Orleans, along the old railroad lines, and stopped
here."

"What about the Taste of Chicago?"

"That festival showcases Chicago cooking."

"But only a limited number of restaurants can participate. Right?"

"We try to accommodate as many as possible."

"But what if too many apply?"

"We try to accommodate as many as possible."

I wasn't going to be able to budge him on that. "Well, tell me how a Chicago event gets started."

"Mmm. Take the cows, for instance. We hope with the Oz Festival to create a totally new thing just as popular as the cows."

"Lots of luck. The cows were a triumph."

In the waning months of the twentieth century, Chicago had been glorified with three hundred and six life-sized fiberglass cows. Placed all up and down the city streets, on Michigan Avenue, the south Loop, north Loop, and River North area, they turned out to be a tourism bonanza. New York later borrowed our idea.

"Indeed they were. They were a triumph of astute business sense and the marriage of civic pride and business acumen."

Oh dear!

"A Chicago businessman," he went on, "saw life-sized street-art cows in Zurich when he was on vacation there. They had brought a million extra visitors to Zurich. A million tourists who would not have been there otherwise! Just think what they could do for Chicago! He took the idea to the North Michigan Avenue Business Association people, who were interested, but they wanted to include more than just North Michigan Avenue. They went citywide. The Department of Cultural Affairs came in on it and soon there was money from the Illinois Department of Commerce. Then the Chicago Office of Tourism came in. Businesses were invited to sponsor the cows and artists were invited to design and paint them."

The cows stood five feet tall. Sturdy, thick fiberglass in composition, the "blanks" were molded in three bovine forms, standing, lying down, and grazing. Once painted, they were installed on the streets from the Board of Trade to the edge of the Chicago River. There was a toreador cow at the Lyric Opera; there were polka-dotted, striped, flowered, and scenic cows. There were cows with wings, hollow cows, cows carrying gourmet foods, cows with shopping packages on their backs, and cut-up cows. There were all colors, including gold and mother-of-pearl and mosaic and one with a window in its stomach. Some of the artists became so fond of them they wanted to keep them. Some of the Chicago carriage horses were afraid of them and would bolt at the sight of one. In a way that makes a weird sort of sense, the horses were especially afraid of the one that looked like a car. Finally a fiberglass cow was assigned to the carriage company and spent weeks in the pasture with the horses, making friends.

After the summer was over, the cows were auctioned off. A "cattle auction," cried the newspapers and TV. A roundup! The proceeds were to go to the charity of the sponsor's choice. And they sold for thousands. Tens of thousands. Two or three of them sold for seventy thousand apiece and one cow brought in a hundred and twenty thousand dollars.

You gotta love a city that is often so pretentious and can still laugh at itself to the tune of three hundred and six cows.

"Still," I said to Pottle, "there must have been some trickle-down."

"What do you mean?"

"Well, who got the license to truck the cows to the spots on the street? Who fastened the cows down on the sidewalks? A city contractor? A private company? Who restored them if they got damaged? Who paid for incidentals?"

"I can assure you that the entire project was on the up-and-up."

"Good. By the way, they've dropped my brother as the principal suspect, you know."

Pottle paled slightly.

"Oh, really? I'm so—ah, glad for you," he said, in tones that made it clear he wasn't.

"It's now known that you and Taubman and Maz-zanovich, singly or together, could have killed Plumly."

Pottle coughed. Then he wheezed. He pulled open his desk drawer and got out an asthma inhaler. He shot the medication into his mouth, sucking in the vapor greedily. When he finally had himself under control, he wheezed out, "Now see what you've done! I'm not supposed to get upset. It brings on an attack."

"Why did you get upset? If you aren't guilty, you don't have a problem, do you?"

He grabbed for the inhaler again, and I left the office.

When I got to my car, I phoned McCoo. It had been satisfying to goad Pottle, but it hadn't taken me any closer to finding out who the killer was.

"Hi," I said, with forced cheer. "Anything new?"

"Cat, you really should talk with the officer in charge instead of me."

"Not Sergeant Hightower. I don't like him."

"Lieutenant Hightower."

"Yeah. And that's another thing. The man is barely competent. He goes by the rules, but he doesn't, as you guys put it, 'bring anything to the table.' How'd he manage to get promoted?"

Silence. I just waited. Finally, McCoo said, "He's connected, Cat."

"Like what? I know he's not the mayor's nephew."

"He's what you might call minorly connected, as opposed to majorly connected. And that's all I'm going to say about it."

"People have been doing that a lot lately. Telling me half a story and then saying I don't need to know the rest."

"Can you wonder?"

"McCoo, is there anything new?"

"We found the gun."

"Really? That's great! Where?"

"In Buckingham Fountain."

"No kidding? That's a stumper. Why wasn't it seen before this?"

"It was in the middle basin, not really visible from the ground. You know there are three levels to Buckingham Fountain, in decreasing size as they go up. A maintenance worker found it when he was cleaning out the basins. Stuff gets into the drains, like leaves and dead birds and bugs."

"Anybody see who threw it there?"

"We're asking. But a lot of stuff gets thrown into the fountain. Coins. Hot dogs. Car keys. I've always wondered how people get home without their car keys. The lower basin gets more stuff than the upper two. Drunks. Strollers. Jackets. Pants. I wonder how they get home without their pants, too."

"Is the gun traceable?"

"Oh, it's got a pedigree. It was stolen in a home invasion three years ago. Our shooter probably just bought it on the so-to-speak open market."

· 20 ·

THE LOLLIPOP GUILD

So the gun was another dead end.

When you get really fed up, you should go to Hermione's Heaven, the best restaurant in Chicago, to be fed up by Hermione.

Her dinners are symphonies. Her lunches are lifesavers. Most of the time, you can't get a table, although more than once she's been kind enough to feed me in the broom closet she uses for an office. It's easier for her, though, if I come in between meals when she can give me a real chair and a normal table. This means early, early dinner, or mid-afternoon dessert. It was mid-afternoon now, and I needed consolation.

Hermione is a queen-size woman and she takes no guff about it. Her view is that her life is her life. Today she greeted me at the door wearing a neon-purple caftan embroidered with silver dragons and a turban a couple of shades bluer than purple. Wow!

"What you need," she said, "is chocolate."

"I'm your slave."

She seated me in the window, an honor not remotely

possible at dinnertime, exited grandly and three minutes later came back with a big cream puff filled with chocolate custard and topped with chocolate-rum syrup and cocoa whipped cream.

"Ah, decadence," I said. "Feeds the human spirit."

"As a matter of fact, chocolate is good for you."

"Oh, come on."

"A recent study has shown that a large percentage of women and a significant percentage of men are chromium-deficient. Chocolate is one of nature's creations that is rich in chromium. You may be self-selecting chocolate to replenish your chromium supply."

"Smart of me. But, Hermione, there's a lot of sugar in chocolate desserts."

"Aha! The *British Medical Journal* reported a study of nearly eight thousand people that showed the ones who ate candy lived longer than people who didn't. Even if they ate candy several times a week."

"But what about the fat?"

"Much as I'm tired of hearing about cholesterol, it turns out that even though the fat in chocolate is saturated, it doesn't raise your cholesterol level."

"That's hard to believe."

"Sorry. What can I tell you? The news isn't always bad. On top of that, there are antioxidants in chocolate. I have been thinking about making up a placard with all these facts, a little card, maybe creamy white letters on a glossy chocolate brown background, one for each table. But then I thought, Maybe it's the forbidden quality of chocolate that makes people love it. What do you think?"

"I think it's pretty damn good either way."

"All right. Don't help me. I'll decide for myself. Cat, why are you so pale and wan?"

"It's too complicated to explain right now. Boiled down,

I got my brother into a horrible jam and have to get him out."

"Eat more chocolate."

"That's a help. Hermione, lately I've been wondering a lot about commercialization."

"You're thinking of going commercial, maybe?"

"I wish. If I could do commercial, I'd do it. No, I was thinking about the commercialization of pleasant, unassuming things. Like children's books. Does it make them less, mm, less a delight? Does it spoil them in some way? If somebody tries to make a buck off a fun thing, does that make the project in some way less sincere?"

"Commercialization of pleasant things! What do you call this?"

"This restaurant?"

"Exactly. I make double chocolate cake. Coq au vin. Snails in puff pastry. Onion soup roofed with the best Swiss cheese baked on top of chewy French bread. These items are *very pleasant*. But I don't give them away. I love to cook but I don't cook for love; I cook for money. And if somebody wants to commission me to teach my recipes to a thousand chefs for a thousand franchises and pay me a million dollars, hey! Let them do it."

Mazzanovich, the contractor, was at the construction site. A man of little politesse, he said, "You again!"

"I suppose you're more agreeable to your constituents. How do you know I don't live in your district?"

"What do you want?"

"Well, I wanted to warn you. The evidence that seemed to show Plumly had been stabbed *after* he left the three of you turns out to be wrong."

All of Mazzanovich's wrinkles came together in the mid-

dle of his face. The man had a frown that would sour a sug-
arplum.

"Whattaya mean by that?"

"Just that what gave the police the idea that only Barry
could have killed Plumly turns out to be irrelevant." I hesitated to tell him I had misinterpreted what I saw.

"Well, listen, Marsala. You're not gonna get me for this.
I didn't kill the guy."

"And I suppose the other two will testify that you didn't
kill him?"

A very odd look came over the rubbery face. It's dangerous to assume you know what a person is thinking, but it
seemed to me his response shifted from confidence to
doubt, to increasingly serious worry.

Finally, he said, "Yeah. They would."

He walked away from me, out into the construction zone.

Still no one had tried to attack me. I hoped that meant I was
right; there was no longer any need. Briefly, I had a terrible
fear that my whole analysis had been wrong and Jeremy had
been the target all along. But that simply didn't make sense.
Jeremy knew nothing that I didn't know. And what he did
know he had told the cops about. Also, it didn't accord with
my observations of the gunshots. Either way, I did my best
to watch my back when I went to the festival offices.

"Barry, you have to talk with me."

"No, I don't."

He was in his office in the Emerald City castle, which
was a good thing because I could stand between him and
the only exterior door.

"Barry, why don't I just put a bag over my head and you
can pretend you're talking to somebody else."

He snorted and folded his arms.

"I'm trying to help you. And before you say I've already helped you more than enough or make some other lame remark, let's just take it as read."

He took a dart out of the desk drawer and threw it at a picture of the Wicked Witch on the plywood wall to my left.

"Whatever helps you," I said. The small children's roller coaster that went around the outside of the castle rumbled noisily to a stop. Barry got up and retrieved the dart.

"First question. Had Plumly been acting different in the last couple of days?"

In a flat but audible voice, Barry said, "Yes. He seemed upset."

"Upset? What kind of upset? Worried? Hyper? Angry? Fearful?" Barry was not especially a word person. He threw the dart at the witch again.

"Huffy," he said.

"Like impatient? Indignant?"

"Indignant. Huffy."

"What kinds of documents on the festival would he have access to?"

"Pretty much everything." He went and got the dart. "This is a temporary office. Hell, it's just a bunch of plywood sheets painted green with a small roller coaster rolling around its outside. We all have other offices. He had. I have. The Park District has. The city has."

"You're saying they all have duplicate documents?" Plumly had told me this as well.

"Sure. The reason we have a full set here is in case something comes up. Say an inspector comes in and says the funnel cakes stand doesn't have a permit. We have to be able to say, 'Oh yes, it has. Here it is.' We need to have all the forms, the insurance, the lawyer's address, emergency electricians, the companies who sent the products, the owners of the merry-go-round and roller coaster, and whatever. We can't go rushing over to some office building for a sheet of paper at ten o'clock at night. So everything was here and he had access to it."

He threw the dart. He was really quite good at hitting the witch in the nose.

I said, "You see what I'm getting at. Could he have come on to a permission form or a bid price for a service or anything like that which would tell him somebody paid somebody else off?"

He left the dart there for now. Sighing, he said, "Cat, I really think you're barking up the wrong tree on this. Let's suppose somebody took a payoff to give out the contract on Porta Pottis. I don't mean the actual brand Porta Potti, but just as an example."

"Right. Like we say Kleenex when we mean facial tissue. Do you remember Aunt Helen used to say facial tissue and nobody knew what she was talking about? Cousin Brenda thought she meant the muscles and fibers of the skin."

He threw the dart hard. He was not going to engage in family reminiscences with me.

He said, "You might be able to find a list of bids, or several sheets of bids, but it wouldn't tell you anything."

"Suppose the committee passed over the lowest bid?"

"Suppose they did. They could perfectly well say that they were choosing the company with the best track record. The most dependable company for the price. What more would you know?"

I thought about that while the roller-coaster cars cranked their way back to the top.

Barry said, "If there are payoffs, they're in cash or cash equivalent, and they for sure aren't recorded anywhere."

The roller coaster started down, making the office vibrate. Kids shrieked. Barry went and pulled the dart out of the witch's nose.

"Did the cops take the festival papers you have here, or could I look at them?"

"They took them. But we brought in a fresh set. And no, you can't look at them. Sorry."

"I'll whine and beg later. Let me change gears. Plumly told me that there were security cameras in the festival area. What do they show?"

"Look in here." He walked over to a doorway with no door in it. The space beyond was small, like the offices. It was the other half of the castle interior. In it were monitors showing different parts of the festival. A man in an OZ security shirt was scanning them alertly. But he was looking alive because he had heard us coming. I saw the edge of a paperback novel sticking out from under a multiline telephone box.

Barry pointed at the monitors. "These four show the four ticket booths, because that's where the most money is. These two show the two first-aid tents, in case of emergency. Plus these eight show the outside of all the different potty areas. That's because if you're going to have sexual assaults, the potties are the most likely place."

"That's all?"

"Yup. And I sure wish there had been one on me Thursday night," he said bitterly, and he stomped back to his office.

"Well, then," I said, standing in the middle of his office, "Barry, how did you get hired?"

"You mean did I bribe somebody?"

"Or know somebody."

"The position of manager isn't glamorous. When things work right, nobody even knows the manager's name. But it's the one position that *has* to work right. There's no arguing, like there is about style or color schemes. The elements— equipment, staff, and all—have to be here, and they have to be here on time, and they have to work. You can believe me or not. I got hired on simple reputation. I do this kind of thing all the time. Corporate weekends, fairs, conferences, you name it. I get hired because I'm good at it, I have a track record, which I'm trying to build up, and one more thing."

"What's that?"

"I'm cheap."

· 21 ·

WAY UP ABOVE
THE CHIMNEY TOPS—

In my early days of reporting, some of the other reporters and I would play a game we called "contacts." The idea was that one person would come up with the name of a real person, known to him but not the player, and the player would have to contact him through a friend of a friend of a friend. You got more points the fewer people you needed to use, but we considered anything over four a bad job not worthy of a real reporter. This is a lot like the "six degrees of separation" idea.

As far as getting close to a person in Chicago is concerned, though, if I couldn't achieve it with just two intervening people, I'd be ashamed of myself.

Actually, it took me one call for Taubman, two for Mazzanovich, and three for Pottle, which averages out okay. I could have done it in one for Mazzanovich, because he was an alderman and I know several aldermen, but the point was to get hold of somebody who would know where the guy went and what he did when he got there and who was willing to tell me about it. Somebody, in other words, who didn't love the guy.

That evening I began to shadow the three suspects. My three suspects, that is, which didn't include Barry. My idea was that they would constantly run into me, which should shake them up. When possible, I wanted to get to where they were going even before they got there. It was a desperation move. But if Barry was innocent, as I believed he was, then one of them must have stabbed Plumly. And only one of them had wielded the knife, whether the others had been in on the plan or had been taken by surprise. Among them, there should be one weak link. I wanted him to freak out and talk.

Did that make me a stalker? Yeah, I guess so.

Larry Mazzanovich's house in Northbrook was impressive. Six two-story pillars ran along the front although they were more for looks than architectural necessity. There was a veranda behind the pillars with several white settees in which no one was sitting and probably no one ever sat.

Large beds of begonias and petunias in sculptured ovals swept down the lawn, flanking the curving front walk. A graceful curving drive led to a three-stall garage.

I drove past, since Mazzanovich wouldn't be home in the middle of the workday. Mainly I had wanted to see where he lived. When he lived here, that is.

His wife spent pretty much all her time here, my informant said. They had two children who were at boarding school someplace. Probably that decision had been made so that they hadn't had to choose between school in Chicago or school out here.

Because Mazzanovich claimed he lived in his aldermanic district. He had a small house there, and he hung around the neighborhood bars. He pretended to live there. He claimed to be a Chicagoan through and through. I guess that was sort of a political fiction.

Well, this certainly was a nice place to visit. But I had to get back to town before dinnertime. I had plans.

Pinning the men down to a time and place was easiest with Taubman, the lighting designer. I had talked to a friend who works for the Civic Opera Company, helping to hire the supernumeraries. A person like that would certainly have to know the Taubmans, and she did.

A string quartet wearing evening dress was tuning up. An evening of music in the Gold Coast apartment of Howard Stoddard would begin in twenty minutes. The glittering crowd of perhaps a hundred music lovers milled around, chattering and checking out each other's clothes.

It was a benefit for literacy, which in my profession I could hardly sneer at, although they could have just donated money, including the large amount spent on white wine, hors d'oeuvres, and the staff of at least seven waiters. My informant told me that the minimum donation was one thousand dollars, and many had probably ponied up more than that. Not me, of course. My friend squeaked me in as a reporter. Making this more believable, I asked for the guest list from Mrs. Stoddard and made notes on the food and the names of the musicians and the music—Haydn, Borodin—even before Taubman walked in. My injured left shoulder was so painful that I had to hold my notebook at about waist level, which was awkward for writing, but otherwise I looked official.

Taubman's wife was raven-haired. Her dress was black

with spaghetti straps, her jewelry was silver, and she looked like a million dollars. She air-kissed Mrs. Stoddard, who looked like a billion dollars.

Taubman saw me and blinked. But I was on the far side of the room and he toughened right up and waved at a man, ignoring me. The two men moved toward each other, Taubman seizing a glass of wine as he crossed the room. I let them talk for a few minutes while I munched pastry stuffed with crab. Then I meandered over to them. Taubman saw me coming and turned away.

A waiter passed near us carrying a tray full of glasses. Taubman leaned over and put his empty wineglass on the proffered tray, taking up another with scarcely a beat missed. Within a few seconds, other people had gracefully but quickly snatched the other glasses on the tray.

Taubman gave me one of those glance-and-look-away things that meant he'd rather I left. I didn't.

"Boozy crowd, isn't it?" I said.

"And no bad thing," said the slender man Taubman had been chatting with.

"My name is Cat Marsala," I said.

"Sumner Britten," he said, holding out his hand. The one without the wineglass.

"It's Dr. Britten," Taubman said, pointedly. "He's chair of the cardiology department at the University of Chicago."

"And you're going to tell me wine is good for you, right?"

He blinked in astonishment. "How on earth did you know?"

"Wild guess."

"Alcohol in moderation is perfectly healthful," he said. "Quite a tonic, in fact. It tends to lower cholesterol and improve cardiovascular fitness. Reduces the incidence of strokes. Alcohol has some effect in preventing peripheral clots, as well."

"No kidding."

"Moderate drinking produces a twenty to forty percent drop in coronary disease. That's about as much as regular exercise. It's as good as Pepto-Bismol for travelers' digestive upsets. And it seems to reduce memory loss in the elderly."

"Well, why don't you doctors tell people this?"

Taubman broke in. "Ms. Marsala, they couldn't possibly do that. Not everybody is moderate."

Britten said, "Some of our patients would start to drink to excess."

"And you know how people are," Taubman said. "They'd take the recommendation as a license to go out binge drinking. And then when they got into trouble, they'd blame the doctors."

"So you're in favor of leaving everybody misinformed in order to prevent a few from making a mistake? Big Brother has made the decision for us?"

"Well," said Britten, "I'm telling *you*."

"People," I said, "are taking away all my vices."

I left the party before the music started. This was no time for idle entertainment. My next stop was a local North Side bar called the Bucket of Blood. That's really the name. It's a very old neighborhood place just a bit north of Uptown.

In the Jeep I had wriggled into Levi's and then out of the skirt part of my all-black Gold Coast ensemble, the writhing doing further damage to my shoulder. My black top, when paired with the jeans, looked a whole lot less expensive than it had with the skirt and sling-back heels. It became more honest, because in fact it was a thrift-shop find, like my sofa. A pair of black running shoes and the switch was done. I keep a box of clothes in the car for exactly this kind of blending in.

Much as I had hoped to get to the bar before Mazzanovich, the chance had been small, so it was no surprise
to me that he was there already. He was surprised, though,
when I walked in.

Making no attempt to approach him, I slid onto a bar
stool and said, "Miller," to the bartender. This was not the
sort of bar where they stocked a hundred brands of beer.

Mazzanovich was sitting with a group of friends and was
now wearing clean clothes, including a pink shirt, navy
pants, and black shoes. There was a blond guy in a plaid
shirt, a little dark guy with slicked-back black hair, and a
Robert De Niro look-alike in a black suit with tan vest, gold
tie, and shiny shoes. I had seen pictures of the little guy in
an article on purported mob figures. Other than me, the
four were the only people in the bar.

Although I was sitting five stools away, Mazzanovich
didn't try to ignore me. He elbowed his friends. He pointed
at me.

Mazzanovich said, "Hey, guys. Know what? This little
lady actually believes that people in Chicago take bribes!"

They all burst into raucous laughter.

"She thinks some people may have *clout*."

They laughed harder. "What? In Chicago?" the De Niro
look-alike said. Everybody laughed even harder.

"And see, she thinks people in the *construction industry*
might get into shady dealings. And politicians and such just
might steer deals. And to get certain jobs, you might have to
be *connected*!"

Now they were not only laughing but kicking the bar
stools and pounding their beer bottles on the bar top.

"And that I would be so bent outta shape to be connected with any such *malfeasance* that I'd murder people
who said so."

Hoots and hollers from the jolly group of guys.

"Gee," I said, very annoyed, "this place sounds just like the cafeteria at Menard when I went there to cover the lockdown." Menard is a maximum security prison in Illinois. Now there was a lot of silence in the place.

"And you know what," I went on unwisely. "The reason I was there was one of the ringleaders was a guy who got sent up, or sent down, depending on how you look at it, because of an article I wrote on him. Not that I'm planning to write about you, Mr. Mazzanovich."

The little guy took out a cigar.

I said, "Mazzanovich, could you come over here for a minute or two and we'll talk?"

"Ooooh," said the blond. "I think she's gonna in-ter-ro-gate you."

"She wantsta come home with me, she can interrogate all she wants," De Niro said.

"Sure, hey, why not," Mazzanovich said. He slid four stools south and smiled in my face.

He said, "So?"

"So who told you I was asking about payoffs?"

He shrugged. "General knowledge."

"You know, I think it's kind of funny that when you or Taubman or Pottle tell me what you were all talking with Plumly about, you tell me the same two problems, flammable cooking stuff and the naked lady on the concession stand. And you tell them in the same order, and you use practically the same words."

"Think that's funny, do you?"

"Yeah. Kind of seems rehearsed."

"Well, hey. We discussed it. What, you think we have our daily three P.M. alibi meeting? Morning after Plumly was knifed, we conference-called and remembered to ourselves what we'd been talking about. Because why? Because nosy people like cops and you are gonna ask. Right?"

"Right."

"And you did, and we did, and there you go, huh?"

"I went to see your house in Northbrook."

He stopped grinning. "So what?"

"Well, see, you live there, not in your district."

"Oh, really? It's my summer house. Mayor Daley has a summer place in Michigan. Couple of aldermen have summer places in Door County, Wisconsin. That's sure a lot farther away."

"Yours isn't a summer house."

"So if you're so smart, why hasn't anybody else discovered this?"

"Well, basically because you're not that important for them to go looking."

"Oh, yeah? Well, what about my opponent in the election? How come he hasn't, like they say, 'ridden to victory' by giving me up?"

"Your opponent is a Republican. In this district you could run a gerbil and get more votes."

"Shit, nobody cares."

"Nobody cares until somebody writes about it."

He went quite still when I said that.

"Not that I want to write about your house. What I want is something else entirely. You know, Larry, if one of you stabbed Plumly, that's not the fault of the other two. Not necessarily."

"That isn't what happened. I hate to say it, babe, bustin' your balloon here, but your brother killed the guy."

"But if one of you stabbed him and covered up for it by giving misinformation to the police, that's involvement. It makes you an accessory after the fact. People go to jail for that."

*   *   *

The next day, at the crack of late morning, I was in the garage under Taubman's building. Now, it's not a new concept that people who are haughty sometimes antagonize people they believe to be underlings. Con O'Mara, who ran the parking garage, had a pink face, beautiful silky pure white hair combed back *en brosse*, bright blue eyes—one of those men who just looks sparkling clean—and a true distaste for E. T. Taubman. A very good thing for me. Especially since I had talked to several other people this morning and had gotten nowhere.

"Both of them," he said, bouncing on very small feet, clad in bright white running shoes. He smelled of Irish Spring soap. My excuse for talking with him had been that I was thinking of writing about Taubman, which was possible, if not strictly true. I had promised O'Mara anonymity and wonder of wonders, he believed me. That part was certainly true. If there is one thing I'm proud of, it's that I've never betrayed a source to write a story. Con O'Mara, though, was all pink and bright and eager to talk about the Taubmans. "She acts more bossy than he does, hon, unless you get to know them. Pretty soon you realize he's just as bad."

"Like what?"

"Ya know how sometimes a person just wants to show you they're so smart they're watching everything? Nothing is going to slip past them, see? I got seventeen men here, taking all shifts and vacation time and all. And see, Taubman decides he's going to pay attention to which ones do the right things with his cars and which guys don't. He's keeping a log, see, of when there's fingermarks on the car. Did I explain that tenants get two car washes a month?"

"No, you didn't."

"Well, they do. Anyhow, I find out that every time he gets the car back, he gives it a grade. How clean is it? Did they remember to wash off any polish residue where the chrome meets the painted part? Like around the lights. Did they wash under the windshield wiper? Clean the ashtrays? And like I said, did they leave any fingerprints? Then he puts the score down next to the name of the guy who did the wash job. Writes it in a little black spiral-bound notebook, no less! At the end of four months he comes to me with the grades, tells me who's bad and who's good. I ought to say, he tells me who's bad and who's acceptable. You ever heard of such a thing?"

"Never."

"Still doing it to this day. Thank God he got rid of the other car. At least now he's coming in with a shorter list. One oughta be due in about another week, I would say. I'm looking forward to that, I can tell you. *Not*, as my grand-daughter used to say."

"What other car?"

"What?"

"He had another car? What happened to it?"

"He sold it. Had a Porsche and a Lincoln Continental. Sold the Porsche."

"Why?"

"Who knows? Why are you so interested? He made some sort of joke that he'd sell the Lincoln instead but his father-in-law gave it to them for their tenth wedding anniversary."

"No kidding? Did he take it to a dealer?" I had visions of locating the automobile agency, tracing the check to their bank, and finding he had signed the check over to whomever he bribed. But that would be too much luck on my part and too stupid on his part. At least I could talk with the dealer and find out the amount.

"No, you know what, hon? He sold it on eBay. First time I ever heard of anybody doing that."

And got cash or a check, which he deposited in his own bank, I suppose. I didn't think I had any way of getting eBay records and finding out the high bid on an item. Damn! But maybe the cops could follow it up.

At least I could get an idea of how much money he got. "How old was this car?"

"Two years. Still in perfectly good condition."

"When did he sell it?"

"This car really interests you, doesn't it? A year and a half ago. No, hon, I'm lyin'. A little less than that. Fifteen, sixteen months."

I called Barry from my car phone.

"When are the decisions made about whom to hire for a festival?"

"I'm busy."

"Come on. Just tell me."

"It varies. I can't just tell you. The Oz Festival had been planned for two years, and the idea first surfaced three years ago. You can't just rush a festival into Grant Park. There's a lot of scheduling. Two years was a tighter schedule than we like. But it was the centennial."

"Well, when are people hired? When were the decisions made?"

"I was hired two years ago. There's a hell of a lot of pre-planning. Then the council worked on what kind of a festival they wanted. And all the advisory committees meet and talk. There are companies that supply rides for state fairs and county fairs, so we knew where to get equipment. Design modifications had to be specified about twelve months in advance. So the artists had to be on board a little before that."

"Well, when were people like Jennifer Denslow and E. T. Taubman hired?"

"Maybe fifteen months ago."

"Aha."

The lightbulb went on over my head. What an idiot I'd

been. I'd been so fixed on the notion that the three "important" men, Pottle, Taubman, and Mazzanovich, had raked in the loot, taking bribes for throwing work to people, that I hadn't realized a major point. Taubman couldn't throw any work to anybody, except maybe an assistant to change a lightbulb. He wasn't on any committee. He didn't have clout. He didn't hand out work, he *wanted* work.

Taubman wanted the prestige and PR of being the lighting designer for the first Chicago/Grant Park Oz Festival. And he'd been a hundred percent right in wanting it. The publicity he'd reaped would be worth many thousands to his business and untold amounts for his reputation. And probably make his wife happier with him, too. From being one of many lighting designers in Chicago, he'd vaulted to being one of the premier lighting designers. What's more, a credit like that didn't go away. It would always be there on his résumé, glowing like a neon strip.

Taubman would be a briber, not a bribee.

Which was why he had sold his Porsche over a year ago. He needed money for the bribe.

But if it ever came out that he had paid people off to get the job, his reputation would be forever tainted. The fact that his lighting was pretty damned good would be smothered by the nasty word that he had stooped so low. And this would be true even if he escaped criminal prosecution for making the payoff.

"So I keep hearing that Taubman is bossy and arrogant," I said to my informant. She was the same one who had told me where to find him the night of the string quartet.

"Absolutely. He regards it as artistic temperament. He's impatient. An ego as big as all outdoors. Doesn't have time for the peons."

"Then why has he been spending time explaining things to me? Guilty conscience?"

"I don't know whether he has a guilty conscience. But I do know why he's been spending time with you. You're the press. He hopes sooner or later you'll write about him."

◦ 22 ◦

POPPIES WILL
PUT THEM TO SLEEP

I sat on a low tiled wall, backed by green shrubs, watching for the right moment. Trying very hard to look like a wealthy young woman whose date would be coming by at any moment, I shifted back and forth on the hard seat.

A couple in evening dress passed by and entered the foyer, but if possible I needed a larger party. A single man hopped out of a cab and went up the walk. No good.

It was Monday evening, and wearing a little black dress, I had approached Edmond Pottle's elegant North Michigan Avenue building. My informant had told me the banker was having a small dinner party for forty of his closest friends.

The slinky dress did nothing to cushion me from the hard tile wall.

But hey! Here came a limo, and there were several people inside. Risking a mistake, I got up and sauntered toward the building. If the doorman saw me come up to the door with a group and then beat a retreat, he'd never let me in later with a different group.

I stopped to fiddle with the clasp on my pseudo-pearl necklace. Sure enough, the limo disgorged five people, one an elderly lady in lavender. Two younger couples accompanied her, the older of the two men taking her arm for support. I fell in next to them.

"Yes, ma'am?" the doorman said, addressing the elderly lady.

"Edmond Pottle, young man."

"Yes, ma'am. Mr. Pottle is on nineteen, the top floor."

He stepped to the elevator and pressed the button to call it. The doorman returned to the front door, while the five of us waited for the elevator. "Oh, you're going to Pottle's, too," the younger man said to me.

"Yes, I am."

"Know him from the bank?"

"No, actually from the Oz Festival." Why not be honest when you can afford to?

"Isn't it nice that Edmond takes an interest in these civic events," the older woman said.

Pottle's apartment was huge. There were only two apartments on nineteen, which meant that each had three sides of the building. Pottle's faced west, south, and east, giving him a full lake view to the east, a view of Navy Pier to the southeast, and the city skyline to the west.

I didn't see Pottle when I walked in. The party of five I had entered with passed through the large foyer and into the living room beyond on the right. A long hall led back from the foyer to a kitchen, which I just glimpsed as a uniformed waitress opened the door and let it swing closed behind her. On my left opposite the living room arch was another hall, presumably leading to bedrooms.

I followed the five into the living room. Pottle did not rush over to greet his guests. The living room buzzed with sound, and Pottle himself stood near a large window overlooking the lake. Beyond him were small tables set with

white tablecloths, and beyond that, the dining room contained a long table, also set for dinner. All the tables were
bedecked with huge bowls of dark red roses, so big that
people sitting across from each other would not be able to
see each other through the flowers. The silver was heavy
and the napkins looked thick.

The rest of the apartment was similar in style. Pottle
liked heavily carved wood. To my eye, the carved mantel-
piece looked as if it had been taken from an old Spanish
church. The sofas were covered in dark red velvet and had
curved backs and carved arms. Several chairs in the living
room resembled thrones.

I made sure I got well into the living room, far from the
front door, before giving Pottle any chance of seeing me.
When he did, unlike Taubman at the concert the night
before, he made an immediate beeline toward me, brushing
past several guests.

"What are you doing here?" he whispered.

"I've come to visit."

"I'm having a dinner party."

"Yes, and I'm dressed for it."

"You can't be serious. You aren't invited. Oh yes, Adrienne," he said to a middle-aged woman who leaned toward
him and cooed in his ear. She and he both smiled toothily.
"I'll be right over and meet your aunt." I had seen Adrienne's picture in the society glossies, but couldn't remember what for. She had something to do with civic statuary. To
me he said, "If you don't leave, I'll call the police."

Four more guests entered the foyer. One said, "Oh,
Emily! Lovely dress!"

"Black, like everybody else, I'm afraid."

"Except for Poppy."

"Oh, Poppy's always different. She always makes a statement."

A woman with apricot hair, presumably Poppy, said,

"I'm not making a statement. Didn't you know red was the new black?"

"I thought beige was the new black."

"Silly! Beige is the new white."

Serving people passed among the guests, making the crowd even more numerous and more confusing. All of the waitresses were young women of about twenty, all of them dressed in black with white aprons, apparently unaware that they should be red and beige.

"Oh, shoot, Mr. Pottle," I said, pouting—something I never do in the normal course of events. "I guess you don't want me here."

"Judge Danvers!" Pottle burbled, ignoring me. "Have a drink and I'll be right there. I want you to meet Adrienne's aunt."

Judge Danvers approached waving his arms. "Edmond! I have some news on *Comerford v. Illinois.*"

"Since you don't want me here, I'll leave," I said, snappishly.

"Well, at least you have that much decency."

Don't count on it, I thought. I sidestepped between a serving person and the judge. Walking swiftly toward the door, I lost myself to Pottle's eye. Just to be on the safe side, I put my hand on the front doorknob, but an elderly man entered at that instant. Glancing back, I couldn't see Pottle anywhere.

I crossed into the side hall, seeing three closed doors, and the open door to a bathroom. I figured the last door would lead to the largest bedroom, which would be Pottle's. I opened the door next to that.

It was a guest bedroom. The bed was made, the night tables flanking it held only lamps and a clock, and the dresser held nothing but two candlesticks. This room was not used much.

Fine. I opened the closet. Extra Pottle clothes. It looked like his winter stuff was in here.

I slipped inside and closed the closet door.

My informant had said Pottle and the Pottle party were going to attend a late celebrity charity auction at Mrs. Marcus Mortimer's estate right after dinner.

I settled down to wait.

The distant hum of conversation was practically enough to put me to sleep, if I'd been in a relaxed frame of mind. But I was keyed up and a little frightened. This foray was illegal, wasn't it?

The best you could say was it was a gray area, ethically speaking.

I'd been let into the apartment. I hadn't broken in. That was good. I'd been told to leave. That was bad.

Well, I was here now, and planning to tough it out.

There was a clinking of glassware and a delicious smell of chicken—and what? Maybe mushrooms and butter and potatoes and other wonderful things. At least they were starting to eat. That was truly good news.

Because sitting in a closet is horribly boring. I mean, there's only so much you can do before even Armani begins to pall.

The group would be going out to that auction. They'd better hurry, hadn't they?

My informant had said Pottle did not have live-in help, as far as she knew. Better be right. She thought he had a cook five days a week and a housekeeper seven days, nine to five. Better be right.

My left shoulder was cramping. There was no position in which it felt pain-free. If I leaned my back against the closet wall and drew my legs up to my chest, the shoulder blade pushed on the wall. If I curled up in a fetal position on the floor—which was carpeted, thank goodness—I couldn't lie on the left side, for obvious reasons. When I lay on the right side, the weight of my left arm pulled the left shoulder down and made it hurt.

Better stop whining. You got yourself into this. Lie there and take it. So I lay on my back, which wasn't great either, since there wasn't much room. I had to push a batch of shoes aside, and I kept reminding myself that they had to be replaced carefully before I left, so that Pottle wouldn't know anybody had been here. If he found signs of an intruder, he'd for sure remember that he never really saw me leave. He was snotty, but he wasn't stupid.

And what if he came in to get something out of the closet before leaving for the auction? Don't even think such things!

When at last I heard an increasing babble of noise, with high-pitched didn't-we-have-a-lovely-time kinds of voices, it was enough to make me weep with delight.

There was still the caterers' cleanup time to get through. But I was willing to bet that once Pottle and gang had left, the caterers would have the china in the dishwasher and be out of the apartment as fast as you could say Brillo.

It was longer than that. But they didn't wait to run several loadings of the dishwasher. They were in a hurry to get home. Probably they had zipped the dinner dishes through the dishwasher while the guests were eating dessert and drinking coffee. They would have served dinner on Pottle's china and silver, so they had to put it away. Their own food-transporting pans and coolers of ingredients they could wash back at the shop. They would probably hand-wash anything else of Pottle's hanging around, while the dishwasher did its thing. Still, it took them an hour. Finally they were out of there, voices fading and the apartment sinking into blessed quiet.

How long did I have?

Sidling silently into the hall, I checked the kitchen. Sure

enough, it was empty. The caterers had left the light on but taken the garbage with them. I quickly checked the other rooms in what turned out to be a ten-room apartment, all of it decorated in dark wood, red carpets and drapes, and lots of dark brocade. Pottle just didn't have a frivolous bone in his body.

I took out a pair of surgical gloves. They had been almost all my little formal purse was able to hold. I slipped them on.

The first search area was the office, predictably a dark wood room, with shelves on three sides and a heavy carved desk under the window. I sat in Pottle's chair and began methodically pulling out drawers. They contained the usual gunk—pens, pencils, paper clips, Post-its, erasers. The two large bottom drawers were file drawers, the left one legal-width, the right one 8 1/2 by 11-inch regular. There were files labeled "car," "insurance," "medical," "products," and so on. They were correctly, not deceptively, labeled. "Products" turned out to be warranties and instruction booklets on all his household products, including the oven, refrigerator, CD player, and other electrical stuff. Also in this folder were bills of sale for his oriental rugs, including the dealer's description of the origin of each rug. Another file labeled "art" was stuffed with letters of provenance of his collection of paintings. In the entire office, there was no computer equipment. Thinking back to his bank office, also free of techno-equipment, I'd bet that Pottle was not computer-literate. Probably he hired people to do his cyberwork for him and had just never bothered to learn.

His medical file only told me that he was being treated for high cholesterol levels, that he occasionally suffered from gout, and had shots for a trip abroad last year. His CBC and urinalysis looked normal to me.

Being this nosy was not nice. Well, hell, I wasn't feeling nice right now.

Did I expect to find a letter from Plumly saying, "I'm on to your kickback scheme, Pottle, you wretch?" Not really, although stranger things have happened. Or a form letter with Pottle's letterhead saying to a vendor, "I'll intercede with the city for you if you pay me" and a line for the "donor" to fill in his name and another line to fill in the amount?

Well, no, but you never knew. If he felt safe here at home, he might file incriminating letters.

I could riffle through all the books on the shelves, looking for hidden documents, but I didn't have time. The last thing I needed was to be discovered here.

What other places did people hide things?

I tried under the mattress in the red-and-black bedroom, but there was nothing. What about the bathroom? Inexpert people thought hiding things in the toilet tank was a clever idea. Nothing there. The medicine cabinet held only medicines. I felt under the drawers in the vanity, next to the sink.

Bingo! There was something taped to the underside. This was very good. If he hid it, it must be important. I peeled one end of the tape from the bottom of the drawer by feel and pulled out a flat package, a bubble pack of medication. They were labeled with their European manufacturer's ID, but were illegal in the United States. He'd put them where neither energetic nor nosy cleaning women nor snoopy female guests would find them.

Rohypnol! The so-called date-rape drug. In two-milligram doses.

"Roofies," I said aloud. "Oh, Pottle, you are a nasty man."

I hit END on my cell phone. McCoo wasn't in his office. He got to the office early in the morning; he was probably home in bed. It was now ten o'clock. I stood on the corner

of Michigan and Chestnut trying to make up my mind. Did
I dare call him at home? Wait a minute. Some innocent girl
might be about to be raped. Of course I'd call him at home.
Let him yell at me if he wanted to.

But he didn't.

"Explain that again, Cat. I was half asleep."

I heard his wife say in the background, "Wholly asleep."

I explained again, ending with, "There was a girl, young
woman I should say, at the dinner. Now that I think back,
Pottle put his hand on her arm and lingered."

"Cat, what do you want me to do?"

"Rohypnol is illegal, isn't it?"

"It's a Schedule III drug, not a Schedule I. The reason is
it has medical uses. It's a benzodiazepine used all over the
world for insomnia."

"Not in this country, right?"

"Well, no."

"It makes people compliant and causes amnesia so they
don't remember later that they've been raped."

"There have been cases, true. It's happened on college
campuses a fair amount. The stuff dissolves quickly in
alcohol—"

"Do something, McCoo. He may be going to rape this
girl."

"Cat, even if this were crack cocaine, what would you
have me do? I can't go up to him and arrest him. I can't
enter his apartment and search. I don't have probable
cause."

"I've told you it's there. I put it back under the drawer."

"Listen to yourself. You did an illegal search. I can't move
with that. Against a citizen who has no criminal record. I'd
never get a warrant."

"But, McCoo—"

"What I could do—" He stopped and thought a few seconds. "I could have somebody go hang around that auction if it's still going on and then just follow your friend Pottle. If the woman he's with seems ill or unsteady, my guy could always call the paramedics. It'll look funny, and Pottle may have fits, but my guy can't really get into trouble if he plays it right."

"Thanks. I like that. Later on, maybe I'll have a serious word with Pottle."

"Well, if you do, claim you know his supplier, not that you tossed his house."

"The heck of it is, none of this is related to the Oz Festival. It doesn't help Barry."

So when McCoo telephoned and woke me up at 10 A.M., I thought I knew why.

"Cat, there's been a serious complication you need to know about."

"You arrested Pottle?"

"No. Mazzanovich is dead."

"What?" I blinked, startled. I had tentatively picked Mazzanovich as the killer, but I stopped myself before blurting that out.

"When did he die?"

"This morning."

"At home? Northbrook or here in Chicago?"

"Neither. On the job site."

"Murdered?"

"Pretty clearly. Apparently his cement trucks were coming, like one every half hour or some such. He's always there to direct them. Although the man driving the truck said he knew where he was supposed to pour, even without Mazzanovich."

"Don't keep me in suspense."

"Guy drives to the place where he's pouring some footings or whatever, and swings his cement tube thing into place, and since Mazzanovich isn't there, he figures he'd better look into the forms, just in case the other truck already poured that particular footing. Because if he had, it would overflow, naturally. Does this make any sense to you?"

"Yes. Go on."

"So he looks in. I guess you pour new concrete onto concrete that's still wet. So he looks in to be sure, and he sees a hand."

"That'd get *my* attention."

"Did his for sure. He calls nine-one-one and they come and they call us and so on. Near as we can reconstruct it right now, somebody shoved Mazzanovich over the lip of the form and into the wet cement and either pushed him down or left him there knowing he couldn't crawl out. The form is like a big square box, maybe twenty feet deep, so I'm betting on the couldn't-crawl-out scenario."

"Good God, that's nasty."

"There were several workers around, but not right near that very spot, and the site is filled with gear and forms and finished footings—"

"Yeah, I've been there. It's a jungle. You could easily be out of sight of other people."

"And there are machines going all the time, so a scream might sound like a lot of other noises. Metal screeching. Well. The investigation is barely beginning. If we're lucky, we may find out that somebody saw Mazzanovich with the killer."

"Wouldn't they have come forward by now?"

"Workmen on the job would have. But maybe some pedestrian passing by saw something. Maybe some delivery truck driver who came and went. There's a lot of shoe-leather investigation still to do."

"Good luck. I didn't exactly like Mazzanovich, but this is pretty ghastly."

"That, yeah. But it also tells you there's somebody very dangerous out there."

"We knew that already."

· 23 ·

DING DONG

McCoo had added that his "friend" had followed Edmond Pottle from the auction last night. Pottle and a young woman, trailed by McCoo's friend, went to a trendy singles bar. There he saw Pottle slip his hand over the young woman's drink while she was watching the action on the dance floor. The friend immediately ordered a very sticky drink, a pousse-café, made of layers of sweet liqueurs. Before the young woman actually drank her drink, he got up, lurched toward the dance floor, and spilled his pousse-café down Pottle's shirtfront. Pottle made such a nasty fuss that the woman called a taxi and went home alone.

McCoo's friend then poured some of her drink into a Baggie inside his own pocket, wetting his jacket but keeping a good deal of the liquid. A chemist could later find Rohypnol in it, if in fact it was there. He would be willing to testify to what he saw.

I thanked McCoo.

I phoned Hal Briskman.

"Hal," I said, "I'm returning your call. Have you heard whether Pottle—"

"You know, I've been thinking a person could do a social history of a culture entirely through its slang. 'It's a doozy' came from the admiration for the Duesenberg automobile, for example, in the days when cars were the latest invention."

"Hal, not now. Can you tell me whether Edmond Pottle's family sent him here to get him out of New York?"

"Mm. Well, yes. That's what I was calling about. There was talk that he'd become something of an embarrassment. Complaints from women."

"And about Taubman. It isn't just his wife who wants him to become a big success, is it? He's more rapacious than he lets on."

"True. He'd go about it differently, though. But I guess you could call him very hungry."

I had to make one more connection. Time to go to the cop shop.

"Lieutenant, things are just too serious for us to be at cross-purposes all the time."

Hightower sat back in his chair and looked questioningly at me.

I said, "We can help each other."

"There's no particular way you can help me. Unless you actually witnessed something—something *that wasn't in error.*"

Low blow. But no worse than I might expect from Hightower.

I said, "Now that Mazzanovich is dead, do you have alibis for Taubman or Pottle for the time he was killed?"

"Not the whole time. There's about an hour's gap when Mazzanovich wasn't seen by anybody. Except the killer. Pottle was in his office, but it's not far away. Taubman was in his studio." He smiled at me. "And your brother was working alone at the Emerald City castle."

Very patiently, I said, "Let me tell you what I've been thinking." He glanced at his watch. "Maybe you could have a cup of coffee while I do, Hightower, so that you won't have to totally waste your time."

"I don't drink coffee. I don't consider it healthful."

"But coffee is good for— Oh, never mind. I'll make this as brief as possible."

"Please do."

The guy should choke on a sea urchin!

"All right. Let's for the moment assume Barry didn't kill Plumly."

"I believe he did."

"Just for the purpose of argument. Can you do that much?" Since he didn't answer, I went on.

"There were three of them there with Plumly—Pottle, Mazzanovich, and Taubman. They were either arguing or talking very animatedly. Jennifer probably noticed that, too."

"Just as accurate, I suppose, as her words that she saw Plumly had an unstained shirt."

Grrrr!

"Does that mean you now accept that his shirt *was* bloody?"

"Only that you couldn't tell one way or the other. And you said you could tell. No, Barry's the killer. We have the fingerprints on the knife to prove it. Plus, he's the only person known to have struggled with Plumly."

"Let me finish. Struggle or no struggle, the three were in heated discussion with Plumly. One of them stabbed him. I think to the surprise, but maybe not to the dismay, of the other two. Why did the killer attack Jennifer and me? Because he thought we saw the blood on Plumly as he ran past us. Not the actual stabbing; they were in a huddle right then and Plumly was facing away from me. Why was I not attacked the next day? Because by then the killer had heard that you very seriously suspected Barry, and soon he heard that in fact you had cautioned him, and he knew you wouldn't suspect Barry if Jennifer and I had told you anything to contradict that. So he had killed Jennifer for nothing." I stopped for a moment in sadness, but went on quickly because I didn't want to lose his attention.

"Once you brought in Barry for serious questioning, the killer thought he was home free. We had not told you that there was blood on his shirt from the time he ran away from the three men. Now, the killer knew that he could always blame the murder on one of the other two, if it ever became necessary. For reasons of their own, none of them wanted to talk to the police.

"But then he hears that there's doubt about Barry's guilt. Suddenly things are not so easy. I'm hanging around asking questions of the three of them. Each knows I'm visiting the other two. If one of the innocent ones tells which one really stabbed Plumly, the other innocent one may go along and the next thing you know, the killer is in jail. He can't let that happen. So he has to reduce it to one man's word against the other."

"So he kills Mazzanovich? Unprovable."

"Maybe. I think he killed Mazzanovich for more reasons than just making it one man's word against another's, though. Mazzanovich was either blackmailing him or on the verge of telling the truth about the murder. I saw Mazzanovich the day before he was murdered, and he was rattled. He was a cheap crook and what used to be called a chiseler. But not a killer.

"Now, with Mazzanovich dead, the killer is left with his word against the other guy's. This is perfectly satisfactory for him, because even if the other guy breaks down and runs to the cops, the killer can just say he's covering for his own crime."

"So you've got three men, two of whom are covering up for the spontaneous murder of a friend."

"Not a personal friend at all. A business associate. And not so spontaneous, either. One of the three came equipped with a knife and an untraceable gun. People don't just do that every day."

"Well, Mazzanovich, Pottle, and Taubman weren't friends, either. They have no mutual history. Why protect each other?"

"No, but they had a mutual interest. Mazzanovich, the contractor, and Pottle, the banker, were in a position to get dirty money from the Oz Festival. The lighting designer, Taubman, didn't have money but he needed recognition badly. He and his wife spend like drunken sailors and they have very little income. He sold his car to get money and personally I think he used the money to bribe Mazzanovich and Pottle to get the Oz job. Mazzanovich had a lifetime history of doing 'favors' for payoffs. He was in a position to throw lucrative contracts to people supplying the festival. He also had a lot of cash going out, with two houses, including an expensive one in Northbrook. And Pottle even more so. He's the kind of guy who can never have enough money. He could grant major contracts to suppliers or unions in return for payoffs.

"If it was made public that they were crooks, they lost big. It would utterly ruin Taubman's reputation, obviously. Mazzanovich would lose his aldermanic position and might go to prison. Pottle as a banker has to be above suspicion."

"This is all speculation."

"Plumly told me he hated payoffs. He wasn't the book-keeper for the festival, but he went over all the festival business papers. For a while I thought he found evidence of the bribes there, but now I don't see how that information would have been in black-and-white anyplace. I think he overheard Mazzanovich, Pottle, and Taubman talking. The walls in the Emerald City castle are three-quarter-inch plywood, and you can hear everything through them. I suspect the three men were alone inside, feeling that they had privacy, talking, and he heard them from outside."

"Conjecture."

"You must be doing serious research into their financial dealings. You'd want to know if they had unexplained sources of income. They're suspects."

"Of course." By his tone, though, I knew he had not given it top priority.

"Then there was the timing. Why was Plumly meeting those three in that half-hidden location behind the pop-corn stand at that exact moment?"

"I'm sure you can tell me."

"He invited them to meet him there. It was the opening night of the festival. The mayor, the police superintendent, and a whole lot of other dignitaries and press were going to be present. He met with the three men. He told them what he knew. And he threatened to walk right on over to the bandstand and make it public unless they all agreed to return the money and admit their wrongdoing."

I paused for him to reply.

"Well, Ms. Marsala, thanks anyway. I think our time is about up."

So I didn't tell him I also knew who the killer was.

I left word for McCoo where I was going, why I was going there, and who had killed Plumly.

· 24 ·

DREAMS REALLY DO
COME TRUE

Seven P.M.

It was a small, shiny gun, an older nickel-plated revolver. Pottle's pudgy hand covered most of it.

"I thought you pitched your gun into the fountain."

"Of course I did. This is a nice fresh new one. Surely you realize there are places you can just about stand on the street corner and yell 'Money for a gun!'"

"Someone will be able to identify you."

"No, not really. I didn't do it quite that way, and I didn't look quite like myself when I bought it, either."

We were in Pottle's office in the bank. Pottle had stopped wheezing. That was surely a bad sign. If his own analysis was right about what gave him an asthma attack, it meant that he was no longer nervous. He'd made up his mind how to get rid of me and he thought his plan would work.

"I've told people I was coming here."

"Indeed. And if they ask, I will tell them you came here. Just in case you really did leave word and anybody outside saw you come in. A secretary leaving work late, the occasional homeless person. Whatever. And I'll tell them you left soon after."

"I told the cops you were the killer."

"Oh, sure. If they believed you they'd be here. So either you didn't tell them or they thought you were a nut. On the whole, I'd suspect the first. But still—"

McCoo would come. But would he come soon enough?

"I must admit, I found it hard to believe you carried a gun to the festival. After all, you're a banker! It was easier to believe a crazy, hungry-to-succeed artist would be a killer. Shows *my* prejudices, doesn't it?"

"Out the door, Marsala."

"But now I know there's something very wrong with you. I guess your family thinks so, too."

"Nice try. You won't make me mad enough to behave irrationally, you know."

I said, "Once Mazzanovich was killed, I knew it was you. Taubman is a lighting expert. He would have known right away that Jennifer and I couldn't have seen blood on a gray shirt in a red light. He wouldn't have needed to kill Jennifer and chase me and Jeremy."

"You're too clever too late."

"And the other reason I knew it was you was this. The man who chased us in the tunnels reminded me of the Tin Woodman. I thought it was something about the way he looked. Taubman was lanky like the Tin Woodman. Mazzanovich had hair that stuck up straight on top. But it wasn't either of them. The similarity wasn't visual; it was auditory. You were wheezing. The Tin Woodman's joints squeak."

"Let's get going," Pottle said, gesturing with the gun. "We don't want to be interrupted."

"I won't move from this office. You can't shoot me here. There'd be too much evidence around. And what would you do with the body?"

"I'd do the same thing I'm going to do with the body as it is. Take you to the basement. I'd just have to use a document cart to move you instead of having you walk there."

"There'd be blood."

"This is a varnished wood floor. I'd deal with it. Get moving. Out the door, please."

Suddenly it seemed like a good idea to do as he said. In this closed room he really could do whatever he wanted. Plus, he was much bigger than I was. He wouldn't really have to shoot me. He could bash me on the head.

Out in the hall, there might be other people around that he didn't know about, or escape routes. I got moving.

The hall was black-and-gray marble, set in a well-bred checkerboard pattern. I couldn't see anybody on this floor. He gestured to the elevator. "Don't yell," he said. "There's nobody to hear you at this time of night."

"Well, then if I yell, you won't mind."

"Yes. I guess that's true."

I screamed "Help! Help! Help!" at the top of my lungs.

He waited, bored. He was so unworried that I decided to save my breath. "What about janitors? Cleaning people?"

"They don't come in until 10 P.M."

"Guards?"

"There's one on the first floor in a soundproof booth looking at monitors of the doors and vaults. There are no monitors trained on the elevators."

The brass elevator door, decorated in a pattern of vines and leaves, slid smoothly open to reveal a marble-and-brass interior. Pottle pushed a button and the elevator descended. Yup, he could wash this floor, too, if he had enough time. And while tests can reveal traces of blood on almost anything, the cops would have to suspect I'd been in here before they bothered to run tests. And even then, how tightly could they tie the blood to Pottle? What's more, I'd be dead by then so it wouldn't help me much.

Pottle was in a position where he really had very little to lose by killing me now and taking his chances later.

The elevator door sighed open on a floor labeled BB, which apparently was the bank's way of saying subbasement. No marble here. The flooring was institutional vinyl.

A long hall led away to the right and left. Pottle nudged me to the left. The walls were poured concrete, painted cream. The hall itself was about fifteen feet wide. There were shelf-lined equipment alcoves along the way. In some were boxed supplies for the bank, mostly reams of paper. A couple of boxes were labeled pencils or pens or erasers, but in keeping with the twenty-first century, far and away most of them were fax cartridges, printer cartridges, both color ink-jet and regular, and so on. I hadn't much time to look. Pottle was pushing me on.

I said, "Don't be so impatient."

"I suppose I'd drag my feet if I were going to die, too," he said with more satisfaction than regret.

We passed janitorial supplies, cleaning supplies, floor polish, mops, brooms, dusting cloths, furniture polish, toilet disinfectant, rest room soap, whole alcoves filled with letterhead paper on shelves with the different letterheads posted underneath each batch. My mind raced, trying to see a possible weapon among all the useless objects.

"Where are we going?"

"Why, the tunnels, of course. Would you believe we never even realized that there were tunnels under the bank until that flood a few years ago? The one where somebody broke through the top of one of the old freight tunnels? We had hundreds of thousands of dollars in damage. All of a sudden the water started to rise in our basement. The maintenance staffers were up to their ankles in dirty water.

Nobody could figure out why at first. It wasn't raining. There were no plumbing leaks. It was utterly amazing. Nobody had any inkling. The tunnels had been down here all along and literally nobody knew. Anyhow, we know now. There's a door down some stairs at the end of this corridor where I can push you into the tunnel."

I had come to a stop next to a storage area for vacuum cleaners.

"I've had it, Pottle. I'm not going any farther. And you'd better rethink this. This isn't going to work for you. They'll just find me, sooner or later. Why don't you come to Chief of Detectives Harold McCoo's office and work out a plea bargain."

"A plea bargain for two murders? Oh, certainly! They'd give me a slap on the wrist, I don't think. This is very safe. For me. Once I pitch you into the tunnels, they probably will never find a body. It's pitch dark down there, and you'll wander blindly until you die of thirst. Nobody will ever figure out where you went in."

I grabbed one of the vacuum cleaners. "Stand back or else!"

Pottle actually giggled. "You're going to hit me with a vacuum cleaner?"

He raised his hand to slap it out of my grip. He could have disarmed me in two seconds, because he was bigger, and also because my left shoulder was so horribly painful. All I could do was hold the vacuum at my waist, while my other hand pulled open the zipper and grabbed at the dust bag.

"No," I said. "I'm going to hit you with this bag!"

"So what?"

He pulled the vacuum and I pulled frantically at the paper-fiber bag, ripping it, which was what I meant to do. Pottle hesitated for maybe two seconds, wondering whether to shoot me right then and there or not. He didn't want to leave a trail of blood if he could help it. And I didn't seem to be doing anything threatening.

"I'm going to hit you with two quarts of dust!"

Then I poured the bag of dust over his head.

His first breath went halfway down. Then the air and dust stuck in his throat. He coughed. He wheezed. He gasped for breath and the gasp just sucked in more dust. Dust ran over his hair and into his eyebrows. Two rivers of dust ran around his nose, across his mouth, and made a little funnel shape as he sucked it in. He grabbed frantically for the inhaler in his pocket.

I was in a fury. I poured more dust over his head, shouting, "That's for Jennifer! And that's for Plumly! And that's for Jennifer again!" She had been a sweet, talented, and kind young woman and now she was dead.

Pottle's face turned red and then purple.

"That's more for Jennifer! And for what you put Barry through!"

I coughed. My eyes watered. My throat itched and partly closed up.

But I didn't have asthma.

As I poured the last of the dust over him, I shouted, "Oh, Pottle. What a world. What a world!"

· 25 ·

REALLY MOST
SINCERELY DEAD

Edmond Pottle didn't die from the dust. So I didn't kill him
directly. In his pocket with the inhaler was a Rohypnol pill
not in its packaging. Apparently he kept it unwrapped and
ready to drop into a woman's drink when opportunity
offered. It had stuck to the mouthpiece of the inhaler and he
sucked it into his windpipe when he sucked desperately on
the inhaler. I actually tried the Heimlich maneuver on him
when he started to turn blue, but it was too late.

I had further damaged my shoulder throwing the vacuum cleaner around, although the injury was well worth it.
With my shoulder immobilized in a fiberglass two-piece
cast held together by straps, I spent the night in the hospital sedated. Sedated but happy.

The next morning, the hospital released me. I wasn't supposed to drive. The taxi let me off at home at nine-thirty in
the morning. Long John was delighted to see me. Sam had
stopped by to give the parrot a change of water, and judging
by the half banana in its skin on the kitchen counter, had

also sat around doling out treats. LJ gets a banana one half-inch slice at a time, as Sam well knows. Birds can't hold bigger pieces and make a mess if they try. LJ takes several minutes to savor each slice.

My answering machine played back three messages.

"Cat, this is Harold Briskman. I have an idea for a snazzy article you could do for us. Call me chop-chop."

"Ms. Marsala, this is E. T. Taubman. My attorney will ring you to discuss your persistent harassment of me." (A click that sounded louder than others, although I knew it wasn't.) This from a man who was happy enough to knowingly let an innocent man take the blame for a murder.

"Aunt Cat?" There was a gulp. "They want to take Lion away from me. They can't do that, can they? Can you help me?"

Shoulder problem or no shoulder problem, I grabbed up my car keys and headed out.

Barry and Maud live in a modest brick house in Oak Park. There's a small front yard with two plots of grass, one on each side of a tan cement crazy-paving path. As I started up the walk to their house, the front door opened.

The woman who came out was about fifty-five, gray-haired, with wings of white at her temples. She wore a light blue knit dress and, given the heat of the day, an unnecessary cardigan sweater, left open. Many women don't believe they can go out without a jacket of some kind.

"Well, thanks. I just feel much better about it all now," she said, turning to face the doorway.

Maud stood in the doorway, flanked by Jeremy, who held a bundle under his shirt. They waved at the woman. She got into a blue Chevy and drove away.

I said, "Hi."

Maud said, "Hi, Cat." She smiled. Jeremy smiled more broadly than Maud, and in fact more broadly than anybody I'd seen in days.

I said, "Who was that?"

"Well, maybe Barry ought to explain."

Barry was lurking in the shadows behind her. She moved aside to let me in.

"Morning, Barry," I said. "I had a call from Jeremy. What's the problem? Who was that leaving?"

"It's like this," he said. He hesitated, and we moseyed into the living room and sat down.

"See, the problem was the collar around Lion's neck. The cat didn't have a name tag or a shots tag, and I know he was a dirty mess," Barry said, "but it still seemed like he wasn't wild, really, but maybe strayed off. He acted kind of tame, you know."

"In other words, his owner might be looking for him."

"Um, yes." He cast a glance at Jeremy, but went on. "So I thought maybe I had a responsibility to put an ad in the paper. So I got the paper to look at how the Lost & Found ads were written. And this is what I saw." He pushed a copy of the *Trib* over to me. A short ad was circled:

Lost cat: A marmalade tom, wearing a red collar with a white diamond pattern. Lost in vicinity of Grant Park Underground Garage Monday. Reward.

It gave a phone number.

"So the person I just saw leaving was Lion's owner?"

"Right. She and her husband were in town on Monday shopping. They left the cat in the car, because it was an underground parking place and they knew the car wouldn't heat up. But they cranked the window down, just an inch, she said, for air."

Maud said, "The woman was horrified that the cat got out such a small opening."

"Cats do."

"And apparently it was her daughter's cat. The daughter had left for summer term at college last month and gave the cat to her parents for safekeeping."

"Cats don't like to be given away," I said.

"The mother was extremely embarrassed and upset."

Jeremy was bouncing up and down. "So that's what you called me about?" I asked him.

"And she talked with me, Aunt Cat, the lady did, and I told her about how Lion had saved our lives, and she said her daughter would be away at college for three more years, and that was too long, and she didn't really like cats very much—the mother, I mean—and we all talked, and you know what?"

"I kind of think I do."

"She said I can keep him!"

"That's wonderful!"

Maud said, "What a relief! I wished he—" We all looked at Barry. She said, "I admit, I told Barry I wished he wouldn't call her."

Barry said, "But I had to phone the woman."

"Because—?"

"Uh—well, it seemed like the honest thing to do."

I said, "Honest like telling the truth is honest?"

"It's not the same."

"No, it's not exactly the same." He had made an honest move, in the face of the possibility that Jeremy would be devastated, deprived of his new cat friend. And Barry knew well how upset Jeremy would be.

"It's not the same," I said, "but it's not entirely different, either. You either have a policy of being honest, or you don't. Wouldn't it be nice if all of life's lessons were right in point? I tell the truth about you and then you have to tell the truth about somebody else. And as a result you tell me you understand and approve of what I did. But then, life doesn't work out that neatly."

Jeremy said, "Well, I think this is neat!"

We laughed.

· 26 ·

THERE'S NO PLACE
LIKE HOME

Saturday afternoon. Closing day of the festival.

We all disembarked from Barry's van in the Grant Park Underground. The van held a rear-facing baby car seat with baby Cynthia in it, a child's car seat for Jeremy, and me and Barry and Maud. We had warned Jeremy we'd only stay an hour or two because Maud still tired easily. Maud and I had talked a long while about whether to bring Jeremy back to the parking garage. I had argued for taking him to the festival, to get rid of any lingering unhappy feelings remaining from our experience, but left the garage decision to her. Once she had made it, I admitted it was the choice I was hoping for.

We simply got out of the van, without making any special fuss about where we were. And Jeremy seemed happy, dancing from foot to foot.

"I'll show you everything, Mom."

"That's the Hungry Tiger, Mom!" Jeremy said as an Oz character ambled past. "You know, the Hungry Tiger who wants to eat fat babies."

You could almost see the warning lights go on over Barry's and Maud's heads. And in balloons like comic book thoughts: Alert! Sibling rivalry! Jealousy! Red alert over here!

"But he didn't," I said.

Jeremy said, "No. Because he was too kind."

"And Princess Ozma asked him to eat something because he was so hungry. And he said—"

Jeremy shouted, "He said it's no use. He already tried that and he just got hungry again."

In Quadling country a Toto look-alike contest was in progress. Yipping and yapping echoed off the Emerald City castle, waking Cynthia. She gazed around and blew a bubble. There were at least seven dogs that looked exactly like Toto. And also three basset hounds, several cocker spaniels, dachshunds and collies and a big Great Dane. Did their owners really think they'd win?

"How do the judges decide between perfect Totos?" I asked Barry.

"They have instructions to give prizes to all of them."

"Oh."

A green clown passed us, juggling green sparkling balls. A Tin Woodman on stilts walked by. There was a woman in a Munchkin costume selling doughnuts. Her doughnuts were piled on a stick stuck through their holes.

A medieval fair must have looked a lot like this.

A bulletin board held big digital photos of yesterday's Wicked Witch look-alike contest, one winner and three runners-up. I remembered the sign. The witch contestants had to be sixty-five or over.

In the distance the official Oz band played "Over the Rainbow."

"Would you believe," I said, "that song was almost cut from the movie?"

Maud said, "No, really?"

"I want lots and lots of popcorn, Mom," Jeremy said.

"Oh, gee, I don't know. It's just a little while before dinner—"

"Popcorn is good for you," I started to say. "It's whole grain and full of fiber." Then I stopped myself. Enough is enough.

"Your dad did a great job with the festival, Jeremy," I said.

"He sure did." Barry beamed.

A fanfare of trumpets sounded from the bandstand near the castle. Loudspeakers blared: "The balloon ascension is about to commence. Ladies and gentlemen of Oz, and miscellaneous visitors, your Wizard will soon ascend into the skies to cross the Deadly Desert." More trumpets.

Jeremy spotted the top of the green-and-gold balloon over the peak of the castle.

"Let's go!" he said. "Hurry up!"

Barry said, "Okay, okay. But it'll take quite a while for him to get airborne."

"Hurry up!"

Laughing, we strolled toward the castle. The P.A. system announced again that the Wizard was about to leave.

The tiny "square" in front of the castle was full of people and many more pressed in as we moved closer. The balloon was a beautiful thing, metallic gold stripes alternating with the bright green. Beneath it was a wicker basket. The balloon lurched woozily, not yet fully inflated.

A little man dressed as the Wizard of Oz stood in the wicker basket, smiling and waving. Dorothy was nearby, holding a tiny wicker handbasket with Toto inside. She was waving good-bye.

The Wizard said to the crowd, "I have put off going away to perform before the crowned heads of Europe, just so

that I could be here with all of you." He sounded more like
W. C. Fields than Frank Morgan. "It's been wonderful visiting this great city on the plains. But now I'm off. Good-
bye, Chicago! Good-bye, Dorothy! Good-bye, children!
Never stop dreaming."

The Wizard stooped and turned up a small gas burner,
which had been kept on a low flame, just barely maintaining
the high, round shape of the balloon. As more warm air
filled the silken globe, the basket and balloon became a living unit. It struggled against the guy ropes holding it down.
When the balloon was fully inflated and pulling hard, the
ground crew of Munchkins untied the ropes. The balloon
rose in a dignified and stately manner into the air. When it
was about ten feet off the ground, the Wizard dropped
overboard three bright green sandbags. Splitting open on
impact, they proved to be filled with gold-wrapped chocolate coins.

The children in the crowd rushed for the coins, gathering
them all in less than a minute. They looked up, and now the
balloon was fifty feet in the air. The prevailing westerly
breeze caught it, and as it lifted, it was borne slowly to the
east.

In a few more moments, it had begun to move at the
same stately pace as several wisps of white clouds.

The balloon, so enormous while it was on the ground,
began to dwindle. The Wizard still waved from the basket,
and the crowds still cheered, but in the cheers there was a
sense of farewell, the sadness of going away.

Jeremy held his father's hand. His mouth was a big round
O. Finally, when he couldn't see the Wizard any longer, just
the balloon like a ball against the blue-and-white sky, he
said to his baby sister, "When you're bigger, I'm going to
read to you about Oz. It's a beautiful place, all surrounded
by the Deadly Desert, so that no bad people can get in.

Nobody ever dies in Oz. It's ruled by a girl named Ozma, who's I guess a lot like you're going to be when you grow up. And you know the best thing of all? There's lots and lots of Oz books and we can read every one."

The balloon got smaller and smaller and became a tiny dot. The green and gold blended into a sparkling green, heading eastward over Lake Michigan, and then the dot vanished.

The Wooden Gargoyles:
Evil in Oz

by Brian D'Amato

. . . the best safety of the frontier settlements will be secured by the total annihilation of the few remaining Indians.

    —L. Frank Baum,
        editorial in the *Aberdeen Saturday Pioneer,*
        December 15, 1890

1. MACATAWA

There used to be steam ferries all over Lake Michigan, the *John Sherman* out of Ludington, the *Chief Wawatam* from Macinaw City to St. Ignace, and the Père Marquette Rail-

way Line's fleet of numbered steamers running from Mil-
waukee and Chicago to small Michigan ports like Benton
Harbor, Muskegon, and Holland. Early in the summer of
1905, my grandfather and his mother were crossing to
Chicago on the PM Line with a group of other summer
residents of the beach resort community of Macatawa Park
in Holland, Michigan, which included Lyman Frank Baum
and two of his sons. As the boat came up on Chicago, Baum
gathered the children in the party together at the prow and
proudly pointed out the first visible words among the riot
of bills papering the wharves and grain elevators that at
that time lined the lakeshore, ornate black and gold letters
painted twenty feet high across the largest of the dock
houses: *What Did the Woggle-Bug Say?*

At this stage in his career, at forty-nine, Baum was already
at least nationally famous for *The Wonderful Wizard of Oz*,
but possibly less for the book, which he'd published in
1900, than for the lavish operetta version he'd written and
produced the year after, and which was still touring to full
houses all over the country. In Macatawa, Baum had built
his beach house, "The Sign of the Goose"—the site of
riotous children's parties remembered fondly by my grandfather—with proceeds from his first success, the pre-Oz
Father Goose: His Book, two years before the debut of *The
Wizard*, and filled it with goose-themed decorations.
According to my grandfather, Baum had also dabbled in
local gossip journalism, and had written, under a pseudo-
nym, a book called *Tamawaca Folks*, a barely à clef novel
about some of the more notorious personages at the
Macatawa resort.

A few years ago I finally tracked down a copy of
Tamawaca Folks: A Summer Comedy. It turns out there are
strong similarities between its plot and that of *The Wizard*,
written only a year later. Jarrod, the hero, is an honest

lawyer from Kansas City who comes to "Tamawaca" for the summer and finds that although it's a place of great beauty—described, more than once, as a "fairyland"—the entire resort community is under the thumb of a pair of fraudulent businessmen: the charming, blustering Wilder—who has double-sold lots, built cottages in the center of public streets, and owns all the businesses—and the elderly, austere Easton, a thoroughly crooked moneyman who "loves to pray for your spiritual welfare while he feels for your pocketbook."[1] In the course of the novel, Jarrod aligns himself with several of the other cottagers; exposes Wilder's subterfuges, false advertising, and misdealings; and serves Easton with an unanswerable lawsuit. Easton, bested in a final confrontation with Jarrod on the latter's veranda, whimpers, "Ruined—ruined! At my age to face the poorhouse! Oh, my poor family—oh,—oh,—oh!," leans backward, throws up his arms, and falls over the rail of the porch "to lie motionless on the soft sand beneath."[2] At the end of the book, Wilder is forcibly reformed and reduced to ordinary citizenship, Tamawaca is taken over by the householders and administered on a new cooperative plan, and Jarrod goes home for the winter to Kansas City. It's hardly necessary to point out that "Wilder" has the same number of letters as "Wizard" and that "Easton" sounds like "East"—although in *The Wizard*, it's the Witch of the West who ends up melting away, not into sand, but "like brown sugar."

Unfortunately, Baum's *The Woggle-Bug*—an extravaganza even grander than the musical *Wizard*, and based on the second Oz book, *The Marvelous Land of Oz* (1904)—didn't equal *The Wizard*'s success. One guesses that one problem may have been the general resistance of insects to what could be called "cuddlification." Enlarged to human size and towering in the footlights, even the jolly, harmless

Woggle-Bug may have looked a bit creepy and Gregor Samsa–esque. The next season Baum had sold his house in Macatawa and moved to Hollywood, California. He made five silent feature films there from his own scripts, each heavy with pioneering special effects, and at one point even tried to finance an Oz-based theme park. But while Baum had certainly sensed which way the media winds were blowing, none of these projects clicked for him the way similar ones would for Walt Disney a few decades later. In 1919, Baum—who by then had written thirteen other Oz books besides *The Wizard*, a number of other Oz-related fantasies, and dozens of other titles under several different names—died with roomfuls of heartfelt fan mail from all over the world but very little cash.

The Oz books have more or less remained in print, with some newer editions reproducing the fine color plates of the originals, and the books subsequent to *The Wizard* still have many devoted fans. But so many millions of people have been so affected by the MGM musical version of Oz that Baum's original work has become something of a victim of its own generative power. I'm quite sure Baum would have loved the movie, not just for its brilliance but because it followed several leads from his own films, for instance the device of having Dorothy's trio of friends appear briefly at the beginning as farmhands. Nevertheless, it's a shame that most people who enjoy *The Wizard* stop there without reading another book in the series, and a bigger shame that many writers and critics—even those who take Baum seriously—tend to dismiss the later volumes: Salman Rushdie, in his book on the MGM film, sums up the standard assessment by calling them "admittedly of diminishing quality."[3]

To me and to many other Oz fans, this seems quite wrong. Like most people I know who were exposed to all the Oz books as children, when I was just old enough to read them (and when my opinion on the genre was certainly worth more than it is today), I preferred the books to the movie, and the later books to *The Wizard*. In fact, as far as I can tell, it seems that few people who read all the books at a young age prefer the first. Gore Vidal, in his essential 1977 essay that revitalized Baum scholarship, said his favorites as a child were *The Emerald City of Oz* (1910), *Rinkitink in Oz* (1916), and *The Lost Princess of Oz* (1917).[4] Suzanne Rahn, in her *The Wizard of Oz: A Reader's Companion,* says her favorites were *The Emerald City* and *The Lost Princess*.[5] My own favorite when I was little was *The Scarecrow of Oz* (1915)—which toward the end of his life Baum himself also said he preferred to the others—although since then I've found more to think about in the fourth book of the series, *Dorothy and the Wizard in Oz*. But each of the thirteen sequels, in which Baum progressively refined his vision, has something singular to offer. Lately a newer crop of articles such as Alison Lurie's excellent "The Oddness of Oz" in *The New York Review of Books* [6] has helped redirect Oz studies toward these later works, rightly returning more of Oz to itself.

2. AN AMERICAN UTOPIA?

Now, as Rushdie points out, the actual dominion of Oz—crystallized in the later books as a rectangular country bordered by impassable deserts, the rectangle divided into five regions whose prevailing colors were green in the center, at the Emerald City, and purple, blue, red, and yellow in the north, east, south, and west respectively—underwent a certain progressive domestication throughout the series. By the last installments it was a land without birth or death, where babies remained forever burbling happily in their cradles, and where even Dorothy and other permanent guests from the standard world would never age, and were vulnerable to death only through accident or violence.

But while this perhaps inevitable drift does make the Land of Oz proper a less hazardous place than it is in *The Wizard*, it never strips the world of the Oz books of sinister elements. There are no stories in a perfect world, and in the later books, the strange lands surrounding Oz (through which the protagonists often have to travel to reach the Emerald City at the end of the book), as well as forgotten pockets of Oz itself, retain characters and themes that are, to say the least, disturbing. My sense is that while they're often thought of as anomalies and outside Baum's generally utopian vision, these darker elements may actually give us a key to Oz's continuing allure.

Lurie recounts how the critical reputation of the Oz books—which is at the moment probably the strongest it's ever been—has varied widely from decade to decade, often because their subversively feminist and pacifist elements scandalize the Christian Right. But almost since the books first appeared, Oz's credibility has also had a more serious charge to contend with, one that for want of a better name might be called the "Narnia Problem," after a typically mainstream attack on Baum that recently appeared in the on-line magazine *Salon*. Feeling that Oz is "infinitely less compelling" than C. S. Lewis's Narnia, the article's author, Laura Miller, tells us that *The Wizard of Oz* "has nothing scary or even unsettling in it" and that "the main characters are never in mortal danger. . . . There is wickedness in Oz but no evil; badness is simply a disagreeable temperament certain people have, not a terrible force in the world, certainly never a temptation to any of the heroes." Miller ends with the charge that "Baum never wrote a deft sentence, while Lewis excelled at them."[7]

Since the subject here is the deeper themes of the books, I'm going to dismiss the attack on Baum's style somewhat airily by submitting that, despite much talk to the contrary, style is still only style, and it's not necessarily the most precious tool in the writer's box. Imagination rates higher, and not only in writing for children. Poe's style was so tabloidishly liberal with adjectives and even adverbs that I doubt whether he'd pass the average freshman creative writing class. But he had Tool Number One, and while there's no shortage of deft sentences in the world, there is always a shortage of imagination.

Which is what, though? Our estimate of a writer's imagination depends not just on the novelty of a writer's inventions, but on their special quality, their "rightness." C. Warren Hollister, in an essay called "Oz and the Fifth Criterion," posits something he calls "three-dimensionality," a quality specific to the fantasy genre—not quite "imagination" as we know it, but whatever it is that makes it possible for the reader to project himself into an unlikely situation, the quality that makes a creation seem for the moment almost possible, solid, memorable, and "right."[8] Baum's plain-speakin' prose would seem to be just the thing for this job, since anything more highfalutin can easily lead to reader resistance, especially from young readers who as yet have no middle-brow pretensions. And beyond that, as Cory Panshin insightfully observes in a letter on the Miller piece,[9] Baum's writing has a directness especially suited to being read aloud— as opposed to Lewis's, which is often oblique and confusing—and this is not quite so easy to achieve as many people think.

But it's the charge that Oz is "sanitized" that does the least justice to Baum's work. It's true that by the last few books in the series Oz has become a near-utopia, and that even writers most sympathetic to the series tend not to mention the country's darker pockets, or to dismiss them with an aside. Ray Bradbury is typical of these, calling Oz "the land of midnight sun, where the day never stops, where noons persist or if they darken briefly, reburst themselves with pure delight." And Baum, in his introduction to *The Wizard*, did profess to have written a "modernized fairy tale, in which the wonderment and joy are retained and the heart-aches and nightmares are left out."[10]

But, as many critics have pointed out, even a quick glance through the first book yields any number of images that show how far Baum fell short of his professed goal: the Kalidahs, "beasts with bodies like bears and heads like tigers" who nearly slash Dorothy and her friends apart before they are "dashed to pieces on the sharp rocks,"[11] the armless Hammerheads, who butt people with heads that shoot out on stalklike necks, or the melting Wicked Witch falling down in a "brown, shapeless mass" and spreading over the floor. James Thurber—possibly more in touch with his child-self than Bradbury—remembers: "I know that I went through excruciatingly lovely nightmares when the Scarecrow lost his straw, when the Tin Woodman was taken apart, when the Saw-Horse broke his wooden leg (it hurt for me, even if it didn't hurt for Mr. Baum)."[12]

Regarding temptations to evil, while it's true that Oz is, usually, a forgiving place, it's a long way from a no-fault zone. In *The Tin Woodman of Oz* (1918), the antepenulti-mate book of the series, our heroes—this time the Scare-crow, the Tin Woodman, and a new "meat" character named Woot the Wanderer—escape from a band of balloon-like inflated creatures called Loons, who, assuming all crea-tures to be of their own anatomical type, had attempted to deflate Woot and his companions with long thorns.

"Every one of them ought to be exploded," declared Woot, who was angry because his leg still hurt him.

"No," said the Tin Woodman, "that would not be just fair. They were quite right to capture us, because we had no business to intrude here, having been warned to keep away from Loonville. This is their country, not ours . . ."[13]

Miller's charge that Baum's protagonists are never tempted to do wrong is simply untrue; in fact, in this case, Woot is tempted to exterminate an entire species (if that's the right term). This sort of temptation doesn't happen only in the later books. In *The Wizard*, the temptation theme goes beyond the Cowardly Lion's famous appetite for Toto; more centrally, the Wizard himself (who is hardly even an antihero, but at worst a "swing character") is a good person tempted by power to resort to "humbug," or fakery—one of the cardinal sins in the ethos of Oz.

The most one could say is that, in general, Baum makes an effort to cage or sublimate his demons while still keeping them on display. Often this process is more subtle than simply creating villains who are easily overcome. Baum said that as a child he was troubled by dreams of being chased by animated scarecrows, and that since then he had "taken revenge" on the figure of the scarecrow for the "mystic feeling he once inspired."[14] His revenge, though, was transforming this hollow, dead, vegetal, Eliotesque specter into the benevolent leader of Oz's pantheon of non-human protagonists. Many if not most of these are equally the stuff of nightmares declawed: the Cowardly, nonanthropophagous Lion, the ax-wielding tin robot who is actually rather meek, or, in *The Marvelous Land of Oz*, the positively Brueghelian figure of Jack Pumpkinhead, whose head is a grinning saw-toothed jack-o'-lantern teetering atop a tall, gaunt wooden armature, but who serves Tip, the hero of the book, as loyally as the more famous trio in *The Wizard* serves Dorothy.[15]

Like, I suppose, all young fans of the series, I tended to imagine myself living in the Emerald City, away from Oz's dangers. But at some point I realized that what I kept coming back to in the books were the sections involving more mysterious elements, a host of strange and grotesque threats to the benign order. Unlike Thurber, I don't remember any nightmares, but I do still remember unique feelings of apprehension and dread. What's most significant to a child's mind is not whether a story is scary enough to be a functional nightmare, but rather in what ways it remains nightmarish. The telling quality of a nightmare is not how obviously it's about danger or death, but its take on life, the specifics of its own particularity—in a word, its originality.

Even the obvious examples above show that Oz is not peopled by the standard dragons and stepmothers that have done duty from the Grimms through Narnia and into the Harry Potter era—what Baum called "the stereotyped genie, dwarf, and fairy"[16]—but by more unexpected constructs. One feels it might almost take a real child to come up with some of them: the Flatheads of *Glinda of Oz*, for instance, who carry their brains in cans, or the characters who accompany Ojo, the hero of *The Patchwork Girl of Oz*, on his own journey to the Emerald City: a Glass Cat, the Patchwork Girl, a living Edison phonograph machine, and the cubistic Woozy, a large, hairless, uniformly rectilinear dog. This sort of whimsy isn't all that far from Lautréamont's famous proto-Surrealist simile of the beauty of a "chance encounter of a sewing machine and an umbrella on an operating table."[17] The same qualities extend beyond the cast to the structures of the Oz books. While the standard fairy tales of the Western canon tend to observe a stately progression, usually with clusters of three characters or events in ascending order of magnitude, Baum's scenarios are less predictable, often organized in ways that could be said to be more representative of real nightmares—with disjunctive changes of scene, inexplicable conflations of character, and an arbitrariness that seems suspiciously purposeful.

In Baum's day this quality was called "nonsense," and its paradigmatic creative genius was of course Lewis Carroll, whom Baum naturally admired.[18] Wonderland and the Looking-Glass World are bleaker and more overtly nightmarish than Oz, so much so that lately the general consensus seems to be that while their reputation among adults continues to grow, Carroll's books are less a favorite among real children than was previously assumed. But I believe that while Dorothy is indeed a less lonely and beleaguered heroine than Alice, much of the oddity she attracts can be compared to Carroll's in its capacity to disturb. There are signs of a dark and secretive genius in Oz, of something that could almost be called evil.

3. THE SITTING BULL EDITORIALS

Like all Oz fans, I'd had only good feelings about Baum the person until I heard about an incident in Aberdeen, South Dakota, where, in 1997, a coalition of Oglala Sioux demanded the cancellation of a planned L. Frank Baum Conference. Their complaint was that when Baum was editing a newspaper in Aberdeen, in 1890 and 1891, he'd written a pair of editorials advocating a genocidal policy against remaining Indians. Since the hate-mongering passages are even more painful when taken out of context, it might be best to quote these editorials in full. The following was printed in Baum's *Aberdeen Saturday Pioneer* on December 15, 1890, shortly after Sitting Bull was assassinated by the Indian Police, a U.S. Army regiment:

Sitting Bull, most renowned Sioux of modern history, is dead.

He was an Indian with a white man's spirit of hatred and revenge for those who had wronged him and his. In his day he saw his son and his tribe gradually driven from their possessions: forced to give up their old hunting grounds and espouse the hard working and uncongenial avocations of the whites. And these, his conquerors, were marked in their dealings with his people by self-ishness, falsehood and treachery. What wonder that his wild nature, untamed by years of subjection, should still revolt? What wonder that a fiery rage still burned within his breast and that he should seek every opportunity of obtaining vengeance upon his natural enemies?

The proud spirit of the original owners of these vast prairies inherited through centuries of fierce and bloody wars for their possession, lingered last in the bosom of Sitting Bull. With his fall the nobility of the Redskin is extinguished, and what few are left are a pack of whining curs who lick the hand that smites them. The Whites, by law of conquest, by justice of civilization, are masters of the American continent, and the best safety of the fron-tier settlements will be secured by the total annihilation of the few remaining Indians. Why not annihilation? Their glory has fled, their spirit broken, their manhood effaced; better that they die than live the miserable wretches that they are. History would forget these latter despicable beings, and speak, in later ages of the glory of these grand Kings of forest and plain that Cooper loved to heroism.

We cannot honestly regret their extermination, but we at least do justice to the manly characteristics pos-sessed, according to their lights and education, by the early Redskins of America.[19]

The second editorial, following the Wounded Knee Massacre—which was naturally then called a battle— appeared on January 3, 1891:

> The peculiar policy of the government in employing so weak and vacillating a person as General Miles to look after the uneasy Indians, has resulted in a terrible loss of blood to our soldiers, and a battle which, at best, is a disgrace to the war department. There has been plenty of time for prompt and decisive measures, the employment of which would have prevented this disaster.
>
> The PIONEER has before declared that our only safety depends upon the total extirmination [sic] of the Indians. Having wronged them for centuries we had better, in order to protect our civilization, follow it up by one more wrong and wipe these untamed and untamable creatures from the face of the earth. In this lies safety for our settlers and the soldiers who are under incompetent commands.
>
> Otherwise, we may expect future years to be as full of trouble with the redskins as those have been in the past.
>
> An eastern contemporary, with a grain of wisdom in its wit, says that "when the whites win a fight, it is a victory, and when the Indians win it, it is a massacre."[20]

Noting the bizarre ambivalences in these passages should not be seen as trying to apologize for them. There is no meaningful apology that could be made. Certainly one can come up with explanations for how the above could have sprung from someone apparently so generous in every other respect. Baum shared a kind of jejune, romantic, all-or-nothing mentality with many Americans of the period; in those days—it seems to us—many people thought about groups first and later about individuals, and were so sold on notions like "national honor" that putting the enemy out of its misery was often seen as (almost) the liberal opinion. And certainly in terms of biography, Baum was something of a perpetual adolescent, a dabbler in everything from performing in musical comedies to chicken breeding, and at this time he was at the low point of his life, at what seemed like the end of a long slide from well-to-do boyhood to the sort of poverty he later described so unflinchingly in the first chapter of *The Wizard of Oz*. Had he witnessed or heard about some Indian barbarity that, combined with his depression, produced a statement he might have repudiated at other times in his vicissitudinous career? It doesn't look as though anyone will ever know. At any rate, the question we Ozians can't help asking ourselves—even though it's not really an intellectual question, not a question of art but one of speculative biography—is whether our knowing about Baum's "genocide editorials" should recolor our view of Oz. Have we been reading the books through emerald-tinted glasses? Is there something about Oz we've been missing? Something sinister?

So far, the usual answer would be no. In the eyes of most people who write about Oz, Baum's world is a sunny one and his outlook on life is enlightened in advance of that of his average contemporary's. Several of the planners of the Aberdeen festival, for instance, responded to a Lakota petition-and-boycott campaign by drafting an "Apology and Pledge" stressing Oz's pacifism and tolerance:

> Baum's books are a sharp contrast to this call for genocide. Difference is valued in his stories; he describes groups of creatures with different characters and beliefs who work out the logistics of living together in respect and harmony. Oz is a multicultural kingdom. How could someone with such a vision have called for the mass murder of an entire group of people?

The fabric of Oz is love, the emotional connection, life-form to life-form, that creates respect, recognition, and acceptance. Baum didn't practice that with the Lakota. Instead he abstracted these people, stripped away their humanness, and turned them into a concept, a "vanishing race," thereby setting up the conditions to think them out of existence.[21]

As Martin Gardner says, "this theme of tolerance runs through all of Baum's writings."[22] This is certainly true as far as it goes. But I think it's also possible to distinguish a subtheme, one that may be equally integral to Oz— not only as a foil to the books' more conscious intentions, but as a component of the fuel that powered Baum's imagination.

4. THE WOODEN GARGOYLES

As Thurber realizes, how nightmarish something is depends to a large extent on the age and impressionability of its audience. A young child, at least, listening to the Oz books before bed, can find plenty to be frightened of. Baum's work doesn't hinge on violent death, like that of Grimm or Andersen, and it has little of Carroll's chilly obscuritanism, but his creations have an eeriness of their own that I think places him closer to Poe. In *The Road to Oz* (1909), Dorothy and her companions—this time a boy named Button-Bright, a Whitcomb Riley–esque character called the Shaggy Man, and a somewhat provocative rainbow fairy named Polychrome—are surrounded by a tribe of gaudily colored figures with grotesque faces on both the fronts and backs of their detachable heads. The Shaggy Man asked them who they are:

"Scoodlers!" they yelled in chorus, their voices sharp and shrill.

"What do you want?" called the Shaggy Man.

"You!" they yelled, pointing their thin fingers at the group; and they all flopped around, so they were white, and then all flopped back again, so they were black.

"But what do you want us for?" asked the Shaggy Man, uneasily.

"Soup!" they all shouted, as if with one voice.

"Goodness me!" said Dorothy, trembling a little; "the Scoodlers must be reg'lar cannibals."

"Don't want to be soup," protested Button-Bright, beginning to cry.

"Hush, dear," said the little girl, trying to comfort him; "we don't any of us want to be soup. But don't worry; the Shaggy Man will take care of us."

"Will he?" asked Polychrome, who did not like the Scoodlers at all, and kept close to Dorothy.

"I'll try," promised the Shaggy Man; but he looked worried. Happening just then to feel the Love Magnet in his pocket, he said to the creatures, with more confidence:

"Don't you love me?"

"Yes!" they shouted, all together.

"Then you mustn't harm me, or my friends," said the Shaggy Man, firmly.

"We love you in soup!" they yelled, and in a flash turned their white sides to the front.[23]

After some trouble, our friends escape the Scoodlers and then destroy them: the Shaggy Man catches their detachable heads and hurls them down a gorge "with right good will," laughing as the Scoodlers' helpless bodies stumble blindly about.

Each book in the series contains at least one or two scenes that are equally unsettling, but I think many Ozians would agree the most unnerving title is the fourth, *Dorothy and the Wizard in Oz* (1908). Gardner says "an atmosphere of violence and gloom hangs over the tale"[24] and more than one critic has pointed out its affinities to Dante's *Inferno*.[25] But the book is also so purely bizarre that one is tempted to wonder whether it reflects a collision of Baum's numerous chronic illnesses with the even more varied patent medicines of the period. At the beginning of the story, Dorothy, a farm boy named Zeb, Zeb's horse Jim, Dorothy's kitten Eureka (Toto has been left at home), and the Wizard—who, since his exile from Oz in the first book, has returned to his vocation as a carnival showman—are caught in an earthquake near San Francisco and tumble through a fault line to the underground kingdom of the Mangaboos, a society of vegetable people. The Wizard gets into a magic contest with Gwig, their great "thorny Sorcerer," and when he wins greater applause for his sleight-of-hand multiplying-piglets trick than Gwig does for his own authentic magic, the Sorcerer begins to cast a spell on him:

> "He will not be a wonderful Wizard long," remarked Gwig.
>
> "Why not?" enquired the Wizard.
>
> "I am going to stop your breath," was the reply. "I perceive that you are curiously constructed, and that if you cannot breathe you cannot keep alive."
>
> The little man looked troubled.
>
> "How long will it take you to stop my breath?" he asked.
>
> "About five minutes. I'm going to begin now. Watch me carefully."
>
> He began making queer signs and passes toward the Wizard; but the little man did not watch him long. Instead, he drew a leathern case from his pocket and

took from it several sharp knives, which he joined
together, one after another, until they made a long sword.
By the time he had attached a handle to this sword he
was having much trouble to breathe, as the charm of the
Sorcerer was beginning to take effect.

So the Wizard lost no more time, but leaping forward
he raised the sharp sword, whirled it once or twice
around his head, and then gave a mighty stroke that cut
the body of the Sorcerer exactly in two.

Dorothy screamed and expected to see a terrible
sight; but as the two halves of the Sorcerer fell apart on
the floor she saw that he had no bones or blood inside of
him at all, and that the place where he was cut looked
much like a sliced turnip or potato. (p. 37)

Fleeing from the Mangaboos, our little band is attacked
by invisible bears:

The horse was plunging madly about, and two or
three deep gashes appeared upon its flanks, from which
the blood flowed freely. . . . As the little Wizard turned
to follow them he felt a hot breath against his cheek and
heard a low, fierce growl. At once he began stabbing at
the air with his sword, and he knew that he had struck
some substance because when he drew back the blade it
was dripping with blood. The third time that he thrust
out the weapon there was a loud roar and a fall, and suddenly at his feet appeared the form of a great red bear,
which was nearly as big as the horse and much stronger
and fiercer. (p. 95)

This sort of thing keys into nightmares and wonderings
that strike me as endemic to young children: waking up in
the night unable to breathe, imagining what might be

inside your body, or feeling there are creatures about that can't be seen.

After they elude the invisible bears, Dorothy and her friends follow a path toward the surface of the earth that leads up an underground mountain, through a high tunnel in that mountain, and out through a series of archways to an ominous land:

"The Country of the Gargoyles is all wooden!" exclaimed Zeb; and so it was. The ground was sawdust and the pebbles scattered around were hard knots from trees, worn smooth in the course of time. There were odd wooden houses, with carved wooden flowers in the front yards. The tree-trunks were of course wood, but the leaves of the trees were shavings. The patches of grass were splinters of wood, and where neither grass nor sawdust showed was a solid wooden flooring. Wooden birds fluttered among the trees and wooden cows were browsing upon the wooden grass; but the most amazing things of all were the wooden people— the creatures known as Gargoyles.

These were very numerous, for the place was thickly inhabited, and a large group of the queer people clustered near, gazing sharply upon the strangers who had emerged from the long spiral stairway.

The Gargoyles were very small of stature, being less than three feet in height. Their bodies were round, their legs short and thick and their arms extraordinarily long and stout. Their heads were too big for their bodies and their faces were decidedly ugly to look upon. Some had long, curved noses and chins, small eyes and wide, grinning mouths. Others had flat noses, protruding eyes, and ears that were shaped like those of an elephant. There were many types, indeed, scarcely two being alike; but all were equally disagreeable in appearance. The tops of their heads had no hair, but were carved into a variety of fantastic shapes, some having a row of points or balls around the top, others designs resembling flowers or vegetables, and still others having squares that looked like waffles cut criss-cross on their heads. They all wore short wooden wings which were fastened to their wooden bodies by means of wooden hinges with wooden screws, and with these wings they flew swiftly and noise-lessly here and there, their legs being of little use to them.

This noiseless motion was one of the most peculiar things about the Gargoyles. They made no sounds at all, either in flying or trying to speak, and they conversed mainly by means of quick signals made with their wooden fingers or lips. Neither was there any sound to be heard anywhere throughout the wooden country. The birds did not sing, nor did the cows moo; yet there was more than ordinary activity everywhere. (pp. 113–15)

The Gargoyles then abduct our heroes, carrying them "far away, over miles and miles of wooden country" until they come to a wooden city, and leave them in a doorless, windowless tower room.

There's something singular about this episode, some-thing that seems inexplicable, a nugget of otherness that has always preyed on my mind. Why *wooden* gargoyles? In Baum's day the word "gargoyle" (related to "gurgle," which is also Dorothy's pronunciation) referred only to sculpted rainwater spouts on cathedrals and other buildings, not to the hobgoblins or succubi they were carved to resemble. Even a living gargoyle would be a new construction, let alone one made out of wood. But if the gargoyles had been simply stone ones come to life, I doubt that I would even have remembered the episode. What is it that's so frightening about their silent wooden world? And is this sort of nightmarishness an anomaly in Oz, or a key component of Baum's vision?

5. MAGIC

For nearly a century, readers and critics have tried to explain what makes Oz so powerful. The short answer, of course, would be "magic." But what is magic, or specifically, what is the characteristic magic of Oz? How were the Gargoyles created, both in Baum's literally magic fantasy world and in the magical operations of his mind? What sort of magic is most essential to Baum's vision?

In *The Fantasy Tradition in American Literature*, Brian Attebery answers this question by positing a set of "magical operations," which Baum employs to shape his world: "animation, transformation, illusion, disillusion, transportation, protection, and luck."[26] This list is a good place to start, but in addition it might be helpful to focus on exactly how Baum's use of each of these types of magic differs from that of other fantasy writers. Regarding animation, for instance, one would want to mention Baum's sensitivity to the personalities of objects before they are animated, and how they retain them after they come to life. One easy example is the Patchwork Girl, who speaks in a sort of unfocused, free-associative homespun doggerel that figures, or is figured by, the patchwork quilts she is made of. Another is the Utensia episode in *The Emerald City of Oz*, where Dorothy finds herself in a principality ruled by a King Kleaver and peopled entirely by living kitchen implements, each with a personality appropriate to its original function. In his descriptions of these and many other vivified articles, Baum always pays attention to where their faces are, what aperture they speak out of, and how they move or hop about—just as when children turn tools or other objects into characters in their games or playlets, they tend to first identify a face or at least a pair of eyes. All this is aided immensely by the clever illustrations of John R. Neill, who not only worked out just where King Kleaver's mouth ought to be, but gave recognizable eyes and noses to the buildings of Oz and many other props throughout the series, to an extent that can remind one of the multiplying faces-within-faces of Northwest Coast sculpture. Children playing with inanimate household objects find they have different personalities, and the objects take appropriate roles in their scenarios. Baum, unlike most adults, remained attuned to this process. Either he paid great attention to the ways children played and imagined, or else he remembered what he had thought and felt as a child.

But he also remembered that childhood has the defects of its strengths. The same power that brings cutlery to life also hatches goblins out of a wrinkled pillow. In Oz, objects often surprise you by being alive and sentient, like the famous talking trees of the first book, which were used to great effect in the Oz musical film. Sometimes Baum recreates the process of a landscape slowly anthropomorphizing around the nervous traveler:

> At first the scene was wild enough, but gradually it grew more and more awful in appearance. All the rocks had the shapes of frightful beings and even the tree trunks were gnarled and twisted like serpents. (*The Emerald City of Oz*, p. 117)

Leonardo wrote about this mental state in his famous passage on how to "wake up the wit": "If you stare at some dirty and stained wall, or variegated stones . . . you will be able to see there diverse things, images of many land-scapes . . . and the gestures of strange figures, impressions of faces and clothes and infinite things. . . ."[27] Children may be more apt to slip into this frame of mind, but I imagine that most people also have had adult moments—and not just during fevers or under the influence of hallucinogens—when anything with roughly two dots above and one below looks like a face.[28]

But although animation operates on the border between whimsy and dread, it doesn't explain why the Gargoyles are what they are. They are animated, but unlike the citizens of Utensia, they aren't objects you'd find anywhere else. How did they get there? Were they originally something differ-ent? Why did Baum choose wood and not some other sub-stance? Is the combination intentionally an arbitrary one, a bit of Carrollian "nonsense"? Or is it somehow significant?

Transformation, Attebery's second category, is the most drastic of his magical operations. Turning something, or usually someone, into something completely different is asking a lot from the reader, and Baum tends to use outright transformation sparingly. When he does, he makes sure that the subject is changed into something contrasting enough to be a surprise, but still somehow fitting. In *Ozma of Oz*, the evil Nome King maintains a sort of prison-cum-salon where his enemies are stored as luxury tchotchkes. In it, the Prince of Ev is transformed into an ornamental pur-ple kitten, and Princess Ozma becomes a grasshopper carved out of a single emerald. In *The Tin Woodman of Oz*, the giantess Mrs. Yoop transforms the Woot, the Tin Wood-man, and the Scarecrow into, respectively, a green monkey, a tin owl, and a small brown bear stuffed with straw. When I was little, at least, there seemed to me to be some sort of mysterious logic at work here, something I'd now describe

as a sort of Lautréamontean "encounter" between the transformation and the transformed.

The most dramatic transformation in the books comes at
the end of *The Land of Oz*, when the boy protagonist, Tip,
is returned to his original identity as Ozma, Princess of
Oz. Lurie, Vidal, and others have discussed the subver-
siveness of this episode—certainly a nightmare for mainstream librarians and PTAs, if not for children—as well as
how the twist might relate to a stage version with an actress
playing the first acts as a breeches role. Personally, I've
always felt this was one of Baum's most Carrollian moments
in that it recalls the promotion of a pawn to a queen toward
the end of a chess game—a theme suggested by other characters in the book, for instance General Jinjur of the Army
of Revolt as the opposing queen, the Scarecrow as an inef-
fectual king, and the living wooden Saw-horse and hastily
animated Gump as knights. But in this case—unlike that of
the Gargoyles—even though Tip's first transformation took
place long before the start of the current book, Baum provides an explanatory backstory. One safe generalization
about Baum's style is that it's invariably matter-of-fact,
never deliberately murky. *Dorothy and the Wizard* may be
his most Dantesque book, but if Baum had meant for us to
interpret the Gargoyles as, say, condemned souls trans-
muted to wood, like Pier della Vigna and his fellows in the
Forest of the Suicides, one thinks he would have at least
hinted at it. The Gargoyles are more blank than that, more
sui generis.

None of Attebery's other categories—illusion, disillusion, transportation, protection, and luck—have much to
tell us about the Gargoyles. There are other things, or procedures, going on here. Maybe we need to add another
operation or two to Baum's magical toolkit.

6. BRICOLAGE

Like many of Oz's distinctive creatures, the Gargoyles seem to be cobbled together a bit loosely. Dorothy, the Wizard, Zeb, and their animal companions manage to escape from their wooden tower prison after they discover that when the Gargoyles sleep, they remove their wings, in which, as the Wizard says, their power of flight seems to reside. Managing to filch a few, our friends lash the wings onto Zeb's cart-horse and flap their way to another hollow mountain that appears to lead to the surface of the earth. The whole episode recalls an earlier one in *The Land of Oz,* when Tip and his semihuman companions similarly escape lockup in a tower of the Palace of Oz by lashing together a flying creature called the Gump out of two sofas, an elk-like taxidermy head, a broom, and a bunch of palm fronds for wings. The Gump reluctantly serves its purpose, but it's incompletely animated—the sofas' legs don't move—and always in danger of falling apart. At the end of the book, it is mercifully dismantled.

There seems to be a tradition in Oz of disassembling and reassembling living beings. The most extreme example is from *The Tin Woodman of Oz.* Before the book begins we learn that our hero, whose real name is Nick Chopper, was originally a flesh-and-blood woodcutter. The Witch of the East became angry with him and enchanted his ax, which kept twisting in his hands and chopping off parts of his body. Each time this happened Nick went to a tinsmith, who replaced the original part with a tin prosthesis. Eventually there was none of the original Nick Chopper left. In the book named after him, the Tin Woodman goes on a quest for his origins and confronts the tinsmith, who explains how, after he'd finished the Woodman (as well as another tin man, a soldier), he happened to create a third man out of their cast-off parts:

"I thought it would be a clever idea to put to some practical use the scraps of Nick Chopper and Captain Fyter. . . . First, I pieced together a body, gluing it with the Witch's Magic Glue, which worked perfectly. That was the hardest part of my job, however, because the bodies didn't match up well and some parts were missing. But by using a piece of Captain Fyter here and a piece of Nick Chopper there, I finally got together a very decent body, with heart and all the trimmings complete."[29]

In a famous scene the Woodman later confronts his own former head, in a paradox of identity that ultimately derives from the well-known philosophical problem of Theseus's Ship. Baum is, it seems, persistently fascinated with decapitation: Jack Pumpkinhead keeps replacing his heads with new pumpkins, which he grows himself; as soon as the current one starts to rot, he buries it in a little graveyard next to his pumpkin-shaped house. In *Ozma of Oz* (1907), the Princess Langwidere keeps a whole wardrobe of heads taken from other beautiful women, to which she hopes to add Dorothy's. When the Princess dons a new head she remains herself, but her personality changes to something closer to that of the head's original owner.

Other creatures in Oz, like *Ozma of Oz*'s wheel-limbed Wheelers or the ostrich-like Ork of *The Scarecrow of Oz*, with its propeller tail and Ping-Pong-paddle-like flipper-wings, combine animal and mechanical elements in ways reminiscent of one of the sculptures of Duchamp-Villon or the early work of Francis Picabia. One thinks of the famous Surrealist game of the "Exquisite Corpse," in which a strip of paper was folded in thirds. One artist would sketch the legs and feet of a figure, fold them under and out of sight, and let the next artist draw the torso without seeing the first part of the drawing, and so on.

Judging by the extent of its use, it might be fair to say that this is Oz's signature magical process: not transformation per se but rather collage, or maybe more accurately what Jean Dubuffet called *bricolage*, a type of outsider-art assemblage using ready-to-hand found objects. It's a destructive as well as generative process, and the pasted-together results always carry a hint of violence, even though, in Oz, the earlier cutting-out phase of the operation is usually only implicit. The result, too, is often disturbing in itself. At least since Leonardo's instructions on how to create an imaginary animal, people have recognized that the fear a monster inspires doesn't come only from whatever frightful powers it might have, but from the disjunction of its components. Simply put, there's something creepy about a Gump. I wonder whether Leonardo, or Baum, would have felt the same queasy feeling I did reading about the Nexia Biotechnologies Corporation's recent announcement that they'd bred a population of genetically-altered goats that incorporated DNA from spiders, which were already producing, instead of milk, long strands of protein-rich web that would presumably revolutionize the high-strength fiber industry. One could argue that something like even this deep-level melding of characteristics occurs in several Oz characters, for instance in the Patchwork Girl, whose brains are an ad hoc mixture of mental qualities in powder form—Obedience, Cleverness, Poesy, and so on.

Bricolage could also be said to be the master paranormality of Oz because its technique carries over into the structures of the books. Several critics have complained that the Oz books don't hang together. It's hard to refute this, since internal inconsistencies and occasional repetitions do show that some of the books were indeed hurriedly written. But either because of Baum's offhanded writing practices or despite them, the disjunctive progressions of many of the books—combined with a feeling of constant forward motion also characteristic of dreams—help create a sense of what the sleep researcher J. Allan Hobson calls "plot incongruity," the pre-logical narrative flow that is "far and away the most common peculiarity of . . . all dreams."[30]

And questioning the overall structure of an Oz book feels like trying to interpret a dream. What esoteric relationship exists between the Mangaboos, the invisible bears, and the Gargoyles? What are the pneumatic Loon people doing in the same book with the Tin Woodman's crisis of identity? Maybe nothing in particular, but when I was little and so many of the world's purposes were so mysterious, it certainly seemed they had *something* to do with each other, maybe something important. Oz felt, I suppose, like the way a myth feels to someone who believes in it, and like a myth a big part of its power lay not in its "universality" but in its most unexpected and disjunctive moments, in the feeling that "you couldn't possibly make that up," and hence the sense that it must have come directly from another world. The trick in creating beings and events with this quality would seem to be like that of writing a good simile or metaphor: the juxtaposed elements have to be disparate enough to combine to something distinctive, but not so far-flung that their combination doesn't seem somehow necessary once it's achieved. The new thing has to feel "right."

7. TRANSMUTATION

The combination of "Gargoyles" and "wood" may well count as an absurdist juxtaposition of disparate elements. But the fact that their entire *country* is made of wood, with wooden birds and cows and wood shavings instead of dirt, goes a bit farther, in a direction one associates with Surrealist compositions like Magritte's still lifes of granite fruit and flowers. Maybe we need one more term, one to describe this specific sort of universal transformation.

Suzanne Rahn comes the closest of anyone I've read when she introduces the term "theming":

> . . . at the turn of the century, color theming was the latest trend . . . a fashionable hostess might give a "Snow Luncheon" in which everything was white . . .. and color theming was only the beginning. Hostesses vied with each other to create original party themes. *Entertainment for all Seasons* (1904) informs its readers how to give a Butterfly Party, a Lemon Party, a Peanut Party. . . . This popular trend and the unaffected pleasure Baum found in it helps explain one of the most distinctive features of his imaginary world—the existence within Oz of innumerable small towns and countries, each based on a single concept logically developed—in fact, a theme. The first of these was the China Country in *The Wizard*, which Dorothy and her friends discover on the way to Glinda's Castle. Here, surrounded by a high wall, is a land whose people and animals are china figurines come to life; even the ground is "as smooth and shining and white as the bottom of a big platter" . . . Dorothy's bedroom in the Emerald City, with its green silk sheets, green books full of green pictures, and wardrobe of green dresses, exactly satisfies children's uninhibited delight in theming.[31]

For entire societies and countrysides made of one substance, though, "theming" may not be a strong enough word. "Transmutation" might be a closer fit.

8. WHITE CITY

At the end of the nineteenth century, the trend Rahn describes went beyond decoration toward a folk craft many people today might consider downright obsessive. Several writers have pointed to the Chicago World's Fair of 1893 as a key to many of Baum's signature themes. Better known as the World's Columbian Exposition, it was the most lavish Fair up to that time, and possibly the most extravagant ever produced. Its main zone, popularly known as "White City," was a vast and ornate Beaux-Arts fantasy of a Venice that never was, with networks of broad canals flowing between courts, fountains, and sprawling domed pavilions, each dedicated to a different category of art, science, or industry. Besides its exhibits of almost every conceivable type of product or livestock, the Exposition featured the first Ferris wheel (its size unequaled until recently), launches of hot-air balloons, and an aquarium that included a tank for demonstrations of submarine diving. At night, White City was dramatically lit with then-futuristic multicolored electric floodlights and thousands of tiny electric bulbs. Outside the main zone, the Fair's "Midway Plaisance"—conceived as a series of re-creations of town squares from many lands— seems to have evolved into something more like a late-colonialist human zoo, featuring pygmies, midgets, families of various tribes of American Indians cooking venison over open fires, and, of course, dubiously authentic "Moroccan" dancing girls. According to Hubert Howe Bancroft in *The Book of the Fair*, the Exposition's leading independent guidebook, the Midway,

> with its stir and tumult, its faces of every type and hue, its picturesque buildings, figures, and costumes, is the most graphic and varied ethnological display that

was ever presented to the world. All the continents are here represented, and many nations of each continent, civilized, semi-civilized, and barbarous. . . . [32]

The Exposition's effect on its visitors, especially those who had never been abroad, must have been overwhelming to an extent that's difficult for us to imagine. Even opponents of the Fair described it with awe.

Baum encountered all this almost as soon as he moved to Chicago, right after his "lean years" in South Dakota and the failure of his newspaper, and the Exposition has been interpreted as having inspired a number of his creations. Certainly White City was one inspiration for the Emerald City. The swift creation of such extravagant splendor out of "nothing," not in Europe or even the East but in the heart of the Plains, on a site that had been a "desolate" prairie fifty years before and which still bore scars of the Great Fire of 1871, might have set one thinking about modern-day magic. The fact that the Fair's imposing-looking buildings were made of wooden frames and plaster of Paris (not only weren't they meant to last, but several of them burned down even before the close of the Exposition) may have informed Baum's recurring "humbug" theme. Several writers have also noted that the Land of Oz, unlike conventionally archaizing fairylands, mixes the exotic, the homespun, the antique, and the breathlessly futuristic in a way that recalls the Exposition. Rahn even sees an echo of Mrs. Potter Palmer, the Exposition's presiding genius, in Baum's matriarchal sorceress Glinda the Good.

But if we twenty-first-century people were actually able to visit the Fair, I think one of the things that would strike us as most unfamiliar is the extent of the transmutational approach in many of the displays themselves. The Forestry Building, to take an obvious example, was

500 by 200 feet, and with its main facade fronting on the Lake; in style of architecture it is of the rustic order, its roof thatched with bark, its sides of wooden slabs from which the bark has been removed, and its entrances fashioned in various kinds of wood. But the most unique and attractive feature in this temple of Forestry is the colonnade which supports the roof of the spacious veranda: formed of the trunks of trees twenty-five feet in height its sides are composed of slabs, the frames of doors and windows being sections of logs with the bark removed. From the roofs of the verandas depend borders, or cornices, fashioned from limbs and saplings into simple geometric figures. Bark covers the roofs of both verandas and main structure, a rustic fence surrounding the latter. In the erection of the building wooden pins were substituted for nails and iron bolts.[33]

This pales, though, next to a glance at the contents of the Agricultural Pavilion. There were ziggurats of maple sugar, towers and log huts carved from Wisconsin cheese, and assemblies of mannequins dressed in evening gowns woven of grasses and willow fronds. The headquarters of a Detroit brewing firm was "fashioned entirely of bottles" and the Illinois beekeeping industry contributed a beeswax house. California products were "displayed in the form of pavilions fashioned entirely of canned fruits, towers of almonds and walnuts, and tier upon tier of boxes filled with prunes and raisins."[34] The pavilion of the Stollwerck brothers of Cologne was

fashioned of chocolate in the form of a temple of the Renaissance period. It is 38 feet in height, and in its construction were used 30,000 pounds of chocolate and cocoa butter, the latter giving to the structure the sem-

blance of marble. Blocks of chocolate form the founda-
tion, upon which rest fluted columns crowned, above the
architrave, by the emblematic eagles of Germany, and
surmounted by a dome, with the imperial crown as apex.
In the midst of the temple is a heroic statue of Germania,
modeled after the figure on the Niederwald monument,
and sculptured from a solid mass of chocolate.[35]

Other exhibits evidenced a more macabre whimsy:

One group contains a stuffed animal [a pig] in a gilded
chariot, with shoats in place of steeds; in another is a
huge hog made of lard, with spectacles on his snout,
and pen and inkstand beside him.[36]

This genre of folly is rare today, although it survives in a
few relics like the well-preserved Corn Palace in Mitchell,
South Dakota, and in some seasonal events like ice-palace
competitions or the petal-covered floats in the Tournament
of Roses Parade. These may seem quaint to us, but Baum—
who at this time was starting his first successful publishing
enterprise, a trade magazine for window dressers—would
have been delighted by such things. In Macatawa, he decorated "The Sign of the Goose" with friezes and murals of
geese, gooseneck railing uprights, and a goose-shaped rock-
ing chair. Even the upholstery tacks were specially made
with heads in the shape of a goose's profile. Baum's cottage
may not have been a masterpiece of naive architecture like
Ferdinand Cheval's famous Palais Idéal in Lyon, but it was
certainly in the same genre, and, as André Breton and his
friends were quick to point out about the Palais, such sites
can turn menacing quickly. What did the wooden geese
look like at night to Baum's young children? Did the empty
goose chair rock in the lake wind? Did his son ever say he'd

seen the geese looking at him, rustling their wooden wings? Baum paid attention to childhood fears, and more than that, to the fact that the line between fascination and fear is often thin. He knew what it was to imagine as a child imagines, and I believe he knew how this imagining can breed violence and terror.

There's an apparently primal fascination with transmutation, or, one might say more simply, with having a bunch of things all made out of the same stuff. There's something miraculous about it, virtuose even when it occurs naturally, as in a group of pyritized fossil sea creatures. But there's also a unique hellishness to the monotony of everything in sight's being of one material. Many people have described extreme depression as variations on the image of a world where everything, including one's own body, seems to be made out of damp corrugated cardboard. Are the Gargoyles under some sort of curse?

Did Baum imagine the Gargoyles as victims of some process of taxidermy or mummification? Were they once flesh-and-blood creatures, now turned to wood by the touch of some craftsman-class Midas or the stare of some unknown species of Gorgon—but, unlike the victims of Medusa and her sisters, still able to live, in fact, as far as we can tell, condemned like the Cumaean Sibyl to live forever?

But if so, wouldn't their substance be something other than wood? Wood can't be cast, which is essentially what goes on in fossilization. It has to be carved, and Baum describes the Gargoyles several times as carved or crafted. By whom?

A child sits on the floor in the center of a room, looks around at the varied forms of the furniture surrounding him, and wonders: What are these things for? Are any of them alive? Who *made* all this?

Who *made* the Gargoyles, besides Baum himself? And

did he have a reason? Was it some demented human, an itinerant carver of cigar-store Indians, maybe, who somehow wandered down into this Tartarean world? Was their wooden land once a vast underground forest? The mute Gargoyles can't tell us. Are they some sort of stringless marionettes manipulated by a puppeteer high above their country on the surface of the earth? Do the Gargoyles count as illusion or fakery and not as "real" magic?

Or could it be their substance that has brought itself to mobile life? Could the choice of wood relate to the Frazerian magical properties of holly or mistletoe, or the broomsticks ridden by witches?

Could it have something to do with the mysterious expression "wicker wings"? The *Oxford English Dictionary* says this feature is "attributed to various sinister creatures," but that "the source of the allusion is unascertained," and quotes Dryden's *Aeneis*:

> The Fury on her wicker Wings, sublime through Night,
> She to the Latian Palace took her Flight.[31]

Or could the choice of wood have to do with properties of wood itself, properties that are much loved, but also sometimes disturbing? Certainly there's something ominous, as well as something reassuring, about an all-wooden room, with its sound-muffling and its overpowering sweet scent of cell rot. Wood exists between the living and the dead, cut from an organism that bridges the gap between animate life and the earth. And a wooden creature in a wooden land calls into question the distinction between the body and the world around it, prefiguring the time when the body will be reduced to the same class of substance as the soil, as "rocks and stones and trees." Earlier in his career, in one of his pre-

Oz fantasies, Baum wrote about a more conventional fairy country called Merryland where the living inhabitants as well as the landscape and buildings are made entirely out of candy. But Baum makes this Land-of-Cockaigne/Rock-Candy-Mountain fantasy his own by mentioning, almost in passing, that the inhabitants also eat the candy, and that although they're immortal, if one of them is broken beyond repair he is eaten by the others. Did Baum think of worlds of this sort as autophagous organisms, like the pig sculpted out of its own reduced fat?

Or should we look for a simpler explanation? Had Baum simply seen something he might have described as a wooden gargoyle?

In Baum's day, it was said that if you'd seen the World's Columbian Exposition, you'd pretty much seen everything. But not everything was good, and there were several dark aspects to the Fair. Twenty-first-century folk would probably identify these as the innumerable monuments to colonialism and environmental rape. However, people at the time— or at least the majority of white people—located the "problems" of the Fair either in the seedy carnival come-ons of the Midway Plaisance or in its displays of the less-enriching customs of less-enlightened nations. The pioneering anthropologist Stewart Cullin singled out a "torture dance" performed in the Algerian and Tunisian Village, where a dancer "ate live scorpions and broken glass, grasped red-hot irons, and drew needles through his flesh, while apparently under the influence of some drug."[38] This sounds even worse than the Scoodlers' Soup Gavotte.

Even some of the more "respectable" exhibits weren't to everyone's taste. The usually voluble and indulgent Mr. Bancroft can barely bring himself to describe the pre-Columbian display in the courtyard of the Ethnographical Building—which included E. H. Thompson's casts of Maya friezes from the ruins of Uxmal, in the Yucatán, and of zoomorphs and stelae from the Highland Maya site of Quiriguá—and turns away with a shudder: "For those who care not for these strange weird forms and faces, there is a gallery of forty large photographs. . . ."[39]

Did Baum tour this pavilion, which also included full-scale replicas of Northwest Coast villages, with their huge "carved posts, fashioned by the Haidas into shapes of beast, bird, and man"? How would Baum have described a totem pole to a child?

Did Baum consciously or unconsciously identify the Gargoyles with American Indians?

Speculating on the experiences that inspire fantasy can be an imaginative dead end. It doesn't tell you what makes fantasy great, and even assuming you've identified the right bit of inspiration, it doesn't explain why the author chose it and not some other. But considering Baum's genocide editorials is investigating a fairly serious charge. Linking them to his Oz work should entail making, at least, a convincing circumstantial case.

9. CAPTIVES OF THE INDIANS

We don't know what direct experiences Baum had with Native Americans, and we can't know what Baum might have read or what was in his long-vanished personal library. But looking through some of the most widely published frontier texts of the period does yield some striking parallels to his description of the Gargoyles.

One narrative Baum mentions[40] in another of his Dakota columns is "Buffalo Bill" Cody's (largely ghostwritten) *Autobiography* of 1879. There are several passages in the book that share the tone of Baum's sketch of the Gargoyles, for instance one in which Cody stresses the variegated dress of a division of Pawnee scouts:

[I]t was very amusing to see them in their full regulation uniform. They had been furnished a regular cavalry
uniform and on this parade some of them had their heavy
overcoats on, others their large black hats, with all the
brass accoutrements attached; some of them were minus
pantaloons and only wore a breech-clout. Others wore
regulation pantaloons but no shirts and were bare
headed; others again had the seat of the pantaloons cut
out, leaving only leggins; some of them wore brass spurs,
though without boots or moccasins. . . .[41]

Cody's book is also suggestive in other ways, especially
in the strange equivalence it suggests between real life
and popular art, with Buffalo Bill alternating between
portraying his own exploits on stage and returning to the
frontier to, as it were, gather more. The perennially stage-
struck Baum was undoubtedly impressed by Cody's feats
in creating his Wild West Show, plundering specimens of
a vanishing world and bringing them to an afterlife in the
arena.

It's also relatively safe to assume that Baum was familiar
with the major works of the preeminent American journal-
ist of the time, Mark Twain, whose depictions of Indians
were often less than enlightened.[42] The following may be a
bit of a reach, but because of the similarity of their name to
the word "Gargoyles," I couldn't resist including Twain's
description of an imaginary tribe in his popular *Roughing
It* (1872):

Such of the Goshoots as we saw, along the road and
hanging about the stations, were small, lean, "scrawny"
creatures; in complexion a dull black like the ordinary
American negro; their faces and hands bearing dirt
which they had been hoarding and accumulating for
months, years, and even generations, according to the

age of the proprietor; a silent, sneaking, treacherous looking race; taking note of everything, covertly, like all the other "Noble Red Men" that we (do not) read about, and betraying no sign in their countenances. . . .[43]

The description of the Goshoots' skin in turn recalls a snapshot of Syrian tribesmen in Twain's earlier *Innocents Abroad* (1869): "These people about us had other peculiarities which I had noticed in the noble red man, too: they were infested with vermin, and the dirt had caked on them till it amounted to bark."[44]

Many other well-published accounts stress the Indians' varied treatments of hair, headgear, and facial features in ways that recall the carved designs on the Gargoyles' heads:

> Like all other Indians, they were fond of ornaments, which consisted of stones, beads, wampum, porcupine quills, eagles' feathers, beautiful plumes, and ear-rings of various descriptions. The higher classes were often fantastic in their wearing apparel . . . . the skin was often inscribed with hieroglyphics and representations of the sun, moon, stars and various animals. . . .[45]

> The hair of the [Cherokee] male was shaved, except a patch on the back part of the head, which was ornamented with beads and feathers, or with a colored deer's tail. Their ears were slit and stretched to an enormous size. . . .[46]

Most descriptions of Indian life east of the Mississippi also include an account of their all-wooden villages:

> The pillars and walls of the houses of the square abounded with sculptures and caricature paintings, rep-

resenting men in different ludicrous attitudes; some with
the human shape, having the heads of the duck, turkey,
bear, fox, wolf and deer. Again, these animals were represented with the human head. . . . [47]

Of course, any number of Old World travelers' tales could
have served just as well as a model for the Gargoyle chap-
ters. But it's important to keep in mind that, as Attebery
stresses, Oz is a distinctly American fairyland—possibly
even an image, in terms of the characteristics of its five
regions, of Baum's conception of the United States.[48]

When Baum lived in South Dakota, at the height of the
Ghost Dance Movement, capture by the Indians was still an
ever-present fear, even if actual occurrences had dwindled
to close to zero. Accounts of captivity among various groups
of Indians were among the most popular genres of frontier
literature, and while we again can't know which if any of
these Baum read, we can assume he was familiar with the
type. One of the most popular captivity narratives, that of
Rachael Plummer—reprinted many times since its first
appearance in 1838—contains more than a few arguably
proto-Ozian details: a cave of glowing crystals, a bear "as
red as vermilion," and Indian accounts of a species of "man-
Tiger" "eight or nine feet high" and with "huge paws and
long claws" instead of hands, which seems to live in sym-
biosis with a gnomelike tribe of little people "less than
three feet high," who dwell in the mountain caves. More
suggestively in terms of the Gargoyle episode, Plummer
tells us that on the day of her release

I had dreamed, the night before, that I saw an angel,
the same I saw in the cave. He had four wings. He gave
them to me, and immediately I was on the wing, and
was soon with my father.[49]

Dorothy's sojourn among the Gargoyles—small, silent hominoids, with barklike skin and inexpressive faces, like the Goshoots—certainly has the flavor of the frontier captivity tales, in which the narrator and his companions are captured, treated roughly but not permanently harmed, moved far away from their homes, and after that (in many of the narratives) regarded by the Indians as something along the lines of pets or curiosities, often with a certain watchful puzzlement that borders on diffidence.

After their escape from the wooden land, things go worse for our friends until they are brought to a complete dead end in a place called the Den of the Dragonettes. At this point, Dorothy remembers that Ozma has promised to look at her every day in her Magic Picture—a sort of universal spy machine—and, if Dorothy makes a certain hand gesture, to whisk her to Oz with the teleportive power of Ozma's Magic Belt. At the correct time, Dorothy makes the gesture, and the next moment our travelers are in the Emerald City.

Why didn't she just do that at the beginning? wonders the frustrated reader. Critics of Baum, even sympathetic ones, have attributed this non-twist in the plot to simple carelessness. But certainly it's of a piece with the absurdist affect of this book in general and evocative of the sense of waking from a dream, which is rarely a feeling of escaping but more one of being pulled unexpectedly to the surface. And while the *deus ex magica* ending could be read as a type of nihilistic collapse of the narrative—showing, maybe, that there's no necessity behind the sort of evil and suffering our heroes have had to endure—it's also suggestive of the ending of Mrs. Plummer's tale. Unlike those used by Dorothy and her friends, Mrs. Plummer's wings can't help her, but the next day her captors, by chance, encounter a band of Mexican traders, who after some haggling buy her.

And so far as I know, this is the pattern in most captivity tales with female authors: instead of evading her captors, or even being part of an assisted escape, the narrator is ransomed out as suddenly as she was captured.

10. ROUGH PLAY

In the early Oz books Dorothy and the other non-Ozians are often in mortal danger, and even in the later sequels— when, as residents of Oz, they've ceased to age—Baum makes sure to remind the reader that they are still vulnerable to death by accident or violence. Saying that Baum's world is "sanitized" is talking about nightmare in terms of degree—a self-defeatingly literal way of thinking. To a child, a single new idea, a new metaphor, or a bit of strangeness, can open up a multitude of elaborate paths, some leading to terrifying destinations. And to an imaginative child, even a mild threat can lead to a fearsome conclusion. As Elias Cannetti says in *Crowds and Power*, any threat, carried to its logical end, is a threat of destruction. The real question is not how violent or literal a nightmare is, but what kind of nightmare it is, what kind of leaping-off point it provides the imagination. If anything is truly utopian about Oz, it's not that there is no danger, but that the characters always conquer danger after a short struggle. I would argue, though, that it's also in this same ease of conquest that Oz's most insidious form of evil resides.

L. Frank Baum, by character and maybe partly by design, was the sort of person who is often characterized as "an eternal child." Without, apparently, much effort, he got at the heart of what educators then called "make-believe" and what today's educators call "play"—without ever showing the children in his books playing at make-believe or, in fact, playing at anything. It seems to me that if his books have a single overriding subject, it's the special powers of children, the ability, say, to put two sofas together to make a flying carriage. Did Baum see his work as speaking to children who are just beginning to grow out of believing in that power, reassuring them that their fantasies have a place in the book-filled world of adults? Did he feel that it also had a cautionary element, coming so close as it does to the often cruel side of "play," the delight in breaking things and the dreadful experiments sometimes performed even on favorite dolls?[50] Are the Gargoyles the result of play? Are they the collection of some rich and overgrown child?

Putting oneself in a child's frame of mind can be a source of great generative power, but it can also be dangerous to others and to oneself, and Baum, at least on some level, knew this very well. He remembered or understood the child's powers of bricolage, the transformations of scale and the transmutations of substance that kids do automatically. He may have understood them better than any other writer. But these same powers that turn a thing into a being can as easily turn a being into a thing, or, as the authors of the "Apology and Pledge" say, into a concept.

Real Indians are not made of wood. But it's not going too far to say that most nineteenth-century writing on American Indians, from James Fenimore Cooper (whom Baum mentions in his first editorial) to Twain and beyond, both sympathetic and unsympathetic, stressed the Indians' extreme stoicism, their indifference to pain, and the perception that they would rather die than submit to slavery. Could wood be simply an objectified metaphor for the Indians' alleged combination of superhuman toughness and their extreme vulnerability—figuratively speaking, their combustibility? In the language of the day, they were eternally defiant, and yet they succumbed to disease and displacement-engendered starvation with bewildering speed. Cut from their roots, as it were, the Indians burned out.

11. THE TROUBLE WITH FANTASY,
OR FAKERY UNMASKED

Over the last hundred years Oz has often had to defend itself against the charges of sentimentality and moralizing. Certainly there are treacly passages, although compared to the general run of late-Victorian children's writing—except for Carroll, Hilaire Belloc, and Edward Lear, as far as anyone I can think of—the Oz books seem positively stark. And although the characters in Oz do talk about what's right and wrong, the talk never seems to be the reason for the story. As in the *Alice* books, there's no identifiable moral or single overriding lesson to be learned from any of the adventures of Dorothy and her friends, besides, maybe, the vague admonition "don't give up." However, while it's hard to say it's ever the "point" of any of them, each of the Oz books contains at least one implied admonition against deceit or "humbug."

Baum was said to have difficulty distinguishing the truth from the tall tales he'd make up to amuse his family and friends.[51] But a hatred of fakery seems to drive much of his work, from the crooked developers in *Tamawaca Folks* to the submersible island in his last book, *Glinda of Oz*. In magical terms, illusion—Attebery's third category—tends to be the province of Oz's villains. Ozma, Glinda, and the other benign, state-approved magic-workers in Oz hardly ever resort to incorporeal projections or disguises, but such things are routinely deployed by the various rogues who try to usurp the rulers' power—for instance Ugu the Shoemaker in *The Lost Princess of Oz*, whose troops of female soldiers prove to be some sort of hologram *avant le lettre*. Disillusion, Attebery's fourth term, is, as far as I can find, deployed only by the good characters to puncture the false fronts of the wicked.

Fakery recurs so often in the Oz books, and is so often humiliatingly unmasked, that it's tempting to comment that Baum's authorial voice may protest a little too much. One hesitates to go fishing for self-reflexivity, but if we did hope to find a representation of Baum himself in the books, we'd obviously have to look carefully at the "swing character" of the series, and the exception to the anti-illusion rule: the Wizard himself.

Oscar Zoroaster Phadrig Isaac Norman Henkle Emmannuel Ambroise Diggs, to use the Wizard's real name (the Land of Oz, he says, was named after his first two initials[52]), is an itinerant showman nearing the end of a long line of semireputable gigs that recalls Baum's own peripatetic career. Baum was an actor, producer, salesman, pitchman, entrepreneur, window-dresser, purveyor of popular but critically ignored stories under a half-dozen different pseudonyms, a loving but never settled family man forever hosting parties for his children and their friends, staging magic-lantern shows and puppet plays and carving wooden geese for his soon-to-be-sold beach house. But it's not just that the Wizard's character and history may reflect those aspects of Baum's own that he had doubts about. The Wizard's favorite turns also recall Baum's characteristic fictional operations. As I've mentioned, Baum only rarely lets us see his process of bricolage in action, but in *Dorothy and the Wizard* he does show the Wizard performing what turns out to be a sleight-of-hand version, pulling a live piglet apart into two live piglets, and then three, and so on, until he has nine piglets, which he then recombines. As a rather run-of-the-mill bit of close-up that nevertheless impresses

Dorothy, the assembled Mangaboos, and even their Sorcerer just as much as the "real" magic all around them, this could be a figuration of writing itself.

At the end of *Dorothy and the Wizard in Oz*, the Wizard is more or less redeemed and comes again to reside permanently in the Emerald City. Eventually, Ozma even allows him to learn a bit of "real magic" to supplement his usual flimflam. But throughout the series, the increasingly kindly and respectable Wizard always retains the hint of something unsavory, a touch of the outcast or even of the sacred executioner. It's clear that he's from a different and more degraded world, and unlike Dorothy and the other children who have been made permanent guests, the Wizard has been worn by it. Certainly he's one of the very few characters in Oz, and the only main character, who is visibly old. And when something unpleasant needs to be done, it's often the black-suited Wizard who for one reason or another ends up with the job—as he does at the end of the encounter with the Gargoyles. Here the Wizard is distinctly less generous than Woot's friends in their escape from the Loons:

> . . .when Jim finally alighted at the mouth of the cavern the pursuers were still some distance away.
>
> "But, I'm afraid they'll catch us yet," said Dorothy, greatly excited.
>
> "No; we must stop them," declared the Wizard. "Quick Zeb, help me pull off these wooden wings!"
>
> They tore off the wings, for which they had no further use, and the Wizard piled them in a heap just outside the entrance to the cavern. Then he poured over them all the kerosene oil that was left in his oil-can, and lighting a match set fire to the pile.
>
> The flames leaped up at once and the bonfire began

to smoke and roar and crackle just as the great army of wooden Gargoyles arrived. The creatures drew back at once, being filled with fear and horror; for such a dreadful thing as a fire they had never before known in all the history of their wooden land.

Inside the archway were several doors, leading to different rooms built into the mountain, and Zeb and the Wizard lifted these wooden doors from their hinges and tossed them all on the flames.

"That will prove a barrier for some time to come," said the little man, smiling pleasantly all over his wrinkled face at the success of their stratagem. "Perhaps the flames will set fire to all that miserable wooden country, and if it does the loss will be very small and the Gargoyles never will be missed."[53]

Does the Wizard's tone in this passage seem quite up to the usual Oz standards? Maybe not. But the sad fact is that Oz is not really so different from the real world. There is, often enough, an "other" in Oz. But after all, isn't it all the fault of the Gargoyles themselves, or rather simply of what they are? The Gargoyles were waiting, long before the book began, for someone from our own world to come along and to eradicate them and their world with the flick of a match.

Ultimately, then, the issue is not whether the Gargoyles are metaphors for Indians, or even whether they recall Baum's notions of Indians, but rather that the Wizard treats them like Indians, using language that chillingly recalls Baum's statement that "History would forget these latter despicable beings": "[T]he loss will be very small and the Gargoyles never will be missed."

Oz's "messages" are, broadly speaking, good ones, and as an instance of the standard admonition "don't give up," the

Gargoyle episode is as good as any other. But if its message includes the notion that you can take care of all your problems with a can of kerosene, we may have a real problem. So far as we know, the Gargoyles had never harmed anyone before our friends' trespassing visit. It's only the introduction of the Wizard and his band into their world that brings suffering, just as the Wizard's opportunistic fakery in the famous first book took advantage of the innocent citizens of Oz proper. Baum's rather disturbing description of his putative alter ego "smiling pleasantly all over his wrinkled face at the success of their stratagem" suggests that he was aware of this, and that, whether or not he ever thought again about his noxious editorials, he may not have been entirely at ease with his self-image. Is there even a submerged wish here that Indians, like (presumably) the Gargoyles, might truly be incapable of feeling pain? Certainly there is at least a hint that it's just not the occasional instances of malevolence one encounters around Oz, but the solutions to them—technological, magical, or simply a bit too easy—that are truly horrific. The childlike powers of imagination breed both good and bad in such proximity that separating them may not be possible. Humbug is not the Wizard's only sin, and the dark places in his character figure a submerged but ever-present evil in the Land of Oz itself.

NOTES

1. "John Estes Cooke" (L. Frank Baum), *Tamawaca Folks* (USA [Grand Rapids, Michigan, n.d.]: The Tamawaca Press, North Dakota [1899, reprinted 1907]), p. 21.
2. Ibid., pp. 144–45.
3. Salman Rushdie, *The Wizard of Oz* (London: BFI Film Classics, 1992), p. 57.
4. Gore Vidal, "On Rereading the Oz Books," *The New York Review of Books,* October 13, 1977, pp. 38–42; reprinted as "The Oz Books" in Gore Vidal, *United States: Essays 1952–1992* (New York: Random House, 1993), pp. 1094–1110.
5. Suzanne Rahn, *The Wizard of Oz: A Reader's Companion* (New York: Twayne Publishers, 1998), p. 79.
6. Alison Lurie, "The Oddness of Oz," *The New York Review of Books*, December 21, 2000.
7. Laura Miller, "Oz vs. Narnia," *Salon*, December 28, 2000, np.
8. C. Warren Hollister, "Oz and the Fifth Criterion," *Baum Bugle* (Winter 1971): 5–8. Also in Hearn, 1983, and Rahn, 1998.
9. Cory Panshin, letter, *Salon*, January 10, 2001, np.
10. L. Frank Baum, *The Wonderful Wizard of Oz*, (Chicago and New York: George M. Hill Co., 1900), Introduction, np.
11. Ibid., p. 60.
12. James Thurber, p.5.
13. L. Frank Baum, *The Tin Woodman of Oz*, p. 64.
14. Baum, interview, 1904, in Hearn, p. 64.
15. See Tim Burton's 1993 film *The Nightmare Before Christmas* for a more intentionally frightening use of the same image.

16. Baum, *The Wonderful Wizard of Oz*, Introduction, np.
17. "Le Comte de Lautréamont" (Isidore-Lucien Ducasse [1846–1870]), *Poesies*, 1890.
18. L. Frank Baum, "Modern Fairy Tales," 1909, in Rahn, p. 28.
19. L. Frank Baum, editorial, *Aberdeen Saturday Pioneer*, December 15, 1890.
20. L. Frank Baum, editorial, *Aberdeen Saturday Pioneer*, January 3, 1891.
21. "Planners and Anticipated Participants in the L. Frank Baum Conference for Aberdeen, South Dakota, Planned in 1997," "Apology and Pledge," np. ("Note: The Baum Festival went on as planned in the summer of 1997. Because of conflicting opinions, the Apology and Pledge were not, in the end, part of the program that took place in the town of Aberdeen."—J. S. Dill, March 11, 1998.)
22. Martin Gardner, "The Royal Historian of Oz," in Gardner and Russel B. Nye, eds., *The Wizard of Oz and Who He Was* (East Lansing, Mich.: Michigan State University Press, 1994), p. 30.
23. L. Frank Baum, *The Road to Oz* (Chicago: Reilly and Buitton, 1909), pp. 108–10.
24. Gardner, p. 36.
25. See Michael O'Riley, *Oz and Beyond: The Fantasy World of L. Frank Baum* (University Press of Kansas, 1997), pp. 147–48.
26. Brian Attebery, *The Fantasy Tradition in American Literature: From Irving to Le Guin* (Bloomington, Ind.: Indiana University Press, 1980), p. 104.
27. Leonardo da Vinci, *Notebooks*.
28. For a clever contemporary collection of objects that suggest faces, see François and Jean Robert's photography collection *Faces* (San Francisco: Chronicle Books, 2000).
29. L. Frank Baum, *The Tin Woodman of Oz* (Chicago: Reilly and Buitton, 1918), pp. 224–25.
30. J. Allan Hobson, *The Chemistry of Conscious States* (Boston: Little, Brown, 1994), p. 91.
31. Rahn, pp. 100–101.
32. Hubert Howe Bancroft, *The Book of the Fair* (Chicago and San Francisco: The Bancroft Company, 1893), p. 836.
33. Ibid., pp. 450–51.
34. Ibid., pp. 445–46.

35. Ibid., pp. 371–72.

36. Ibid., p. 266.

37. *Oxford English Dictionary*, entry, "wicker"; John Dryden, *Aeneis*, vii. p. 478.

38. Stewart Cullin, "Retrospect of the Folk-Lore of the Columbian Exposition," in *Journal of American Folklore* 7 (8): 51–59, quoted in Robert Cantwell, "Feasts of Unnaming: Folk Festivals and the Representation of Folklife," in *Crossroads*, Virginia.edu.

39. Bancroft, p. 636.

40. One feature Baum wrote for his own Aberdeen newspaper was a humorous serial narrative called "Our Landlady." In the installment of December 6, 1890, the eponymous heroine walks into Indian country alone to assess whether the Sioux are actually a threat, taking Cody's book with her as a guide.

41. William Frederick Cody, *The Life of Hon. William F. Cody, Known as Buffalo Bill, the Famous Hunter, Scout, and Guide: An Autobiography* (Hartford, Conn.: Frank E. Bliss, 1879).

42. W. W. Denslow, the illustrator of *The Wonderful Wizard of Oz*, also contributed illustrations for Twain's *A Tramp Abroad* (1880).

43. Samuel Langhorne Clemens, *Roughing It* (Hartford, Conn.: American Publishing Co., 1872), pp. 146–49.

44. Samuel Langhorne Clemens, *Innocents Abroad, or, the New Pilgrim's Progress* (Hartford, Conn.: American Publishing Co., 1869).

45. Albert James Pickett: *History of Alabama* (Mobile, Ala.: 1851).

46. Henry Timberlake, *Memoirs of Lieutenant Henry Timberlake* (London: Printed for the author, 1765), p. 49.

47. William Bartram, *Travels* (Philadelphia: James and Johnson, 1791), p. 454.

48. See Attebery, pp. 90–93.

49. Rachael Plummer, *Rachael Plummer's Narrative of Twenty One Months Servitude as a Prisoner Among the Comanche Indians* (Houston, Tex.: 1838), np.

50. For a contemporary treatment of this theme see the 1995 Disney film *Toy Story*, which turns on the idea of abused toys, naturally coming down solidly on the side of children who never do such things.

51. Eunice Tietjens, quoted in Gardner, pp. 27–28.

52. L. Frank Baum, *Dorothy and the Wizard in Oz*, p. 193.

53. Ibid., pp. 160–61.

OZ BOOKS BY L. FRANK BAUM

The Wonderful Wizard of Oz, 1900
The Marvelous Land of Oz, 1904
Ozma of Oz, 1907
Dorothy and the Wizard in Oz, 1908
The Road to Oz, 1909
The Emerald City of Oz, 1910
The Patchwork Girl of Oz, 1913
Tic-Tok of Oz, 1914
The Scarecrow of Oz, 1915
Rinkitink in Oz, 1916
The Lost Princess of Oz, 1917
The Tin Woodman of Oz, 1918
The Magic of Oz, 1919
Glinda of Oz, 1920

TWENTY QUESTIONS IN OZ:
AN OZ QUIZ

1. Oz is called Oz because . . .
   a. O.Z. are the Wizard's first two initials
   b. it is short for Ozmandias
   c. it is Often Zany
   d. its ruler's name was always Oz

2. Before they cast Judy Garland in the movie, Hollywood considered using . . .
   a. Sonja Henie
   b. Margaret O'Brian
   c. Shirley Temple
   d. June Allyson

3. How many different characters did Frank Morgan play in the MGM movie?
   a. 2
   b. 3
   c. 4
   d. 5

4. In the book, the Wicked Witch melts away like . . .
   a. wax
   b. sand
   c. brown sugar
   d. ashes

5. Which of the following L. Frank Baum projects never got past the planning stage?
   a. an Oz theme park
   b. an Oz Sunday comic strip
   c. an Oz silent movie
   d. an Oz stage extravaganza

6. The Shaggy-Man carries
   a. an iron
   b. a sandwich
   c. a love magnet
   d. a sewing kit

7. An Ork is somewhat like an ostrich, but has
   a. metal feathers
   b. a propeller
   c. green plumes
   d. skis

8. In the MGM movie, the initial scenes in Kansas are filmed in
   a. black and white
   b. Technicolor
   c. emerald green
   d. sepia

9. You can escape from Pokes by
   a. running
   b. dancing
   c. calling for Glinda the Good
   d. singing

10. The Hungry Tiger wants to eat
   a. emeralds

   b. chocolate

   c. fat babies

   d. broccoli

11. In Bunbury, houses are made of

   a. Rice Krispy squares

   b. green cheese

   c. crackers

   d. gingerbread

12. Kalidahs are beasts with

   a. heads of tigers and bodies of bears

   b. bodies of tigers, heads of hawks

   c. no heads

   d. sharp beaks

13. Polychrome lost her

   a. emeralds

   b. rainbow

   c. magic mirror

   d. blue and red

14. How tall is Mister Yoop the Giant?

   a. 2 inches

   b. 21 feet

   c. 210 feet

   d. as tall as you want

15. In the MGM film, the idea of Glinda's using snow to neutralize the effect of the poppy field came from

   a. L. Frank Baum's original book

   b. L. Frank Baum's Oz musical comedy

   c. L Frank Baum's Oz silent movie

   d. The MGM screenwriters

16. The Lonesome Duck lives in a
   a. diamond palace
   b. emerald castle
   c. cave of rubies
   d. wicker basket

17. What was Billina the Yellow Hen's name before Dorothy renamed her?
   a. Lisa
   b. Bill
   c. Eggstraordinary
   d. Chick-chick

18. Old Mombi plans to turn the boy Tip into a
   a. pumpkin
   b. goldfish for her pond
   c. statue
   d. stew

19. The Glass Cat is transparent except for her
   a. heart
   b. heart and brains
   c. heart and brains and eyes
   d. a mouse in her tummy

20. Haughty, cruel Queen Coo-ee-oh was changed into a
   a. rutabaga
   b. diamond swan
   c. stuffed tiger
   d. goldfish made of gold

Answers: 1) d 2) c 3) d 4) c 5) a 6) c 7) b 8) d 9) c 10) c 11) c 12) a 13) d 14) b 15) b 16) a 17) b 18) c 19) c 20) d

ABOUT THE AUTHOR

In addition to her nine Cat Marsala novels, Barbara D'Amato is the author of the Anthony- and Agatha-winning true crime book *The Doctor, the Murder, the Mystery: The True Story of the John Branion Murder Case*, as well as a mystery novel, *On My Honor*, which was nominated for an Anthony. Her *Good Cop, Bad Cop* won the prestigious Carl Sandburg Award. Her other novels include *Help Me, Please* and *Killer App*.